To Drown in
Dark Water

To Drown in Dark Water

Steve Toase

UNDERTOW PUBLICATIONS

TO DROWN IN DARK WATER

First Edition
All Rights Reserved
ISBN: 978-1-988964-27-0

Undertow Publications. Pickering, ON Canada

Publication history appears at the back of this book.

To A & C

You're my world. If anything in these stories is a bit too unsettling, remember it's probably just an elephant in disguise or a cheese sandwich.

Table of Contents

Call Out

OPENING THE FIELD GATE, Malcolm sensed something born wrong sheltered in the old cattle shed. The sickly sweet smell of decay spread across the hillside. Round his feet, half-blind, featherless jackdaws cawed. Malcolm hesitated, not wanting to cross the grass, to make those final steps on this late-night call out. Bill Hoden had already started over the field. He lifted up his left hand and beckoned Malcolm on, holding a damp cigarette between two remaining fingers.

"Never seen owt like it, veterinary. Not in fifty years of farming. Knew something wasn't right when it hit the cobbles. Birth waters scorched the floor stone-white clean." He coughed and spat a mouthful of phlegm into the mud.

"How was the mother?"

"Cooked from the inside out. Like she'd been in one of those microwave ovens."

Malcolm pulled his coat tighter.

Bill undid the padlock on the double doors. The broken boards scraped on the floor. Malcolm waited for Bill to go first, but the old hill farmer just stood there.

"Aren't you going to show me the animal, Bill?"

Shaking his head, Bill stayed exactly where he was.

"Seen it once. Don't need to see that again."

Malcolm noticed an old leather-bound book under Bill's arm,

King James in faded gold on the cover.

Reaching into a pocket for his torch, Malcolm stepped into the shed. The smell was worse now. As a country vet, he was used to rot. Hoof infections, orf, or abscesses, his work year was filled with the scent of decaying flesh. This was something else. Like bathing in abattoir waste.

Inside, the temperature rose, first to a pleasant glow, then more furnace-intense as he walked deeper inside. His eyes stung and his throat gagged.

Hilary had taken the phone call, scribbling the details on the Welcome To Yorkshire writing pad and shouting up the stairs. Malcolm had come down, wrapped in a towel, roughly drying his hair. Squinting to decipher her writing, he read the note, making out Bill's name and the farm, Crop Hill, underlined three times.

"You haven't written down what the problem is," he said, walking to the living room door.

Turning the sound down on the TV, Hilary turned round on the sofa.

"Bill never told me. Before you say anything, I did ask. He just said for me to get veterinary up to the farm fast."

Malcolm sighed, already getting cold, and went upstairs to find some warm clothes.

Using an old cloth handkerchief, Malcolm covered his face and walked deeper into the barn. The remains of the mother slumped in the corner, steaming in the cold, limbs half-gnawed.

None of his training had prepared him for this. None of his training had prepared him for being a rural vet full stop. He'd learnt how to recognize ringworm and deliver a calf. Learnt about anatomy. But his studies never covered how to translate Swaledale dialect and how it differed from Wharfedale, or how to keep your fingers working at three in the morning in a fierce moor wind. No, you picked that up as you went along. He wiped his forehead and turned the torch on. The light caught on the air. The bulb faded until the flimsy filament glow was the only thing visible and he remembered not picking up the newly charged batteries before he'd left the house.

He could hear the creature breathing, creaking out each broken lungful of air.

Malcolm creased his ammonia-burnt eyes. The beast's hide was sticky with amniotic fluid, membrane caught between yellow teeth. Fur tar-black, apart from the ears, stained clot-red.

Malcolm started breathing again – shallow, though. He knew what waited in the corner. Not from Stickland's book on anatomy or Cunningham's *Veterinary Physiology*, but tales told over pints of sour beer, in polished wood taprooms.

Only a handful of days had passed from arriving in the Dales for him to hear the first tales of bargests, the red-eared, shape-changing hell hounds that skulked the stones of Troller's Gill and the streets of Thirsk. There were stories of them hunting travellers across High Moss and carrying trusting cattle herds into tannin-stained water. Of course, they were just one of a cast of thousands, alongside boggarts, giants, cursed chairs, all used to scare children to bed and incomers from the fields. He'd paid these folk stories little attention. His countryside was one of dirt tracks and distemper, not hell hounds and hauntings.

Malcolm could do nothing here apart from become food. He kept the creature in line of sight and backed up to the door, reached behind him and pushed. The thick planks gave then held.

"The door seems to be stuck, Bill," he said.

"Not stuck, veterinary. Locked."

"Well, unlock it, then."

"Can't do that, veterinary."

"What do you mean, you can't do that? Open the door, Bill," Malcolm said, trying to keep his voice even.

"Got family to think of. Yon beast needs feeding," the farmer said, pausing. Through the boards, Malcolm could smell tobacco burn as Bill sucked on a hand-rolled cigarette.

"Stop messing about, Bill. I've got family, too. Open this door," Malcolm said. The creature's eyes started to open.

"Not my problem," Bill said.

Malcolm undid his jacket and reached into his pocket for his mobile phone from under old receipts. Tissues fluttered to the floor like anemic, torn butterflies. With his right hand steadying the left, he turned the phone on, the small screen pulsing faint light. The stack of lines in the top corner refused to appear. No signal. He waited, staring, not wanting to look around, giving the phone screen all of his attention. It stayed blank, no service provider name or 'Emergency Calls Only' appearing like a hidden portal to transport him out of this place. His fingers went numb. The phone clattered, back popping off, spitting the battery across the dirt.

He collected the phone up and dropped the shattered plastic into his pocket, then banged on the door.

"Bill? Are you still there?" he asked.

"I am, veterinary. I'm not going anywhere," the old farmer said. Malcolm could picture him leaning against the wall, cap pulled down low against the ice that laced the air up here, no matter what the time of year.

"I know you're not going to let me out, but can you do me a favor? Can you get my vet's bag out of my car? The door's open," he said, trying to keep his voice steady.

"Don't think I can. I know what you carry in that black bag. Surgical tools, syringes, tranquilizers. Get that for you, and you'll try and stop the beast. You're too good a bloke. I don't want you suffering, thinking you can get out. Just go over there. Let the creature do its thing. All nice and quick-like."

Malcolm checked his pockets for bubble packs of ketamine, finding two, both empty.

Crouching low, he looked round the shed. The walls looked ramshackle, but the planks were thick and soaked with a hundred years of creosote. There was no way he was going to break out by hand. Squinting, he scanned the walls for tools. A rake or a silage knife, anything he could use to prise his way out.

"You still there, veterinary?" Bill said.

For a moment Malcolm thought about not answering.

"Yes," he said, still scanning round for tool racks.

Slipping on the cobbles, Malcolm walked to a side wall and got his fingers behind one of the planks. The wood stayed where it was, pushing a splinter the length of a scalpel into his palm, blood pooling. He wiped his hand on his jacket and sat down, back against the wall. The bargest was in no rush to move, its eyes not leaving him once. Damp from the floor seeped through Malcolm's trousers, turning his skin to ice.

Try as he might, he couldn't rationalize this. Here was just another creature. Shaped by story and drunken bragging but a creature of flesh and bone, nonetheless. Even so, the cunning burning in the newborn, thousand-year-old creature's eyes charred his marrow with fear.

It was hopeless. He was stuck in here with this animal. Animals were his work. His life. He'd spent the last ten years tending them, keeping them alive, even when he knew most of them were destined for the slaughterhouse. He pulled out his wallet, hand shaking as he undid the clasp. His hand spasmed, tipping coins and credit cards around him in a fan. Reaching down, he picked up a photo, now coated with half-rotten straw. He tried to clean the dirt off, so he could see Hilary and Tamsin properly, but they just became more obscured under a fine brown film of decay.

The photo was of Tamsin's graduation. The proudest day of his life, watching his daughter follow in his footsteps. He stared at their faces. Every few moments, he closed his eyes to try and recall them, but they stayed out of sight, reluctant shadows of a past cut off by these wooden walls. After a while, he kept his eyes shut and sobbed his throat raw.

Outside, he could hear Bill mumbling to himself. He sounded as scared as Malcolm felt.

The beast acted like it had all the time in the world, sitting on its haunches. There was no need to rush. Malcolm was going nowhere.

A drunken memory surfaced through the panic and under his breath, Malcolm thanked Old Marley. Cut hand cradled in his lap, he pushed himself up from the floor, cramp bringing him tumbling down more than once. Crouching, he let his fingers drift across the floor like dangled puppets. Straw stuck to the cobbles in patches, layered and thick. It came away in strips, each laminate clouding the air with the stench of animal waste. Using small movements, Malcolm worked his way across the barn, pulling up decades of trampled bedding and dung, piling the fragments in stacks behind him. All the time, the creature watched, steam condensing against Malcolm's skin.

Not many listened to Marley. Not many understood the creased shepherd, anyway, much less when he was on the outside of half a bottle of scotch, but Malcolm took the time and paid for the drinks. Marley cared for his animals more than anyone Malcolm had met. Get past the slurring and he could tell a good story, for the price of a single malt, of course.

Marley was the first to mention the bargest to Malcolm, first to describe the red ears and the culling stare. He didn't know if Marley's story of being pursued over the moors was true. He didn't know if the whispered story of keeping one side of Moor Gill, the beast the other, was an embellishment. At the moment, he had little to lose and little left to try.

Outside, he could hear Bill stumble his way through the Lord's Prayer. If it weren't so serious, it would be funny. Dale gossip whispered the only time Bill saw the inside of church was to dip the collection plate.

Shifting along the ground, Malcolm carried on pulling fragments of dirt from the floor, slowly revealing the channel. Only shallow, the drain carried water along the barn to a stone slab trough at the other end. Now out of sight of the creature, Malcolm reached under the wall and pulled away 50 years of mud, the dirt pushing nails away from his fingers.

Only a trickle came at first, water the colour of port. He wiped his face, leaving a stain across his forehead, scrabbled back and banged against the door. The creature looked up at the noise, spit dripping onto the floor.

"Don't be struggling, veterinary. If it were me, I'd be scooting across that barn. Get it over and done with," Bill said, his voice close as if he were trying to peer through the gaps.

"Well, I'm not you, Bill," Malcolm said, his teeth grinding as he tried to keep from shivering.

"Ay, you're right at that, veterinary. I'm outside; you're stuck in there."

"Might get out, yet."

"Might be pigs fly. I'd rather bet on that than you making through the night," Bill said.

Malcolm listened to him pause as he took another drag of his cigarette.

"Don't drag it out. I know it's not fair on you, but I don't want you to suffer more than you have to, veterinary. I'm not a cruel man."

Malcolm ignored him.

He knew time was running low. His movements had been slow, trying to disturb the fetid air as little as possible. The creature might be less than twelve-hours-old, but the thing that clung inside was older than the hills themselves. The bargest blistered with cunning.

Cold mud coated Malcolm's hands up to the knuckles, all feeling gone. He pressed on, scooping up handfuls of muck, throwing them over his shoulder, getting careless. Outside, Bill stopped stumbling his way through scripture and listened to the dirt slip down the walls.

The folk tales never came with specifics, or volume tables. Never said how much liquid needed to flow. Whether a river or a stutter. Malcolm kept digging the channel free.

The water was sticky, more sludge or soup, but it flowed,

nonetheless. He watched it creep across the floor, rivulets spilling between the cobbles until the stone submerged below the neonatal stream.

An expression passed across the creature's face, one Malcolm had never seen on an animal; confusion. Not the dislocated confusion of pain. Genuine wonderment at the lack of its own comprehension of the situation. Then anger.

Malcolm watched the creature's skin dragged in through its mouth, now turned to a raw wound. Ribs and muscles glistened on the outside of its torso, like offal on a butcher's slab. Malcolm's brain protested, breaking down in the face of this. In that moment, he knew that if it couldn't kill him to feast, the bargest would kill him with fear.

Somewhere deep inside, in the place that cocooned stories, he realized he must turn his back. If he didn't, and soon, his heart would turn itself inside out of his chest in sympathy.

With effort, he pivoted each footstep. Outside, Bill started on the Psalms, sung in a discordant tenor to no tune a congregation would recognize.

Eyes closed, Malcolm faced the wall, whispering childhood stories to himself. The bargest's breath scorched his jacket, wax running from charred cotton and dripping on the floor. Every nerve was telling him to turn. He stayed the other way, elective blind.

The whispers started. Fears and memories dragged from childhood. Voices of dead people Malcolm had buried deep squirmed their way out. His back was soaked with sweat, now. Then the promises of wealth and debauchery started. The offers of gold and power, if only he would turn. If only he would look just once. He didn't even need to open his eyes, just peek. Just peek enough to step over the little, tiny stream bisecting the barn.

His throat was full of sand. He couldn't speak, even though every inch of skin wanted to let the air burn his lungs and turn it against the walls, like Joshua against the walls of Jericho. He wanted to scream till his teeth powdered and tongue rotted at the root. He wanted to open his eyes and see the sun stream through the oak tree, outside his childhood bedroom, to sacrifice every minute of his adult life just to wake up from this stained and bitter nightmare in the cocoon of his childhood.

Malcolm stayed silent because he knew, deep down, even when the lies delivered in Hilary's voice were at their most persuasive, that to survive the next few moments, he must not turn around.

Even when something brushed his cheek or took his hand. Even when he could no longer feel the cobbles beneath his feet or know if he were asleep or awake, he still did not turn round.

Malcolm never knew how long he stood facing that wall before his legs gave out, crumpling to the floor, head catching the straw and bringing a dreamless sleep.

Daytime had arrived when he came to, a dull, grey light visible through his sore eyes. He looked over the trickle of stream. The back wall of the shed had gone, broken planks littering the hill beyond, tufts of thick, black hair caught on the rusted nails. Still, he didn't cross the water, instead smashing his shoulder again and again into the padlocked door until the wood gave, spreading a bruise across the top of his arm.

He half-expected to find Bill slumped on the grass outside, or mauled beyond recognition, but the field was empty apart from a pile of half-smoked cigarettes, a ripped-up copy of the King James Bible, and a flock of half-blind, featherless jackdaws cawing in the mist.

Streuobstwiese

KATE'S BEEN OUT ON the roof again. She's drawn her finger through salt the colour of wood ash, the sigils barely holding together on the terracotta slope of the tiles. The gutters are clogged with yellow fat, and dead hares whose eyes are gilded in gold leaf. Across the valley a field of barley whitens with mould and blight.

I coax her back through the casement and hold her while she whispers curse words into the damp cotton of my shoulder. Her breath smells of bonfire smoke. She does not sleep.

I know where the artist's bones are. Deep in the clay below the Gravenstein apple trees. Root-wrapped and smeared with grease. The fruit tastes slightly of marrow and damp cloth. It is not an unpleasant flavor.

Something has been killing the hoopoe, leaving their plucked bodies in the orchard's long grass. Their scorched beaks have been torn free and sealed tight with honey. Kate does not come down here often, though she can see the trees from the house. I pick up the corpses, the loose feathers, and drop them into a burlap sack, the one I normally use for harvested fruit. Later, I bury their small bodies in shallow graves.

"I didn't mean to," Kate says, and I know she's telling the truth. "He scrubbed out the salt. I don't know why he scrubbed out the salt."

I look at the line going around the house. A single footprint has worn through the white powder, tread still visible. He lies on the corner of the porch, eyes wide and blinded with mould erupting through his jaw and across his tongue. Even though the cartilage in his throat has turned to dust, he still tries to speak.

"You need to finish what you've started. It's not right to leave him like this. To leave him for me to deal with," I say, but even as I finish speaking, I know she can't. She never can. We keep two large apple presses behind the house. I use the second one, and later burn his uniform down at the far end of the orchard. The wind will carry the char of smoke down the valley, away from us and the town.

Kate sits, her back against the pollard's bark while she knits. I watch bees flit from blossom to blossom. The day is calm and bright, her needles clattering against each other. I'm glad she's come down amongst the trees. The air is full of the scent of fresh grass, crushed by our footsteps. I force the scions into the cleft cut in the rootstock, take out the chisel and seal the graft with wax from a single red candle.

Afterwards, I'm not sure how she distracted me to get at the tree, but she managed to. The glyphs are small and precise, carved with the tip of her knitting needles. I know she has good intentions. She sees the gaps in the world, and needs to close them. I'm grateful. How can I not be, but I wish she would tell me. Speak to me. I dig up the tree and the surrounding soil. There are still unburnt scraps of uniform on the warm embers. I push them deep into the flames as the dirt-covered roots start to smolder.

We are low on food, so I take some of last year's crop to the village to sell.

"Had a bonfire?" Carmen in the grocers asks. I know what she wants to know. I stay silent. I've hidden most of the scrying ingredients in the house, but Kate is inventive. Instinctive. I can feel her watching even when she isn't.

"Burning old scrub," I say, putting the basket on the counter. There will be extra cash, too, but I will stash that away for the winter.

"We've seen the hut again, Rachel. Glowing between the trees," Bill says. He stands by the window and does not turn as he speaks to me. I have not seen the hunting lodge appear, but it does not surprise me.

I notice the clattering first. Hundreds of barbed fishhooks fall from the sky onto the road outside. This is not Fortean, but a threat. I step outside, and the downfall pauses long enough for me to get to the car before intensifying once again to trap Carmen and Bill inside the store. I see their faces pressed against the lettered glass.

The sky glitters. Kate has done it for me. Setting the clouds on fire and letting them fall like forgotten fireworks.

"This won't last, you know," she says, slipping her arms around my waist. "We just need to make the best of it."

The streamers of light twitch as they hit mist rising from the river.

"Already fading," I say, and she sighs, unhooking her fingers and walking away.

I arrive back from the orchard and cannot get into the house. The porch is covered in wax bees, their wings fluttering against the rotting wood. The day is warm, and the wax soon melts. The insects inside fall to the ground, suffocated. I try not to step on them, but there are too many, and they rasp as I make my way inside. The hives will be empty now, and many of the trees will not fruit.

The artist only ever gave Kate one piece of art. An old installation never taken by a gallery. She keeps it in the cellar, no other room big enough to display it. On the day he delivered it, he pulled up the lane in a battered white van. With our help he dragged out the hospital gurney, ants and beetles already suffocating in the thick smear of honey across the metal.

After he left, Kate would eat the sweetened insects, dedicating each death to a goddess whose name only she knew.

In the morning I scour the river bank, collecting torn shrapnel from a plane's fuselage. The registration number is scorched beyond reading. There is no-one to tell.

I take Kate by the hand and she leads me down to the orchard, though I am the one who asked if we could go. Paperweights of dew slide from the grass, glisten on the skin of her bare feet, and for a moment I am transfixed. We reach the orchard, and it is worse. Even Kate gasps. The elm trees are no longer seedlings, their granite branches resting on the crowns of the apple trees, crushing the Berlepsch and Weirouge to pulp.

"There are two thousand," she says. She reaches up and plucks a leaf, lets it fall. Silica in the rock glistens like dying stars.

"There need to be zero. They are killing the apple trees."

I do not ask where the stone has come from. Whether she grifted it from some family quarry in a nearby village, or erupted and cooled a volcano far through the earth. I think I can smell bone in the rock. I do not ask.

Someone has been to the house. Aftershave lingers around the porch, a light reek of citrus and alcohol. I let my hand rest on the door handle, peering through the frosted glass for any bundles in the hallway that do not look like they belong. Kate is sitting on the stairs.

"The visitors went away," she says. Her knuckles are red-raw where she's torn skin to lace. I nod. It was lucky they did. I know what she was planning to do. I'm glad she didn't feel she had to.

She has found the artist's cap and is wearing it, long hair bunched up inside. Sat in the dark. The room is heavy with the reek of sweat-stained wool and all his lies.

When he was alive, he never took it off. The thing with lies is they have power. He knew that and wore them like ribbons.

Kate uses them to create other things. These falsehoods smell of mildew. I glance at her arm in the little light coming from the window. She is sprouting jackal fur in the crook of her elbow. I reach into my pocket for the tweezers, ready to pluck it out hair by hair. Root by bloodstained root. It's the only way, or it will spread and she will be his by morning.

Later that night I take the hat down to the meadow and try to burn it to ash. The flames dance across the weave. I wedge it into the crook of a pear tree. I know it will be back in the attic by morning.

They're not taking our apples in town anymore. They say that the crop is tainted. Kate wants to come to the town, to support me. I can't let her. The way they'll react to her. The way she'll react to them.

I wake up in the middle of the night and go to her room. She's sitting on the edge of her bed, window open. I can hear flies buzzing across the fruit as their offspring burrow through apple skin. The scent is sweet and warm and collapsing. I walk across to shut the window and she says nothing.

"You need to stop," I say.

"What will happen, will happen," she replies. Her face is turned toward the floor, shadowed and hidden. I cannot tell her reaction. There is a scent of burning willow and pine. Sap bubbles out of her fingertips and drips to the floor.

I tell Kate that after enough blossoms have fallen in the meadow, the artist will find his own way back through the soil to knock on the door. She asks about all the wasps that drink themselves to death on apple-rot cider, slipping between worm castings and mole burrows. I do not have an answer for her that is not a lie, so instead I tell her a truth: Wasps never stay under the earth for long, dead or not, before they steal skeletal leaves for wings and return.

We drive into the town. It's the first time Kate has left home in five years. She sits in the back, the window closed even though the day is one of the hottest of the year. I can smell myself on the recycled air inside the car.

I turn us down the main street. People are sitting under parasols, drinking ice-crowded drinks and eating chemical- flavored ice cream.

"They're staring," Kate says, shrinking down in her seat.

"They're not," I lie. "It's far too warm to pay attention to anyone else."

But she does not believe me. My lies are brittle children, and they do not live long around her.

The beetles are small and black and crawl out from inside the doors, up over the car's windows, scratching the glass with their feet. Soon they obscure the view outside, the temperature inside climbing as the sunlight bakes their carapaces.

I put on the wipers to clear the windscreen, but there are too many, and they smear as they are crushed. I slow down. I can hear them crawling along the petrol pipes, drowning in the fuel and filling the tank. Their dying bodies clog the air vents, sealing us from the world.

I could explain that this spectacle of death is draping us in attention. That people who had not noticed our progress through the town center are now leaving their houses to watch. To stare. I do not. Cars are not the only things that can be suffocated with dying insects. We abandon it beside the road and walk home through the orchard.

"We need to make the circle bigger," she says. I am too distracted by looking after the fruit to pay any attention. To give her any attention.

The salt crosses the track up to the house, crystals fresh. Along the ditch are two rows of salt pans, evaporating in the sun, stone tacky with clots.

There are two people on the back porch. She has slit their throats with sharpened oak leaves. Wrapped them in blankets that do not cover their injuries. Through the fabric I see bones like larch poles snapped and splintered. The last of their blood, the little she did not harvest for crystals, has seeped across the floor. Flies from the rotten apples sip their fill.

"What was I supposed to do?" she says, I take her arm and lead her back in. Her hands are stained with yellow pollen. I do not know which flower it comes from, but I wash it down the sink.

"It was very quick," she says as I scrub her hands with the nail brush. She winces as the bristles catch her knuckle scabs. I say nothing.

I did not want to leave her for the night, but accountants don't come where we live. Carmen and the others must have seen my car go. Took their chance to try and stop Kate. They did not succeed. From a distance it looks like the visitors got together to help manage the orchard, but Carmen and the others aren't pruning the tree. Accelerated branch growth has woven its way through their veins, splitting their muscles from their bones. Their teeth will be the fruit harvested in autumn. I find Kate amongst the windfall, arms around her knees.

"We need to make the circle bigger. All the way around the fields," she says, but I know that no salt circle will ever be big enough to keep the world out. Maybe we're two faces of the same monster, me and her. I hold her close and ignore the sound of shattering jaws from the canopy above. I lace my fingers through hers and lead her back to the house.

Kate has covered all the furniture in calico, thick and muffled. Mice tug the fibers loose and hoard them behind the wooden slats in the walls. I stand in the middle of the room and look around at the chairs, the sofa, the cupboards. The piano. She brushes past me and sits down on the stool. Her hair is curled with honey that drips down the back of her dress. I try not to gag at the sweetness. She rests her hands on the covered keys and underneath, hammers strike taut, muffled strings.

"When he made the original one, he meant it to be silent."

I've barely finished speaking before I know I've made a mistake. She stands and walks over, placing each foot with grace. Running a finger through her hair, she coats my lips with honey. The sugar turns to skin and I have no mouth. She returns to the piano stool and continues to play.

Later that night she wakes me and runs a fingernail across my face. The mouth is not mine, her memory is not that precise, but I am glad to be able to speak.

"I'm sorry," she says, and I want to answer, but even with my speech returned I cannot bring myself to reassure her.

Wilted blossoms fall around us as we stand in the middle of the orchard.

"They're dying," I say, and she nods. The trees can take only so much grief. Absorb so much death before their roots wither in the ground.

"I can make them come back," she says, and I appreciate her offer, because it is truly given, and comes from sadness, which is her most powerful ingredient, but I shake my head.

"Even if they do, there are no bees," I say, and before she offers to fix them too, I hug her, and we sag against each other like two trees planted too close.

There are routes she does not know. Routes I have masked from her with honeysuckle and knots of uncarded wool buried in old lemonade bottles, the necks sealed with glass marbles and apple pips. I buried them long ago, pressing them down into the dirt of the path, below stiles and between hawthorn trees. The fog of them gets lost in the fog of her thoughts.

The basket is heavy, and split-willow rods rub away the skin of my forearms. Kate is having a good day.

"I can come and help, Rachel," she says. She never uses my name. There are only two of us. It sounds crystallised on her tongue.

"I'm fine," I say. "I'll be back for dinner. I have my lunch in here."

She smiles, and I do not notice at the time how brittle it is.

I should not have drawn her attention to the basket. There is food in there, but not for lunch. Enough to get me beyond the hills.

The route is blocked with brass rods running from thorned branch to thorned branch. She is sitting on the fence, wrapped in calico. The trees reach out and entangle me before I can move. Blood beads along my arms and hardens to ladybirds that scratch far more than the thorns.

"I couldn't carry on," I say.

She nods and strokes my arm between the wounds to give me ease.

"I know, and I'm sorry."

I wake up in the fruit cellar, lying on a metal gurney. It is dented beneath my spine, and I cannot get comfortable. Across the room she has arranged the artist's bones, a pile of wet soil on the concrete where she has sifted for his fingertips. Without moving, she drags the gurney toward her. The hare is nestled in her lap, blank-eyed, gold-leaf crumpled against its lashes.

"I won't be him, you know," I say.

"I know," she says, smiling. "I will have the best of both of you."

This is a lie she speaks with the full knowledge of its nature.

His skeleton doesn't quite fit in my skin. Splinters of bone embroider my muscles, which are too short to stretch across the new femurs. My own are a fine powder coating my diaphragm and lungs. Already, infections are spreading from the clay she did not clean from the time-pitted surface of his spine. Vertebrae are in the wrong place. I do not know if this is intentional or carelessness. There is pain, but I cannot scream. She has stitched my mouth shut to stop my face slipping from his skull. She has kept my hands free to make the new artworks he never finished. The fingerbones are too long for me to hold the tools she has prepared. Soon she will strip me back to her artist's bones, and I will be little more than fat clogging the drains.

The Kromlau Gambit

THE ROOM WAS TOO HOT and too small, and the black haired man was coming up fast on the fly agaric he'd ingested in preparation for the meeting. Sand flies crawled across his scalp and over his eyebrows. He let them find the warmth of his mouth, dedicating each small death to a different perished god. Blood sacrifices were still blood sacrifices, no matter how small.

The door opened and two men walked in, shadowed against the fluorescent lighting in the corridor beyond. The first, in his fifties and uniformed, stood to one side. Saluted. The second man sat down opposite, draping his white coat over the back of the chair. One hand went to the other wrist again and again, seeking out a patch of bloody and scabbed eczema. Soft skin trapped under the man's fingernails as he scratched.

"Thank you for joining us," the soldier said. "My name is General Vasiliev. I have oversight of this facility. Doctor Kuznetsov is our scientific director."

Finishing, he offered his hand. The black haired man stared at the soft pink skin for a moment and ignored the gesture.

"I hope the journey from the airstrip wasn't too demanding," General Vasiliev continued.

The black haired man smiled. Leaned back in his chair until it tipped onto two legs.

"The catering was lacking. I almost dined on the driver until I realised there was no map in the vehicle for me to make my way here alone."

The two Russians looked at each other, unsure whether to laugh or not.

"And what should we call you?" Kuznetsov asked, nails still working a hole into his arm. The black haired man licked his lips for a moment as he thought about the answer.

"You can call me Papa Yaga."

"Papa Yaga?" Annoyance shadowed Vasiliev's face as he spoke and Papa Yaga smiled.

"It seems fitting, don't you think?"

"I do not," Kuznetsov said. "It seems like folklore and myth."

Papa Yaga stood and walked up to the large emblem that hung on the wall behind him.

"Do you know what they represent?"

"The hammer and the sickle?" The General said. Papa Yaga nodded. "The industrial worker and the peasant."

"And the red?"

"Socialism, of course," Kuznetsov interrupted.

Papa Yaga shook his head and ran a finger down the curved plaster blade, wincing as if it was freshly honed.

"The hammer is to represent those sacrificed to the three crippled gods. Their skulls crushed to spill their blood into packed dirt floors of ancient wooden temples"

General Vasiliev looked amused

"And the sickle?"

"Those beheaded in the cornfields to bring a good harvest. If the edge was sharp, and the wound deep, the spine severed first time."

"And if not?"

Papa Yaga stared at Kuznetsov until the scientist looked away.

"A lot of peasant children grew up with the burbling of cut throats as their first lullaby." Opening a pocket, Papa Yaga took out a pipe, packed it with a selection of crushed leaves and lit the mixture. "Would you like to know about the colour red?"

"Shall we get on with the reason we've convened here?" Kuznetsov said, standing and waiting for Vasiliev to join him. "Rather than getting distracted by this outdated superstition."

Papa Yaga smiled and held his arms wide as if ready to embrace both his companions.

"Unfortunately for you, my man of science, outdated superstition is exactly why we're here. Did you manage to collect together the resources I requested?"

Kuznetsov opened the door.

"Please, follow us."

The hangar was vast. Corrugated ceilings held back tons of concrete and the desert sands beyond. They stood on a balcony overlooking the working floor, Papa Yaga between the General and the Scientist.

In the centre of the room a large crate waited unopened, surrounded by several smaller boxes.

"We have not begun processing the organic material. There was some uncertainty about whether you would require input at this stage."

Papa Yaga nodded, taking in the scene. Smiling to himself. His word had brought these rare artefacts across the globe to this Soviet facility in Kazakhstan.

"Shall we go and inspect them?" he said.

Down on the working floor Vasiliev gestured for a soldier to come over with a crowbar. Papa Yaga took the tool, turning it over in his hand and levered open the first crate.

"Just like Christmas," he said, shrugging when no-one else smiled at his joke.

A scent like old wet leather spread around them. He reached inside and lifted out the piece of skin, running a finger across the elk tattoo.

"The offering of human flesh," he said, showing it to the two Soviets. Handing the fragment to the waiting soldier he opened the next crate, lifting out the tied bunches of herbs inside. Their fragrance did nothing to counter the reek of rotting meat still spreading out across the hangar.

"Perfect. I like working with you gentlemen. You're very good at following orders. Now for the big one. If you wouldn't mind helping."

Kuznetsov clicked his fingers and several more troops came to stand around the large crate. One took the crowbar from Papa Yaga, working his way down each rough wooden panel, prising stamped designations apart as he opened the side.

The Mammoth was upright and defrosting. Pools of dirty water collected in pale tubs underneath, placed there to stop leaks during transit. Papa Yaga took a small metal shot glass out of his jacket and dipped it in the melt-water, swallowing it in one go.

"And the ancient mastodon for strength. If you can convene to clip the hair and remove the tusks it will be much quicker than me attempting to do so by myself."

Kuznetsov nodded, and scribbled a note on a piece of paper.

"What about the meteor?" Vasiliev said, picking up the curved fragment of iron from the final crate.

"You had the metal prepared to my specifications?"

"Of course."

Papa Yaga sat cross legged on the floor, laying bunches of herbs out in a fan before him. The fly agaric was blossoming inside him now. Spreading mycelium through his veins. He exhaled and smiled.

"The meteor is a key."

"The key?"

"Quite literally a key. Over many centuries man has pigmented the earth with religion and magic and superstition. The taint of ritual has settled against the upper atmosphere, replicating a protective magical circle around the globe."

In the dust he drew a rough sphere, marking around the edge in symbols.

"This keeps out many, shall we say, problematic entities, but also prevents anything living escaping into the vastness and horror of the void."

"And the meteor can overcome this?"

"The meteor has entered our world from exactly that vastness and horror of the void. It will be recognised as it returns."

"Why do you need the rest of this?" Kuznetsov said.

"Everything needs a little ritual comrade, everything needs a little ritual. Now, if you don't mind, I wish to confirm my fee."

The Cosmonaut sat alone in the sealed chamber, a book open on the desk in front of him. Papa Yaga tried to read the paragraphs but the thick glass blurred the Cyrillic text.

"Senior Lieutenant Bragin. Awarded the Order of Alexander Nevsky, the Order of Glory 2nd class, and The Order of Lenin."

"Fascinating. Will he be missed?"

Kuznetsov and Vasiliev looked to each other.

"Missed?" said the General.

"Does he have family?" Papa Yaga said.

Kuznetsov opened a file and searched for a piece of paper.

"Yes, a wife and two girls. Seven and Nine."

Papa Yaga nodded.

"Under ten but old enough to appreciate the loss of a parent. Their grief always tastes the sweetest. Why did you select him?"

"We have our own criteria obviously. Competency as a pilot. Reactions in a crisis. Loyalty to the CCCP."

"No scandals? No whores or mistresses? No gambling debts or narcotics habits?"

"We were able to accommodate your requirements."

"You see gentlemen. If we work together we can achieve great things. A pure soul is a delicate flavour. One to be savoured. Like fine caviar. Something I'm sure you gentlemen, as loyal party members, will be familiar with. A good untainted soul settles on one's tongue. Nip the edge with an incisor and the flavour slides down one's throat."

Neither man looked at Papa Yaga, instead fixing their gaze on the small isolation cubicle where Senior Lieutenant Bragin continued to read his book.

"If you would be so kind to take me back to the hangar, clear it of your men, and seal the doors against intrusions, I will prepare the materials. I'm so excited that I will play such an important role in the first living thing venturing beyond the planet."

General Vasiliev and Doctor Kuznetsov said nothing.

Alone in the vast hangar Papa Yaga chewed the final piece of fly agaric and opened his bag, taking out a knife, a glass vial and a desiccated toad. The soldiers had piled the fibres of Mammoth pelt beside the crate, arranging the tusks in a semi-circle. With the knife in his right hand he drew the flint blade across the palm of his left, then swapped it over, waiting until the blood seeped from the cut into the handle. Once the connection was made and the white fibrous mycelium knitted themselves into the darkened wood he started to carve the first piece of ivory.

The fragments fell away until he held a single yellowed staff, carved over with forgotten letters. Depictions of flayed gods and hollowed out ghosts. Using the tip he pushed the fibres into a circle, placing inside the tattooed skin, a single pound of Mammoth flesh and the meteorite iron. Balancing the toad on top of the metal, Papa Yaga retreated beyond the circle, struck the flint blade against another fragment of iron, and started whispering an invocation as the Mammoth fur ignited. The flames flared as his voice rose, jaw distending and tongue splitting to spatter words that shattered the microphones left in the hangar by his Soviet observers.

When he finished speaking the flames extinguished themselves and the blade tumbled from his hands. He walked across the circle of ash and picked up the dome-shaped fragment of meteor. The surface had melted and was now covered in twig-like symbols. Papa Yaga read them, ignoring the bulging in his peripheral vision as he did. Satisfied, he knocked on the hangar door and waited until he was let out. The guard tried to hide his fear at the blood dripping from Papa Yaga's eyes and as yet unhealed jaw.

"Install this piece of meteor in the space vessel's nosecone and your cosmonaut will be the first living creature to bridge the gap between earth and space."

"And our business is concluded?" Kuznetsov said. His nails were worrying the scab on his arm once more. Blood dripped to clot a trail on the concrete.

"Once I collect my fee. I'll make all the arrangements for that. You just provide me with the launch time."

The scavenged electrical equipment looked out of place in the centre of the ritual. Tripod legs rested on the inner circle, each point marked with a precise sigil drawn in ash. Bones of the three sacred animals lay spread underneath, the vessel to hold the cosmonaut's soul balanced in the centre. The air smelt of solder and burnt wiring. Papa Yaga inhaled the fumes until they filled his lungs.

Leaning against the wall of the bunker, he waited for the launch. The monitoring devices crackled, empty of any signal. With his eyes closed he surveyed deeper levels.

When it came, the launch sent ripples through all the planes, corporeal and non-corporeal. Acoustic waves picked up by devices in the earth, and ethereal echoes from the extra charms he'd placed on the meteor iron. There were only ten minutes until the capsule reached space. Papa Yaga stood, stripped and prepared himself.

Those ten minutes passed in a flurry of activity. Chants, invocations and inhalations occupied his time. Then he waited. The primitive monitoring devices picked up the communications. He fitted the consumption mask to the vessel. Readied himself to feast.

Somewhere above him the first living creature to venture into space died, and his preparations snared the soul, funnelling it back to earth. He listened to it squirm and strain against the constraint of the fleshed tunnel that guided it through the atmosphere. Down into the small glass bowl. He checked the seal on his mask and waited.

The taste was the first sign something was wrong. The lack of delicacy. Of nuance. He recognised the flavour. Had consumed it in a more controlled manner many decades before.

Severed of flesh and earth, the dog's soul remembered. It remembered wolf and jackal. Becoming rage and anger, it remembered death carried in saucer eyes and cunning carried in seven tails. It remembered howling the hunt while wearing clot red ears, and circling those found outside the boundary fence. And as it remembered, the dog's soul attacked every muscle, organ and ligament inside Papa Yaga.

Papa Yaga tried to prise himself away. The ritual was too far along. Claws and teeth still embedded in the soul tore at his throat and stomach in fear. Soon the organs and muscles inside his torso were little more than gristle. Now hollowed out, he recovered his balance and tore the mask from his face. Turned on the primitive radio in the corner of the room.

"The Union of Soviet Socialist Republics announces today to the world that it has successfully sent the first living creature into orbit. At 5:30 PM Moscow time a craft was launched with a dog as a passenger to test the viability of manned spaceflight. In light of the huge advances represented by this successful mission the Union of Soviet Socialist Republics will continue with its space programme and maintain its position as the world leader in off planet exploration."

Curled on the floor Papa Yaga waited until the last of the animal's soul dissolved and as it faded to aftertaste on his tongue he screamed until the concrete around him cracked in two.

Dry Land

THE MEN DROWNED though they were nowhere near the depths of the sea. Their chests filled with salt heavy water. Bloated with ebbing seaweed that swelled in their throats.

The women tried to clear the lungs of the choking. Turned the men on their sides. The recovery position remembered from school. On their fronts. Ribs splintered against cobbles and kerbs.

Still the water came. Torrented past shattered teeth. In desperation the women clogged mouths with towels and torn shirts. Closed them with cotton wool and stitches. They no longer cared to bring the men to breathing. They were past saving. Now they just wanted to stem the flood they knew was coming.

The pressure was too great. Water split the skin of the men's gullets. Overwhelmed the gutters and backed up drains. Rose up the walls of shops and homes alike. Took breath from sleeping families. The drowned floated on the surface of the flood. Floated above bones splintered and smoothed and polished by seawater. Seawater so far from the sea.

Winter Home

THE WALRUS BEGAN TO HEAT UP in the late summer sun, reeking of lightly roasted blubber. Lena leaned forward, away from the vast dead mammal, and tangled her legs in the garlands of corn-flowers decorating the truck's flatbed. On her lap she balanced a small container of herbs and held it tight in both hands.

The truck rounded the corner into Sofia Straße where the crowds became denser, and Lena tried to spot her parents, but could not see them anywhere in the press of people. The walrus's scrimshawed tusks rattled against the tailgate as the vast wheels below her clattered over the tram lines. Spinning lights of the police escort glinted everything the blue of lifeless skin.

From the airport to the city centre had taken over four hours. Now in the shade of the tall town houses the temperature dropped. Lena pulled her jacket tighter, though the traditional costume did nothing to keep out the chill.

Beside her one of the other attendants reached out and put her arm around Lena's shoulders.

"Not far now," she said, trying to reassure the younger woman. Lena's back ached. She dare not stretch back too far in case the vast sea mammal's decaying flesh tainted her best outfit.

Lena knew it was an Atlantic walrus and that it weighed one-thousand kilos. She knew the blubber layer was 15cm thick and knew the exact ceremonial knives the City Butcher would use to bisect the torso. She knew the smell of the gases that would expel when the body was opened, and the scent of sawing through the walrus's rib cage. Though her only role was to carry the herbs to the Ceremony of Opening, the seminars and training events had been thorough.

Lena braced herself with one hand as the truck clipped a kerb. Down the street she saw the town hall come into view, pulley ropes gasping back and forth in the breeze.

Lena remembered standing in the crowds, watching the truck carry the walrus through the city streets, and the vivid blue glacier ice cut from between its organs, impossibly large, paraded back toward the outskirts the next day. The feeling of awe to know that one had been cut from the other and winter was just around the corner.

Now she was part of the ceremony, the small jar of ground rhodiola root ready to be smeared into the creases of the vast creature's skin. She would get to be in the room when the City Butcher cut through that slack skin and the Gletscherverein lifted out that pure block of ice to be lowered back down into the street.

The truck parked below the pulley chains. As the driver climbed out of his cab to start looping the hooks through the steel eyelets, Lena and her companions climbed down to race for the Town Hall Entrance.

The first to the room would be handed a bouquet of cornflowers by the City Butcher. Lena knew she had no chance of outrunning the others, most involved in the Winter Home celebration for many years. Instead she buried herself in the middle of the melee and concentrated on making her effort seem real.

Upstairs and out of breath she followed the stream of people into the echoing ceremonial room, pausing to shake the hand of the

Mayor, The City Butcher, whose apron reeked of previous years' festivities, and members of the Gletscherverein who looked far from comfortable in their traditional outfits of leather shorts and woollen jackets.

The window casement lay against the wall, removed to allow the walrus to be swung into the room and onto the scarred wooden table. Around the room hung portraits of previous officials who had overseen the Winter Home ceremony, stretching back to the 15th century.

Outside the window the pulley creaked until finally the platform swung against the building, clattering the old timber frame.

Lena took up her position against the far wall and watched the Mayor open an old sea chest, take out two hemp ropes, passing one to the City Butcher, and the next to the members of the Gletscherverein. With knots tied too fast for Lena to follow, they secured the platform and dragged it in to rest on the old operating table. Once untethered from the pulley, they used the same ropes to drag the table across to the centre of the room to stand next to its twin, a second wooden table, just as old and just as scarred. The men stood around red-faced and sweating with the effort.

A few moments went by while they caught their breath and then the City Butcher nodded to the attendants in turn. Each one carried their small jar of herbs or oils up to the walrus, opened the lid and rubbed the offering into the dead creature's skin.

Lena was halfway along the line. While she waited she stared at all the tusks mounted to commemorate the Winter Home celebrations of previous years, each one decorated in scrimshaw showing scenes of the sea and winter. Below them were photographs of city officials standing around blocks of glacier ice, the opened walrus behind in the background. She could not explain why, but this did not sit well with her, as if the animal's sacrifice, stranding itself upon the beach, was the least important part of the whole celebration.

The person to Lena's right returned to stand beside her, and it was Lena's turn. She adjusted her hat, making sure the yellow ribbon was positioned just right, tucked under the brim, and walked forward toward the dead walrus.

Opening the small jar, she poured a generous handful of rhodiola into her palm and held it to the air.

"With this offering we prepare you to gift us with the beginning of winter," she said, and rubbed the powdered root into the animal's back. The skin felt greasy from the other offerings, tufts of hair scratching her skin as she smeared the root into the folds and pores.

Once she was sure the root was all used up Lena stepped back, bowed to the walrus, bowed to the Gletscherverein, Mayor, and City Butcher, then once more took her place against the wall.

Over the past decade there had been protests about the annual ritual, so much so that observers now accompanied the collectors to make sure that a live beast wasn't hunted from the waves. It never was. One was always found washed up on the beach, as it had been for many generations. Only ever one and always at the right time.

Her hands smelt of the pungent herb and the creature's skin. She tucked them behind her back and waited for the preparation stage of the ritual to be finished.

The final attendant walked back from the table, and with a signal from the Mayor everyone closed in for the opening of the beast.

All bowed their heads while the City Butcher drew his flensing knife and cut through the walrus's skin, and the blubber underneath. Reaching into the cavity he peeled back the layers that kept the sea chill from the walrus's heart and lungs.

The smell coated everything, and Lena knew that her dress would be good for nothing apart from the ritual in the coming years.

She could not help but peek, watching the City Butcher reach down to his belt for the bone saw and begin to cut through the exposed ribs. Small bone clouds rose into the air with each stroke, and the room filled with the scent of burning hair. She carried on watching, waiting for a glimpse of translucent blue, the purity of ice that lay hidden under the skin of the mammal that sacrificed itself each year.

Sweat dripped from the City Butcher's face into the walrus's chest. He paused to wipe his brow with a bloodied cloth from his belt and continued sawing. Lena had no idea how long they stood there while he worked, but eventually he climbed onto the table and straddled the creature's corpse. With two hands he reached inside and snapped each bone in turn, the sound echoing around the room and loud enough for those outside to hear and cheer in response.

The final rib cracked apart and Lena looked up waiting to see the ice emerge for the first time, an honour for any child born within the city walls.

There was no ice. As the City Butcher wrenched the final rib, sea water—dirty and stained with shit and plastic—gushed out in a torrent. It cascaded down the walrus's flanks leaving behind streaks of diesel. It hit the scarred wood of the table, and splashed across the attendants.

The wave hit Lena full in the stomach, soaking her with rotting sewerage. Winded, she looked down at her skirts and apron, now tainted with old cotton buds and ribbons of baby-wipes.

She tried to catch her breath but could not. The stench caught in Lena's throat and made her retch, but she held her stomach and did not add to the mess collecting on the floor around her feet.

Looking up she stared at the others in the room. No-one seemed the least bit surprised. Still straddling the walrus the City Butcher wiped his hands on his apron, glanced toward the Mayor, and shook his head. The Mayor said nothing, folding and un-folding his hands as if the movements would freeze the sea water lapping across the tiles. Lena watched him turn and nod toward the members of the Gletscherverein.

She hadn't noticed the double doors in the far wall, the frame perfectly matching the ancient wooden panelling. Two men took one each, opened them, then rolled away the empty table. They reappeared moments later with a second table bearing a large block of glacial ice.

The perfect blue was as beautiful as Lena knew it would be, glistening as the facets reflected the lights above. No beauty could counter the stench of sewerage and betrayal in the room.

"You knew this was going to happen?" she said, looking at the other people stood around the dead walrus, no longer the bringer of Winter. The creature was now just another victim of the choke of life on land creeping into the sea.

No-one spoke. A fellow attendant grabbed Lena's arm and put a finger to his lips.

"This isn't the first time, is it?" The realisation tasted worse than any of the human waste drying on the floor.

The Mayor sighed, and placed his hands on the walrus's flanks.

"It's not the first time," he admitted. "But the people need a sign. They need to know winter is home, and they need to see the ice. Tradition must be upheld."

"They need to know the truth."

The City Butcher shook his head. He cleaned the bone saw with the old rag, taking his time over each metal tooth, and tucked it away in his belt.

"The truth is what we tell them. The ice will be displayed on the platform until the morning, and then at dawn it will be paraded through the streets on the truck. The tusks will be mounted on the walls here," he said gesturing toward the scrimshaw mounted in velvet cases. "And Winter will come home."

"For how long?" she said, her voice even.

"For how long what?"

"For how long will winter still return? This is not a sign. This is a deception."

"It's been five years since the walrus carried the ice to us, and winter still arrives each year, now if you've finished interrupting may we get on with the important business of hoisting the ice for the people to see?"

Lena had run out of words. They dried on her tongue and choked her, so she stood aside while the Gletscherverein and the Mayor dragged the second table across to the window, fixed the pulley's hooks to the four corners of the metal plate, and let the ice out into the city sky.

A cheer went up from the crowd outside, and somewhere the town band started playing. Attendants rushed to the window, waving to relatives and friends, trying to reach the garlands of flowers woven in ropes around the pulley's struts.

Lena hung back. While everyone else was distracted by the celebrations she dragged her hand through patches of bone dust staining the table where the walrus lay, and rubbed the powder into the back of her dress.

The Mayor glanced back, and saw her lingering. Gestured for her to come over to the window.

"I'm sure your parents are in the crowd waiting to see you here, this being your first Winter Home as an attendant."

Trying not to look too reluctant she pushed her way to the front and waved, though she had no enthusiasm for spotting the faces of those she knew.

⁂

Using the back streets to avoid the crowds she could not face, Lena reached home.

She was alone, her parents still out on the streets celebrating the Winter Home that she now knew to be little more than a con.

Her clothes were still sodden, wool clasping the dirty sea-water like an old friend. In the bathroom, she turned on the light, placed the mop bucket in the middle of the bath and stripped. First she took her dress and squeezed it over the plastic container.

The water kept coming, oil-stained and thick with grease, until the bucket threatened to overflow. From the laundry basket she pulled on a jumper and pair of jeans. Unwashed, but still cleaner than the clothes on the floor. Still cleaner than she felt now she was party to the deception. The grime and pollution had crept into her as guilt, and she could not shake the stain of silence.

She found two more buckets in the storage room and continued to wring seawater from her clothes. Once her dress was dry, she moved onto her apron, shawl, jacket, and tights, each one giving up far more water than it should have been able to hold.

She remembered her parents hanging on to empty plastic containers, putting them in the cellar just in case they needed to stock up on drinking water in the future. Using an old funnel she decanted the pollution heavy seawater into them, filling four to the brim. It would take two trips to complete the plan hastily forming. Two chances of getting caught.

No-one paid Lena any attention as she walked through the streets, a container in each hand, stopping regularly to rest when her arms ached. Each stretch between pausing shortened as fatigue set in, cramping her arms and shoulders.

The truck was unguarded. Above, the ice swung from side to side, high enough for all to see. A symbol of the brilliance and cycle of returning winter. But all that was a lie, and she would not lie.

Only secured by a thin chain, the fuel cap was easy to undo. Lifting the water container was harder, but by balancing the base against her leg she was able to tip the water into the tank.

Water displaced the diesel. As each container emptied, the stench enveloped her, clinging to her skin once more. After the first trip she showered, but no matter how much she soaped or scrubbed nothing she did shifted the stench of sewerage.

The second trip was no easier. The two containers felt heavier, as if the secret burden was getting bigger the longer she stayed silent. She knew that it was fatigue that weakened her arms, increasing the number of times she had to pause.

Drunken revellers stopped her and she pretended she was taking drinking water to the crowds, and that, no those who interrupted her mission could not take just a cup. Eventually, though it took much time, she arrived once more at the truck and emptied the second pair of containers into the diesel tank.

The walk back home through the crowds felt like an endless hike through a dying forest. A place where there was no-one to speak to though she was surrounded by people. No-one who could understand. They were drunk on cheap wine and occasion. If she told them they would blame her. But tomorrow? Tomorrow was a new day.

Lena walked to the Town Hall with her family. Her father held her hand, and she tried to hold her nerve. They pushed their way through the press of people until they stood before the red-and-white barrier that now ran around the truck. High above, the block of ice swung back and forth on the platform, melt water splashing to the street below.

The window was back in place now, and she watched as the casement swung back, the town's brass band in their uniforms. Buttons as polished as their trumpets and trombones to catch the early morning sun.

They started playing the traditional march 'Welcome Home to the Coming Winter,' and as the tune reached the middle section the platform was lowered, steady and slow, each rope held by the Gletscherverein.

The tune ended with a crescendo, and the platform came to rest on the flatbed, metal scraping against metal. No need to secure it with ropes or chains. The weight of the ice was enough to hold it in place.

Lena squeezed her father's hand. He looked down and smiled with pride. She wondered if that pride would still be there by the end of the day. Maybe he could take pride in her for doing things differently. For telling the truth. Maybe she would never let him know at all.

The driver climbed into the cab, and switched on the ignition. The engine turned over but did not catch, a cough like some vast sea creature choking in waste. As the engine failed to start, heat from the struggling metal warmed the mixture of fuel and foul water heavy with salt and shit and pollution, spreading the stench through the crowd. Around her, people held sleeves and scarves to their faces. Lena squeezed her father's hand once more, and with her head held high walked away toward home.

Green Grows the Grief

BY THE END HIS BONES were like peeling paint on iron. Sophie had lifted him into bed when they'd eventually sent him home from the hospital. He weighed less than the blanket-wrapped urn she carried in her arms.

Behind her, Simon followed; stepping only on the grass she'd already flattened. Since they were kids she'd always taken the lead. Always clearing the way for him.

Sophie glanced behind. He was too hot in his suit but would never admit it.

"It's a sign of respect," he'd said, looking her up and down in her day clothes which he thought weren't even suitable for going to the shops in, never mind scattering their Dad's ashes.

At the back the cousins followed in a snaking trail, seeds and meadow petals snagging on their t-shirts. Their children had played together so long and so close for the past ten years it was hard to tell where one family began and the other ended.

She rounded the corner of the small copse of trees. The greenhouses alone, the buildings they were once attached to long since gone. Somehow the fragile structures of metal and glass still stood when stone and alabaster had fallen. Something like grief caught in her throat and she swallowed it before she had a chance to pay it any attention.

Her Dad had worked in the greenhouses as an apprentice

gardener, and though his working life took him all over the county, he always returned when he could. Even when the estate fell into ruin. She wondered what he would think now. Whether he would weep at the chaos of trees and plants, pressing glass out of rotten window putty, or whether he'd rejoice in the vibrancy of life. She didn't care. He wasn't alive to ask. Another question that would go unanswered.

She stopped. Simon stopped behind her, not wanting to face what they had to do shoulder to shoulder. The children had dispersed into the overgrown meadow like so many seeds.

"Am I going to do this on my own?" Sophie asked without turning around. A breeze caught the sky, then caught the branches. They rattled against the remaining glass.

"I'm here, aren't I?" Simon said. She shook her head, partly in disappointment. Partly so her loose hair would hide her grief.

Shifting the urn from one arm to the other she walked to the greenhouse. Roots and grass had long since knotted the door shut. She knelt down, ripping the plants free of rusting metal. When she looked at her hands, her palms were sliced and smeared with blood. The world taking another payment from her. The urn stood cushioned on a pad of meadow flowers. A metal vase of bone and ash. Nothing more. The door finally moved enough for her to enter. She picked up her burden and went inside. Simon did not follow.

She thought the heat would hit her under the magnifying roof. Roll over her skin, snagging it and drawing sweat out of every pore. Enough glass was still above to turn the air humid. Bonsai ponds in the top of book-sized leaves. No, it wasn't the heat that hit her first but the smell. The smell of damp soil. Of leaves browning to smears beneath her boots. Hidden flowers that shook free their scent as she brushed against knots of vegetation. The reek of rotting plants transformed to taste in her mouth. She swallowed and tried not to think of spores and seeds and decay, but instead the urn and her Dad and the pile of ash he now was.

Pine trees rose through the canopy, their branches holding them in place. Vast untended tomato plants blazed with yellow, around their stalks fruit crawling with flies. Across the building, metal troughs full of soil and rotted stems. Each step she took unleashed another eruption of flavours. Plums and apples. Lilac. Under her feet she ground away blackberries, glancing behind at the trail of skins.

Without looking she took off the lid and reached inside, feeling the larger pebbles of bone fall through her fingers. Scooped them up again. When she took out her hand she stared at the grey streak filling the lines of her palm. Staining the calluses at the base of each finger. They would go with the next wash.

There was no perfect place in the greenhouse to scatter his ashes. No matter where she spread the burnt and caramelised bone, her Dad would still be dead.

She took out a fistful of powder and dropped it around some sugar snap peas, then some more into a container of ferns. After each handful she scattered she moved faster. It would never be easy, but it could be quick. The only thing to do was to make the process short. There were no words to say. No words to hear from him anymore. Just dust and dirt and silence. Soon she'd forget the sound of his voice. She'd already lost what he sounded like before the choke of cells and the surgeon's blade. Her only memory was the slashed croaking at the end.

As she found paths around root-mats she came closer to the windows and ran her finger down the glass; through the warm smear of algae. Outside, the children ran through the grass, their location visible by the clouds of seeds rising to be carried away on the breeze. Simon stood staring in the opposite direction, as if he couldn't bear to look at the greenhouse in case he caught sight of her.

Another handful of ash. Sophie wondered if she held her Dad's hand or his head. Over the past few months she'd cradled both as he struggled to speak, too weak to use a pen to write when his voice failed. The one time his eyes brightened was showing him pictures of the greenhouse. Seeing the joy on his face she knew what his last wishes were. How important they were to him. Dreams and choices the only thing distinguishing him from the malfunctioning meat he was trapped within.

The tree was in the centre of the greenhouse. She had no memory of the curling path that took her there, as if recollection was rationed and she could not waste it on something as meaningless as paths.

Bark rough and root splayed, the tree had shattered its home, a glitter of splinters upon the ground around her feet. Upending the urn she tipped the remaining burnt bone upon them. There was no breeze to carry them away. She wondered if, when high summer scorched through the dirty glass, the bone would char once more.

Outside she did not speak to Simon, did not call to the children. She walked the path back across the field, knowing the place she arrived at would not be the one she left. That home did not exist.

It was July when Sophie returned to the greenhouse, and as she crossed the field the heat lifted blisters from her skin. By the time she stood beside the steel and glass she was ready for the relief of being out of the sky's glare.

There was no relief. No sanctuary from the heat. True, the sun no longer scraped one layer of skin from the other. Now the scent of rotting palm leaves and ferns filled every pore. The stench of lilac as it baked under glass. The sweetness of tomatoes rotting on the vine. It seeped into everything. It had been a mistake to come.

She sat on the floor and crawled under a potting bench, not caring if decades old compost stained her skin. Beetles and aphids crawled over her legs. Caught in her hair. Beside her feet she found fresh falls of broad bean pods.

The urge to feel the cool of the velvet inside was too much and she picked one up, running her nail down the seam as her Dad had shown her many years ago.

The beans were shrunken and withered, velvet absent. Instead the inside of the pod blackened and scored. Rotten. She put it down and opened the next. This one had also succumbed to blight. The third she almost didn't open. Didn't want to see the bloated decay. Swallowing down bile in her throat she opened it anyway. The beans were perfect, plump and pale. She popped one into her mouth and chewed, feeling it turn to paste against her tongue. In that moment she was five again, sitting on the back-step, stealing as many beans as she put into the bowl. The memory was so strong she did not notice the grit until she opened her eyes, breaking the spell.

It tasted of charcoal and dirt. She spat the mess into her hand and stared at the charred bone in the centre and carried on staring until the sun went down.

Back home Sophie spread the remaining beans on a sheet of newspaper then went into the back porch and found the plant pots. Nothing special. Cheap terracotta with a hole in the base for drainage, but her Dad used them every year, never breaking them even when he himself was broken.

She had no soil to plant them, only realising halfway through. When she returned from the garden centre with a bag of potting compost, she walked back into the kitchen, saw the chaos on the table and expected to smell cigarette smoke coming from the open door. It took her two hours before she was in any state to finish the job.

"Funny isn't it," he'd said, before his voice was stolen from him. "Spent all my life looking after plants and a plant is going to kill me. Maybe they're getting their own back for harvesting them with pinching fingers and knives." She'd watched him tip the packet of tobacco into the bin. "Seems a waste, but I can't have anyone else feeling like this."

She remembered the concern. The sadness. Her memory edited out the coughing and the hollowness within him.

The ghosts did not come until the beans sprouted, arriving as the leaves unfurled from the split of skin. Just shadows on the stairs. At the corner of the landing. She never saw enough to know for certain. The scent gave him away. The reek of tobacco and soil and the rich velvet tang of harvest. She carried on planting.

Sophie paused for a moment before opening the door, standing aside to let Simon in. He did not say anything about the seedlings lining the stairs and hallway. Not until they were sat down with a cup of tea.

"We don't mind looking after the boys, but we're worried about you."

So many lies in so few words, she thought.

"I'm fine. I just need some time to get back into a routine."

"He's not here anymore," Simon said. "You can't replace him with this."

After that first time she'd returned to the greenhouse to collect what seeds she could. Tomatoes, courgettes, potatoes. It did not matter. There were traces of him in all of them.

"I need to keep myself busy."

"You could keep yourself busy looking after your children."

Sophie shook her head.

"I don't think I'm the best person for them to be around right now."

"So you expect other people to pick up the slack, while you try to do what? Become Dad and ignore the people who are still alive and need you."

She snapped around to stare at him. What she wanted to say was, "Maybe if you'd helped a little more when he was alive I might have space left for the living." What she said was, "I think you'd better leave."

"This can't go on," he said on the doorstep. "You need help so you can care for your responsibilities."

"Good bye," she said, shutting the door in his face.

Alone in the house, she opened the windows and as the breeze stirred the plants she was sure she heard a tar-coated lung rattle amongst the leaves.

After that the ghosts came often, hidden in the branches and stems. Sometimes Sophie thought she caught words in the dance of leaves. Late at night she woke and heard a trowel digging through loose compost. Draping herself in her dressing gown, she walked along the landing. Sat at the top of the stairs with the carpet scraping her calves. She did not venture down. Just stayed there listening to the sound of secateurs that were not there, smelling tobacco smoke floating up from the kitchen.

Every time a ghost appeared the others did not vacate the house. They accumulated like the plants. Anchored to the spot as if roots of ectoplasm spread under the floorboards. She walked through the living room, past half-potted seedlings, and charcoal seeds tipped out of pockets onto unread newspapers. There was no shortage of those. She harvested them from the unopened mail beside the door. The house smelt of burnt bone and soil, and she did not want to erase either.

Once a week she listened to Simon knock on the door, ignoring the sound until he went away, then watching him walk down the path, leaving her to the plants.

There was plenty to eat. Tomatoes. Beans. Sugar-snap peas. Sophie did not bother to cook them anymore. Just tore them from the vine and placed them on her tongue. Crushed them and felt the tiny lumps of grit stick in her throat. Mourned once more with each meal.

It was his birthday. She almost missed the day, its significance lessened by the date that bookended his life. Only noticed it by the old calendar still hanging in the kitchen. That last birthday, gathered around his bed. Simon put a party hat on him like he was a dress up doll. Held out a cake knowing he couldn't blow out the candles or eat the icing. This is what you could have won. She would never forgive her brother for that. She would celebrate her Dad's birthday for her. For him.

Sophie sat down at the table; soil-covered newspapers all over the stained tablecloth. The salad covered the whole plate, vegetables plump and ripe. Picking up her fork she pinned a tomato in place and cut it in two. The knife was not sharp and the bruised red skin tore. Inside, the finger bones were held in place by damp pith. Taking a piece she chewed while chopping down on the courgette, lifting the knife when the blade scraped against the vertebrae growing inside. She ran her tongue along the tarnished metal, pushing the fine dust against the ridges in the top of her mouth. Still hungry, she bit into the runner beans, stopping only to spit out the half-formed teeth. The noise of them rattling against the plate sounded like rain on glass. She continued to prise and pull the edible from the dead until hunger no longer gnawed at her and the table was covered with too many bones. The ghosts were close. Stood around her as she ate. She continued eating, walking around the house and tearing fruit from plants and forcing them into her mouth. Feeling the bones settle in her bloated stomach. Outside in the yard she scraped away at the potato plants, not bothering to wash off the soil as she chewed, feeling the smooth lengths of ribs stick in her throat. Each plant she stripped, swallowing peas and beans until there was no space left within.

She woke surrounded by bones. Different sizes. Different ages. Some were bare and fresh, the rounded ends not yet fused, others raked and scored by disease. Teeth freshly erupted. Still more yellowed with nicotine.

She arranged them all around her. Grouping them by size and rot. Twenty individual collections. All the same person.

The younger ones smelt of baby powder and sour milk, the older ones, the ones most twisted and damaged by the rot of cancer, those smelt of hospital disinfectant. The ones in-between? The partial skeletons. Fragments of skulls and finger bones. Those reeked of tobacco.

The knocking came as she knew it would, and when it did, the sound was so loud she thought the glass would shatter.

"Open this fucking door, Sophie."

She heard Simon pressing the doorbell over and over. There was no longer any electricity to power it and he started hammering on the door once more.

"I'm coming back tomorrow. With Police. With doctors. We're not looking after the children any more. That's your job."

He didn't know if she was actually in the house. Neither did Sophie. She did not move or respond. Just laid there amongst the ghosts and bones and her own regurgitated food.

The house would not flesh the bones. The carpets and wallpaper, brick and cement. None of these would cord muscle or spin nerves. The house was not the place for these remains.

The bag had carried his tools. Not the bag he took when he was working on other people's gardens. The one he used in his own plot. All the bone just fitted, and only with the zip unfastened. Every femur and finger bone. The newborn and the dying man. Sophie did not question this. It was a time of miracles. A time for magic that was clay-dry and knotted as any root.

The greenhouse was barely standing. The summer growth shattered the remaining panels. Everywhere, plants filled frames where once glass magnified the sun. She rested her head against the door and closed her eyes. Whispered a liturgy, whether for the greenhouse, her Dad, or herself she could not say.

By the time she cleared enough space upon the floor Sophie needed to rest, and when she woke the only light was second-hand, gifted from the sun to the moon.

She laid the bones out around her. Her knowledge of anatomy was less than her knowledge of plants but the bones themselves knew where to be placed. When she finished she lay face down in the dirt, her eyes turned from the light. From the memories she tasted on the air. From what was about to return.

When she woke, Sophie smelt them standing around her. Smelt the reek of unburnt amber leaf. Knew the greenhouse had clothed the bones in skin of leaves and nerves of vines. Knew to look up for her Dad to be returned to her once more. Gaze on him and not lose him again. She opened her eyes.

From where she lay on the floor she saw their legs. Their calves of bone and plant. The decay of heat and humidity rotting the vegetation as it clasped muscle and tendons, and in that moment Sophie knew her Dad would not return to her. The only thing to come back would be decay and the slow sliding apart of memories. Without looking up she crawled across the floor of the greenhouse. Behind her the figures walked in her trail. They did not speak. Did not try to convince her. Just followed. Remained out of sight but present as her Dad always would be now. At the door she crawled through, pushed it closed against the press of plants.

Climbing to her feet she stared across the field. It would be a long way back, but the ghosts would not follow her any more, just the memories she chose to take with her. She opened her hand. In her palm was a single piece of burnt bone. It was enough.

Not All The Coal That Is Dug Warms The World

WHEN I TURNED 44 I knew I would never be well again. A dense erosion in the depths of my bones that I curled up around saw to that.

My daughter, Lou, came in every morning and placed a cup of tea on my bedside table, just within reach. If I'd left my book open, pages splayed, she picked it up, slid a piece of torn paper in as a bookmark, and tucked it down the side of my bed. Later, she came and took the drink away again, trying not to spill the now cold liquid down her dress.

Sometimes she tried to open the curtains. Let the light in as if the glow itself was an elixir. Annoyed, I waved her out of the room. She pretended not to be upset. I pretended not to hear her cry, leaning against my bedroom door. Shallow sobs making the door handle rattle.

Morning brought more tea I could not face, and a small pile of letters. I placed the cup to one side and worked through the mail. Personal, pastel, envelopes of concern. Brown, windowed letters like anonymous offices. At the bottom, plain white bank envelopes hidden amongst the junk mail.

I slit the envelope with my nail, watching the paper tear to a fringe of gills. Inside the columns of numbers cascaded down the bottom of the sheet until there was nothing left, a single digit held in place by a minus sign.

For the next few moments I stared until they became another language and put the bank statement on the empty pillow beside me.

Today the cup was a simple white, porcelain thing, with a clump of poppies printed on the front. Not the sort of crockery I would ever buy myself. Probably a gift from a pupil who had long forgotten me.

The tea's surface was slick with tea oils, leaving a tidemark on the inside of the cup as I placed it back on the bedside table.

Careful not to catch the cup's handle I ignored the dull ache in my joints and opened the drawer, taking out the form and a pen. I knew this day had been coming and had already read the instructions. Read all the clauses. Clause 4.2 about sanctions. Clause 10.8 about how my family would be supported if I died during the period of my benefits. I made sure the pen was black and filled in the rest of my details in capitals.

Lou came in and picked up the cup, wrapping her hand around the side, lacing her fingers through the handle.

I passed her the letter, steadying my left arm with my right hand.

"Find an envelope and post this," I said.

She took a moment to read the official name at the top before taking it, sliding the paper into a pocket of her jeans.

"There must be another way. Something else we can do," she said.

It wasn't a question, but I answered as if it was.

"My savings are gone. I have no options left." I shrugged and winced. "It will work out."

⌇⌇⌇⌇⌇

The medical assessor came a week later, visiting on a bad day. Rather a bad day than one when the symptoms had shrunk back to nothing.

I struggled out of bed, Lou standing by, not allowed to aid me as I raised my arms, was bled and measured. While they watched I leant on the wall, coughing up against the wallpaper. Lou moved forward; her help stayed by the cold hands of the assessor.

"You do want him to get some money don't you?" he said.

Lou looked to me. I closed my eyes and tried to ignore the smell of damp.

Twenty minutes later he left, opening the bedroom door for Lou to lead him out with three cups held in her hands, two empty and one full. I heard them talking on the landing, though they whispered.

"Will he get some help?" Lou said, the cups clinking together as she rested her arms against the bannister.

"I can't say for definite. There are algorithms and numbers to be crunched. It's all done on a points system by the computer."

I pictured Lou's face crumple. The same expression whenever she got bad news.

"I'm sorry I can't give you more information Miss Jackanelle," he said, trying to keep to the official line.

The letter arrived two weeks later. Recognising the red ink franking on the envelope, I placed it to one side. The experts said all along that my condition wasn't stress related, but the pain spiralled down my limbs to burn fish-hooks into my marrow.

I still opened the other post first, leaving the government letter to the end. Not wanting to know. Either way, yes or no, it wasn't good.

The first food package arrived two hours later, jars and tins stamped with a government arrow. I read the ingredients on each one, mouthing the syllables to myself. They all had one ingredient in common.

Lou must have been at the back of the house. I called down the stairs until I tasted stomach acid in my throat. A few minutes passed, then I heard her footsteps on the stairs.

She came in, shutting the door behind her. Reaching down she held my bowl out as I wretched. Placing it on the ground out of sight she leant back against the door.

The jar was heavy in my hand. It wasn't important which one I showed her, just that she saw the symbol.

"Anything with this symbol on in the cupboards," I said, turning the jar until she could see the thick, black arrow embossed on the surface.

"Never eat anything from here, no matter how hungry you get."

She peered at the label.

"Don't eat peanut butter?"

"No. Never eat anything with this arrow symbol on. No matter what is in it. Baked beans. Sauces. Bread. Don't touch it. You still have the cash card?"

Lou nodded.

"They give us a little bit of money. Use that if you get desperate."

"And you?"

I held up the jar. "Whatever they give me."

Truth be told the food wasn't too bad. Bland and nondescript, true. Never going to win MasterChef, but edible. That first night Lou cooked me pasta and sauce. I kept most of it down. Once out of the container the food looked just like every supermarket own brand. The added ingredient didn't add anything to the taste.

I slept well that night, not having to worry about the house for the first time in months helped. So did a full stomach.

In my dreams I saw the fine, fibrous webbing forming in each organ. Stretching across my stomach and curling inside my gall bladder and kidneys. Gritty, streams of mineral settling out of my recently digested food and collecting like dying fish in the mesh.

When I woke there was no difference. I still had pain in my limbs like crushed concrete every time I moved, yet for the first time in months I didn't start the day hungry.

The cereal was bland, and fell apart in the UHT milk supplied. Lou sat on the edge of the bed, watching me eat, parent child roles reversed. She never spoke, just sat, hands folded in her lap, scared to say the wrong thing.

When I'd finished the bowl, she took it and placed her hand on mine.

"How are you feeling?" she said. I kept my fingers moving so my knuckles wouldn't remember to hurt.

"Better. Full stomachs heal minds," I said, smiling, trying not to picture the grit forming and catching on the nets.

Of course I knew they weren't like gillnets, woven by fishermen's crushed fingers, the minerals nothing like the haematite surfaced pebbles I saw in my mind's eye. We'd all watched the documentaries showing the fibrous strings, thick strands of mucous, the minerals like fat cells.

A substance discovered in a lab that could replace lanthanum. A mineral that could be cultured in the human digestive system. A failing economy. Large scale unemployment.

The home-helps made their first visit that Friday. While one stayed downstairs, tidying rooms Lou never got around to, the other sat on the edge of my bed. She ran a hand across my duvet, the dried skin of her fingers catching on the material.

"How're you doing?" she said. "Feeling any better?"

I held my arms up, sleeves falling back. My elbows creaked with friction as I laid them on my lap. She ran a hand across my swollen joints and I winced. Smiling, she patted her hand on my wrist.

"Are you ready?" she said. I nodded and lowered myself back to the mattress, shuffling until my head felt comfortable on the pillow. She rested her surgical bag by my feet, opening the top, the room filling with the scent of pine disinfectant.

Staying silent she took out a yellow sharps box, another the same size coloured industrial green. With a flourish she spread out a candle-coloured disposable towel, laying out an aerosol, syringe, scalpel and something I couldn't identify. A length of fabric.

"Before you start," I said. "Can you turn that photo around?" I pointed at the picture of Maggie on our wedding day, the cheap paper slightly warped due to the damp of the room and lack of glass. My only daily reminder of how she looked.

The home-help nodded and pushed the photo onto its face.

"Ready?" she asked again, stroking my upper arm.

I nodded. She folded down the bedding and pulled up my top, buttons catching on my ribs. I watched her pick up the spray and closed my eyes as the cold mist settled on my skin, then the pressure as the syringe evacuated its contents into me.

My torso became a haunting I was only vaguely attached to. Never really squeamish I opened my eyes and watched her pick up the flint-bladed scalpel and draw it across my midriff, the blade morphed to the press of gravity.

She picked up the strip of material, the length of her hand, one side covered in minute fabric hooks. She lowered it into me, lifting it again, the mineral drawn out like strands of roe. Tugging the final strands free she detached a length of my stomach lining, redder than the rest, like gristle. I felt a moment of loss, a second of grief for its amputation.

Holding the minerals in one hand, she loosened the lining with the other, dropping it into the sharps box.

She stapled me back together, the clicks far too loud in the room.

"No need to be too neat," she said. "Just to stop you emptying yourself in your sleep. We'll be opening you again in two weeks."

"Why don't you fit a zip?" I said, wincing as I tried to find a comfortable way to lie. I couldn't. She paused in dropping her gloves and swabs into a surgical waste bag as if seriously considering the idea.

⁂

Every morning for the next week Lou stripped the bed when she brought in my cup of tea, trying not to look at the yellow scabbing dried to the sheets. I stood, holding onto the wall as tides of nausea came through my insides. There are marks on the wall, stained with my blood, where I slipped and fell while trying to get to the lowest point I could.

The fortnight passed in nights of waking with bedding stuck to the open wound, pulling away as the fever caused me to swipe the sheets away in my sleep.

Then the day was here again and the home-helps were here again, one tidying downstairs, the other spreading out her implements alongside my legs on the bed.

After the spray she injected the anaesthetic, then pliered the staples free. I felt my skin tear, even through the numbness. Once my midriff was open, she dipped in the strip of hooks, fishing around to clasp the precious strings.

Cat's cradling the minerals between her hands she tutted.

"Have you been eating properly?" she said, draping the strands into the green box and beginning to refasten my wound.

"Is there a sanction if I don't produce enough?"

She smiled a professional smile, and fastened in the next staple. I winced as the anaesthetic started to wear off.

"Of course not. We just need you to stay healthy," she said, clearing up her tools and taking off her gloves.

And then the cycle of weeping and healing started again, each morning Lou bringing in the cup of tea hot. Each afternoon taking it away cold with the second set of soiled sheets stripped from my bed.

Two weeks later the home helps visited again. Lou sat on the far side of the bed, holding my hand. I didn't ask her to. The night had been long and disturbed. The home-help crouched on the floor beside my bed, rolled up my t-shirt, grimacing at the scar running diagonally along one side of my torso.

"That's not healing well," she said, swabbing it clean with soaked cotton wool. "We'll have to go in on the other side. Time to earn your lance corporal stripes."

Lou leant across and put a hand across her mouth when she saw the line crusted with yellow and unhealed skin.

"Can't you miss this week. Let him get better. Come in two weeks."

The home-help stopped what she was doing and stood up.

"If that's what you want," she said, stripping off her gloves and getting a folder out of her bag. "You'd not get any money for this fortnight though."

"No money?" I said.

The home-help nodded. "You'd still get food, but it would be the basic rice and oats. Enough to keep your system distilling the minerals."

From her top pocket she took out a pen embossed with a mobile phone company logo, and started to fill in a form with my details. When finished she placed it beside me and slipped the pen into my hand.

Lou snatched the form and started reading.

"Your sanctioning him for non-cooperation?"

The home-help shrugged.

"Obviously, because he isn't cooperating."

"But when you come back, in a month, the minerals will still be there. You won't have lost anything."

Taking the form back the home-help shook her head.

"It doesn't work like that," she said, placing the paper back by my side. "So, if you want to miss today's collection then sign the form. I have eight other visits to do."

I shook my head and crumpled up the form. A look of relief crossed the home-help's face and she opened her bag, spreading the instruments out on the edge of the bed.

⚬⚬⚬⚬⚬

Mrs. Fredricks from down the street came to visit, trying not to look uncomfortable at the stench in the room. Lou brought a chair in from the lounge, setting it down at the foot of the bed, then bringing us each a cup of tea. She waited for me to pull myself up, not saying anything as I winced. Underneath the bedding I felt one of the wounds weeping, the sticky liquids seeping down my midriff.

"So, how are you keeping?" Mrs. Fredricks said, more for something to say then really wanting to know.

"How are the family?" I said for the same reason. "Have you seen them recently?"

"Our Sue had a little boy," she said, brightening up. "They called him Sammy."

From her pocket she took out a mobile phone, swiping through the gallery to get to the latest, proud grandparent, photos. Leaning forward to show me her enthusiasm overrode any discomfort she had.

I stared at the phone not even seeing the photographs. I almost smelt the flesh scorched off the minerals to process them before building the phone. Did this handset include minerals cultured in stomachs, grown like farmed salmon? Was this fake carbon fibre-cased phone related to me by blood? Did my bezoar enable Mrs. Fredrick to speak to her relatives, view the photos of her innocent grandson?

With a start I pushed myself away, the sheet falling down to my waist revealing the diagonal scars. Mrs. Fredricks covered her mouth with her hand, then composed herself again. The embarrassment was replaced by something else, I couldn't quite identify. Then I recognised it. Disgust. Not with my scars, but me.

"Well," she said, opening the door with one hand, trying to balance the phone. "If you'd made proper provision you wouldn't be in this situation."

I listened to her walk down the stairs, stopping to talk in hushed tones to Lou.

Cautious, I touched one of the scars and a burning sensation harrowed through my ribs into my back. I breathed deeply to dissipate the pain, not noticing until later that Lou had come in to get the cups, Mrs. Fredrick's empty, mine still full.

Over the months my torso became a scratch pad of scars, some never healing, others fading against my skin like contrails in the early afternoon. Each visit started with a treasure hunt to find a clear area to enter the cavity under my skin.

Occasionally, the home-help took out her mobile phone and photographed me, sending the image through the ether for a second opinion. Waiting for it to twitch and beep an answer on where to slice into me next. I stared at the device, the glossy surface, corners rounded like bone terminals. The black glass screen reflected some peeled paint on the wall.

In the obscured mirror I saw flesh decaying, scorched by the heat of the lithium battery, the fumes curling out of the side vents. A hand-held crematorium.

The phone vibrated against the sheet. The home-help picked it up, stared between me and the answer, then shook her head.

"I'm sorry about this, but we're having to go in through the back. Can you turn over?" she said, reaching out to hold my hand as if that would calm my fears.

With my free hand I moved the blanket and pulled up my t-shirt, wincing as fibres caught and tugged at the open edges of the wounds.

"I can't lay on my front," I said. "Not until these are healed."

She lifted up her glasses on the lanyard around her neck.

"And that will be another two weeks," she said, reaching into her bag for a form. "I'll have to sanction you, I'm afraid."

I watched the pen move across the paper. I heard Lou moving around in her bedroom, trying to clean the black mould from the walls. The sanctions wouldn't affect me. I would still eat.

Slowly, I turned myself over, cheek against the pillow, cotton scratching at my eyes. I listened to the home-help slide the paper back in her bag and pick up the anaesthetic.

"This will be cold, then a sharp needle," she said, fussing over turning my skin to marble, then draping a strip of tiny hooks, like upturned teeth, into my opened organs.

Lying there unable to move I turned my head to where she was cleaning up.

"What if," I started saying, then stopped not wanting to finish the question.

She took off her gloves, dropping them into the medical waste bag, then crouched down beside me.

"What if what?" she prompted me.

"What if I can't carry on? What if my body just can't take any more?"

She closed her eyes for a moment, gathering her thoughts.

"The simplest thing is to come off benefits."

Quickly she held her hands up. "But we understand that's not an option for everyone. Not for you in any case."

"And if it isn't an option?"

"Someone else in the family has to take over the obligations."

Her eyes flicked to the wall. In the silence I listened to a scouring pad trying to clean black spores from rotting wallpaper.

"Is that the only option?"

As feeling returned to my back I closed my eyes.

"I can't crouch for long these days. The knees go after a while. Read your information notes," the home-help said, standing up. "All you need to know is in there."

I heard the door shut, and turned myself toward the closed curtains.

Next morning Lou came in with a cup of tea, placing it just in reach. She didn't look at me at all these days.

From the floor she picked up a pile of dirty towels and left. Pulling myself up straight I leant back against the headboard, then arched away from the wood, the slight contact tearing a chunk of raw flesh out that caught on my skin as I shifted around. I retrieved the form listing the clauses from under the pillow and read them again. At the bottom I found what I was looking for. Clause 10.8.

The cup of tea felt heavy in my hand. I tried to remember the last time I'd held anything heavier than a spoon.

Lou always put the milk in first. I hated the way it turned the tea insipid. Devoid of flavour.

The first mouthful made me want to throw up, but I kept on drinking, pausing between each sip.

Reaching across I stood Maggie's photo back up. I saw so much of our daughter in her face. Lou was an echo of her. With the photo facing me it was like they were both in the room to witness I was doing this for the right reasons.

Using all my strength I smashed the cup against the bed's metal frame, selecting the sharpest sherd. I could have just poured the tea into the carpet, but it seemed disrespectful of everything Lou had done for me since her mother died.

Closing my eyes I pressed the ceramic edge between my wrist tendons and made the first cut.

Children of the Rotting Straw

THE SKY WAS MADE OF STICKS, narrow woven and distant. Vast hurdles that covered the world. When the rains came they scented the ground with bark rot and leaf mould. I crouched to the soil catching droplets in buckets and watched the water seep out faster than the containers filled. There was not much time. The scarecrows would be coming soon.

The creaking was the first sign, a slow scraping of timber against timber as they dragged themselves through the mud. A noise that drowned out even the sound of rain. Sarah was playing across the other side of the yard.

"Time to go in now," I said, picking up the buckets. Above us sunlight slanted through the deluge and wicker clouds.

"I like it out in the rain," she said, not looking up. Around her fingers she wove daisies and meadowsweet, fingers stained with pressed petals

There were no trees to shelter under anymore. Not now the sky was sticks. The scarecrows were getting closer. Down the lane, their single feet ground and splintered along the cobbles.

"No time for that now. Come quick but steady. Bring your flowers with you, pretty things that they are. We can weave them around your mirror."

"Then when I get ready I will wear my summer garland?"

"Then you'll wear your summer garland."

Her hand was heart-sized in mine. I walked as fast as I dare. Too quick and the scarecrows would think I was running. I risked a glance to the sky. The storms always washed new ones from between the branches. There were two behind me, gazing over the garden wall, their mouths filled with rainwater, but we were soon in, the bolts across. I watched them through the window until they lost interest and moved on down the lane.

The next day the yarn fell. Vast strands of sheep's wool, feathered as it draped to the fields through the sky of sticks. The scarecrows stayed away. They always did when the air filled with colours. Maybe it was the sensation of the fibres upon their ragged skin, maybe the scent of lanolin on the breeze. I stood at Sarah's bedroom door.

"Get dressed. We have to harvest the sky today."

We wore thick suits stitched from shed scarecrow husks found on the lanes, stained inside with our sweat from the weight of their discarded skin. Cracked with use. Gloves to protect our hands.

Sarah followed me down the lane. I listened to her breath against the inside of her mask, and could not help checking the seams of her harvesting suit once more.

The fall was thick that day, the dense corrosive strands of wool curled upon the meadow flowers. I parked up the cart and ran my glove along the edges of Sarah's clothes.

"I made sure I sealed it properly," she said. "Just like you showed me."

I knew she was telling the truth, but I'd seen what untreated wool did to skin. How it blistered and peeled flesh. Scars that never healed.

"I like to check," I said. "You know that."

She nodded and clasped my fingers, reassuring me.

We started in the top corner, where the drystone walls met each other. I hauled the wool into the cart while Sarah wound it onto the bobbins. The yarn-fall continued throughout the day, and we continued to harvest under the slatted sun.

The message was hidden under a knot of fine madder dyed wool. A tiny thing made of paper and written in charcoal. There were only two words. 'Help Me'. I had never seen anything else arrive with the yarn, beyond scorching and scars.

Pulling the message free I folded the edges like butterfly wings and pressed it inside my glove. The dye pressed onto the paper seared my palm and I gasped. Sarah looked over, but could not see my expression behind the mask, as I could not see hers.

She slept well that night. The day's harvest was more tiring than usual with several trips back and forth to the house, each time the cart loaded to the top with yarn. The colours were more varied than usual too. Madder red, onion yellow, and dogwood blue. No greens. No nettles or larkspur, but it had been a long time since either had torrented between the sticks that arced the sky.

Sat by the window, I flattened the piece of paper in one of Sarah's old books, opened it and spread the note out on the sill.

It would be a few days before the wool was dry enough to weave. For now there was nothing else to do but wait. I stared at the two words, blurred by the heat of my hand, but still legible. Help Me. I looked out into the night. The scarecrows were there again, leaning against the garden wall, their arms loose by their side, showing they were awake. Watching. If they were asleep their arms would raise, waypoint stiff, showing routes no-one wanted to walk. If they saw me looking they did not react. I stared at the tear of words once more.

Sarah would sleep through and if she woke before I returned, there was enough work to be getting on with. I watched her in her bed for a few moments, curled up under abandoned tapestries we had not finished. Half formed unicorns and knights in loose weave. Edges frayed from the lack of finishing. The absence of one or another colour needed to complete a design.

I glanced out the window. The scarecrows had left. Now there was time to wait. I sat in the dark, the stench of wool drifting in from the weaving shed. She would be fine if I left for a couple of days. She would be fine.

The scarecrows were easy to track, twinned ruts from their single feet as they dragged themselves in parallel to their nest.

They leaned against each other while they slept, shoulder against shoulder, their bulbous faces turned outward and toward the sky, arms outward pointing to places that did not exist.

No-one ever saw them return to the place beyond the sky of sticks, but everyone saw the beds left empty of children.

I walked light, circling the meadow grass where they stood. Their expressions did not change between rest and wake. They did not scent me. Did not react to my presence at all. I moved in closer, but kept at arm's reach. I'd not seen scarecrows attack, but I'd seen the results. Circular splintered wounds piercing rotting corpses. The struggling bodies, still alive, hoisted on loops of yarn, their skin scorched and scraped.

I moved quick. I could when I needed to. Slid the flensing knife into the back of the first scarecrow and stood back as mould-spotted straw spilt out. The second scarecrow woke, trying to turn to where I crouched. I ducked under the arms, escaping the grip that would not open once closed. My knife flicked up, slicing away button thread, then the stained shirt underneath. All the time its stuffing continued to empty it continued to reach for me, until there was so little left it crumpled to the ground.

I'd never gutted a fresh one, normally harvesting the skins from roadkill or husks found out beyond the fields. Reaching into the wounds I dragged out vast handfuls of straw, trying to ignore the urge to vomit as it crawled across my skin. Pushing my hands into the head I carved out the inside and tipped the seeds into the soil, crushing them below my heel.

Once empty both skins fitted in a rucksack, compressed as

I tightened the straps. For a moment I thought about torching the insides left scattered around the clearing. Burning the straw and the seeds and the flesh, but I did not want to remain there anymore. Above me the sky of sticks sliced the moon into razors of light.

It was normal for a yarn fall at night to follow one during the day. I did not return to the house to check on Sarah. If she woke then my words of explanation would not be effective.

Instead I sheltered in the weaving shed and slid myself into the scarecrow skin. The inside was still damp, reeking of winter haystacks, dying rats and putrid fruit spoiling in the fields. A smear of flesh stuck to my lips and pushed against my tongue. I hooked it out and watched the beetles crawl away over the stone floor.

The yarn draping from the sky was thigh thick. Wide enough to bear my weight.

I knew the husks could keep the corrosive dyes at bay while we harvested and lowered the fibres into the fixing pits, but to protect me as I climbed? There was no certainty, and for my hands to start burning halfway up? Either the fall or the scalds would do for me.

I chose the thickest strand I could find. Even in the dark the vivid purple of hibiscus glowed. I reached up and wrenched the yarn. It held. I wrapped my legs around, and dragged myself up.

There had been something in the curl of the letters that looked familiar, a recognition that intensified when I placed the note beside Sarah's schoolbooks.

My daughter was up above the sky of sticks. Not my Sarah as she was now, asleep and unaware, but my Sarah in the future. Maybe the scarecrows would take her from my care in two hours, or two weeks or two years. I did not know for certain. The only thing I knew at that moment was I had to rescue this Sarah. I held the note tight, even as I clung to the yarn.

Though the fresh scarecrow skin kept the dyes away from mine, the fumes still seeped in through the mouth, stinging my nose and eyes. I tried to hold my breath. The hand over hand climb needed more air than I cared for and so I had to hope that the steam rising from under my hands was less corrosive in the air than to touch.

The climb was long and didn't get any easier. Above me the sky got closer. So near they were no longer sticks, or branches, but vast trunks, woven together. Each new growth wrapped around the last. The yarn draped down through the gaps. Hundreds of them like vines of colour, burning away the bark to the heart-wood below. The blood of the trees stuck to the second skin I wore and seared scars into the hands and arms. I ignored the scent of cooking meat and continued to pull myself up, dragging myself around the rough branches.

I glanced down through the sky of sticks to the ground below. I could just make out the fields. A patchwork of land that smeared at the edges.

I rolled onto my back then sat. Every metre of the sky of sticks was covered in bark huts, silver birch and oak plated together into walls and roofs. Some were barely big enough to fit a single person, others so vast they obscured the second sky above. From the larger huts cables of yarn evacuated through open doors, finding the spaces between to drape to the ground below. The smaller ones were quieter, doors bolted from the outside, most attached to the larger houses like tumours. Between everything moved the scarecrows, their single legs uneven and unbalanced on the rough trunks underfoot.

I waited, letting my breath still as much as I dare while I re-covered. While I decided where to start looking. The air itself stung my eyes. Everything floated through tears and sweat.

The scarecrows ignored me as they walked their rounds, fixed expressions unchanging, mouths always open. Even if they saw they seemed not to care that my legs did not narrow to a single point or that my chest moved.

I leant forward to stare back to where my home should be. I watched the nearest hall opened, thousands of strands of yarn pushing across the wooden floor. Moving slowly I walked up to the door and leant around the corner. Wherever Sarah was it was not in there.

Scarecrows stood around roof high wheels twisting wool, bringing fibres together into vast strands before it fed out of the door to fall like solid rain. There were no people, no-one taking breath, just the children of the rotting straw.

If Sarah was not in the spinning hall, she must be nearby. Near enough to slide the note between the fibres that passed under the scarecrows' fixed stares.

I took the first hut, opening the door with care. The room was tiny and reeked of rotten meat. The figure inside was not a scarecrow, not anything at all anymore but food for the thousands of insects that swarmed over mould-covered bones. I moved closer, trying to ignore the stench. At least these scents didn't scorch my mouth.

The girl slumped forward over a pile of wool, the fleece itself sodden and growing its own forest, the line between person and product of no consequence to the creatures that feasted there.

Sliding my skin-covered fingers through the hair, I turned the strands over, searching for something familiar. A perfume or knot to tell me this was my daughter. There was nothing.

I heard scarecrows passing the door and waited until they had gone. They did not speak to each other, so I did not worry about them asking me questions. Maybe they scented the rain-ruined straw. I hoped enough was smeared within my disguise to distract them from my blood and bone.

Once they passed I moved onto the next, empty of everything except a single pitcher of water, and the third, crammed so high with the dead that the flies blacked out any light.

The fourth hut was larger, stood on its own a slight distance from the spinning room. From inside I heard a scraping noise, the sound of fine combs meeting each other and pulling away. Standing outside I listened until I heard breath and opened the door.

She was older than the Sarah in the world below, and the look of fear she wore upon seeing me aged her more. I reached behind my head and unstitched the scarecrow's face.

"You got the note," she said. There was exhaustion in her voice, her fingers bleeding. In her hands she held dried teasels, the spikes thick with off-white fibres.

"We need to get out of here before the scarecrows notice," I said, unpacking my bag and holding out the second skin. "Put this on."

I looked at the tiny amounts of wool in the room, small bins full of carded fibres ready to be spun. I tried to imagine the amount needed for a single length. I pictured all the huts I would not find with stolen children. I pictured how big the sky was, and despite the need to rescue my daughter I wept for all those who would not be saved.

"I can't wear that, Mum," she said, shrinking back against the far wall.

"Then I cannot save you," I said. "I cannot get you away from this place and back to the land below."

She was at least ten years older than the Sarah I'd left sleeping below, and I had to bite my tongue to stop myself asking about what filled in time between the two daughters I now had.

She turned to face the wall and I fastened up the back, watching the skin knit itself together. Though she stared out of the face, the eyes were not hers, but those of the scarecrow I'd ambushed.

"We have to leave soon," she said, her voice sounding fearful even when muffled. "They will come soon for the wool. They're always coming for the wool."

I nodded, tying my own disguise back in place, hiding any fear I might hold myself. I reached out a hand and she took it with a fist far bigger than a heart. I opened the door and waited.

The yarns were still falling to the ground below. Finding the vivid purple strands was not hard, and I went first, wrapping myself around, clasping it as I would clasp Sarah when we were safe.

She followed and we slid back down to the ground, away from the sky of sticks. The scarecrows paid us no attention.

Returning was faster than the climb, the friction of the fibres burning against our covered limbs. I kept glancing up to check Sarah was still above me, and tried not to flinch every time I saw a raggedy man following, reminding myself it was my offspring, my flesh, no matter what disguise she wore.

Reaching the ground, we both tumbled away, toppling in the meadow grass until we came to rest, vertical and upright.

This was the time for reassuring words, the time to embrace her and tell her everything would be ok. That no-one would take her again. That not a single fibre of wool needed to pass through her hands. I spoke the words but none came. There was no sound. Not a single syllable no matter how loudly I tried to shout. Reaching around the back of my head I searched for the stitched seam to free myself from this dead skin.

I looked over at Sarah. She was pointing at my legs. I did not look down, but pressed my fattened fingers into my mouth. Felt the rotten straw within. Now, when there was nothing else to do, I lowered my gaze and stared. Sarah's legs were gone, replaced with a single wooden pole, stained and splintered.

I did not know where else to go. Sarah followed, as trapped as I was. She had no other destination, and kept pace as I dragged myself through the lanes, and over the cobbles.

The younger Sarah was playing across the other side of the yard.

"Time to go in now," my earlier self said, picking up the buckets. Above us the sunlight slanted through the rain and the wicker clouds.

"I like it out in the rain," the younger Sarah said, not looking up. Around her fingers she wove daisies and meadowsweet, her fingers stained with pressed petals.

Ruby Red and Snowflake Cold

THE SISTERS HAD NO HEART of their own. They asked the flowers for advice and the flowers took the sisters' eyes in payment, enwrapping each in skin thin petals.

"To make a heart," the flowers said, "consume the winter. Eat it like a banquet. Suspend days of snowfall in the air and let them drop against your tongue until your mouth is full of ice and pine needles."

"And then?" the first sister asked.

"What then?" the second sister asked.

"Then breathe," the flowers said, before they became too distracted, shuddering at all the sisters had seen with their now severed eyes.

The first born sister ate all the days, when spirals of clouds froze skin and metal alike. The second born sister ate all the nights, when the stars themselves became snowflakes to be crushed into drifts by the weight of cold on the wind.

And then the sisters breathed, and they breathed muscle and blood. They breathed valve and nerve. They breathed atrium and ventricle, and as ice formed around the pulsing heart the sisters opened their mouths.

The veins tethered to the inhalations of the first born sister, the arteries to those of the second born. Through a winter of no nights and no days the heart pumped all the colour from the sisters, turning them to ash, until, ruby red and snowflake cold, the heart was the only living thing left.

The Taste of Rot

I AM SO FOCUSED on putting Marylyn's affairs in order that I do not notice God arriving in the rotted corner where summer and winter meet.

My sister's apartment is street level and street facing. A single room with a single window looking out onto what the floods left behind. She is in every brushstroke, on canvas and wall plaster, though she has not been seen since the height of the deluge.

Softened by rust, my alarm wakes me early. I abandon sodden sheets to dress in clothes damp to the touch. The waters have forgotten the city. The city cannot forget the waters. I cannot forget Marylyn.

Every time I take a breath in that single room I ingest damp loosened pigment from her portraits. I know that I will not find her. Too many bodies are not recovered. I have no way to sort the silt softened flesh clogging the river into sibling and stranger. I am there to collect what remains. Box it up. Throw out the unwashed paintbrushes and half used tubes of acrylic. I cannot help but hope that she will put her key in the door. Let herself in.

The streets have flooded so often in the August heat it is hard to tell anymore where the three rivers end and the city begins. Every time the water recedes silt and sewerage stays, stuck in gutters and drains. A fresh tidemark up the side of sandbagged shops. Pavements are clogged with water damaged furniture, home to rats and mosquito larvae. Incubators of a different kind of rot.

The café on the corner has left the board across the doorway. Now laminated and split, it has done little to keep out the water. I step over and take out a handful of coins. All the time I walk between the tables, the owner watches me over smeared varifocal glasses. His gold braceleted and tattooed arms rest on the counter as he slowly turns the pages of a cheap newspaper, pages returning to pulp.

By the door is a cork noticeboard, swollen and distended. Photos of the missing held in place with plastic-coloured pins. I almost don't notice Marylyn's photo amongst all the others, then try to convince myself that I haven't.

All the drinks on the chalkboard have been erased, though their ghosts remain where the cloth can't quite shift them. Only one item is listed on the menu. Inundation Coffee. No price. I check my change. Place the money on the laminate worktop. The owner sorts through, picking up more than I think is fair. Each coin leaves a slight dent in the condensation.

The coffee has hints of mildew, like spores have been sprinkled into the hot milk as some kind of new seasoning. I try to ignore the aftertaste and sup it for the caffeine rather than the flavour.

"I want to show you something," the owner says, standing up. I look toward the cup. Drain the coffee in one mouthful. Follow him behind the counter.

"It's getting worse. Started last week, and is just getting worse."

The mould is patchy, spreading above the skirting like a map of some imaginary atoll. I reach out and touch the infestation, watching the crust disappear into my skin. Faint stains remain on the paint.

"Clean them away," I say. "Bleach and water."

"I've done that," the owner says, kneeling beside me on the tiles. "They keep coming back and spreading."

"Probably will do until the city dries out."

"If the year carries on like this, then the city will never dry out. Come here," he says, and holds onto my sleeve so I have no choice but to follow.

The kitchen is at the back of the café. The buckled door opening onto a narrow alley is drawn closed, air heavy with the scent of rotten food.

The owner opens two cupboards, then three more. Lastly he swings open the rusted door to the fridge. Everything is furred with mould, green and off-white.

"As soon as the delivery van pulls away, all my supplies start to rot. If I don't sell everything with the morning rush it's inedible. Has to go in the bin." He shuts the fridge door. "And there is no morning rush anymore."

I hold my hands up. Shake my head.

"I don't know what you want me to do."

"I don't want you to do anything. I just needed to tell someone."

The two children have built a counter from driftwood and sit on the pavement, their clothes stained by the gifts the receding waters leave. The girl has some kind of infection in her tear ducts, cheeks swollen and bulbous from the pressure. The boy's mouth is covered in sores. Every so often his tongue flicks out to lick away a flake of skin, jaw twisting as he chews. Only the girl speaks.

"Fragment of the holy garments," she says.

On the counter are squares of curtains, duvets and coverlets. Each is torn and stained, host to several types of fungal infestations. I pick one up. Several beetles scatter for the dark.

"Not today," I say, restacking the pile.

The girl makes a sound that I think at first is her replying, then I see she is tearing more fabric into squares. Her hands are red raw and covered in tiny fissures.

"You do not want to receive communion? That is so sad to hear."

She is ripping strips from the boy's shirt. Short lengths of cotton snag in the cracks of her skin. She stares at me until I blink "Such a shame."

Inside the library I taste mildew in the air. The sixth flavour. It taints everything. Books are stacked in piles along the floor. Pages warp as if repelled by the touch of paper. I walk between the shelves looking for the librarian. She sits on the floor, surrounded by piles of the worst affected. As I watch she takes a book and opens the cover. The letters slide off the paper, diluted ink staining her skin.

"Today?" I say, holding my sister's library card in my hand. The volumes I need are in the attic, far from the devastation. I stare at the undulating stain running around the once pristine wooden shelves.

"Not today," she says, pulling a length of velvet from her pocket and wiping her hands clean. I recognise the pattern from the children's stall.

"You can't save them you know," I say.

She puts aside the rotten book in her hands. The cover looks familiar but I have no chance to read the title.

"I'm not trying to save them. I'm trying to find something."

She picks up the next one and runs her hand across the spotted paper, fake leather binding split and curled upon itself. Holding my fingers by the tips she draws a shape with the derelict ink on my palm and pushes it toward my face.

"Taste it," she says.

"I think I need to go," I reply, and look toward the door. Nearby I hear two of the three rivers meld and dance together. I wonder how many books pulp to the rocks under the surface of the confluence.

"Taste it," she says again, and swipes a little of the black stain across my lips.

Like some rare cheese it does not taste as it smells, the flavour raw and delicate. I run my tongue across my teeth and let the tang spread through my mouth before licking clean the palm of my hand.

The flavour of ink and mildew lingers, and I do not want it to end.

In Marylyn's apartment spores create galaxies that pause in the air. When I walk through they settle on my skin, dressing me in a potential to life that lives in death.

Condensation collects in the corners of the window, tiny echoes of the city floods.

I open cupboards to make myself something to eat. The bread is spotted. I cut away the infection. Crumbs spray across the worktop as I slice and whittle. When I finish there is barely anything left. Opening the fridge I take out the cheese. Untouched, it has absorbed the taint from something else nearby and reeks of rot. Though I do not eat any, my gut churns. The bacteria inside me resents the potential invasion, or wants to invite it in.

I walk beside the river, placing each step with care upon the cobbles. Gnawed faces gaze up through the silt-heavy water. No-one has recovered them. The cemeteries are still too sodden to take the dead. Better to leave them and feed the pike. Bones scrape free when the dredgers pass through. No-one cares. I pause and stare at the water. I know that I will not see Marylyn. Will not recognise her if I do.

Something unseen swims through. Unsettles the corpses. Gases bubble up. Pop against the surface. Fill the air with the scent of dying. I hardly notice. The scent of dying is everywhere.

The priest takes my hand as I walk past, his surplice stained as if a pen had snagged on some rough vellum and spotted him with cochineal.

"Come into the temple, my child," he says, and I do not pull away.

The stairs inside are unlit. In the dark I imagine I can see thick brackets of fungus latched to the walls. He leads me up and up and up, finding the next step with the toes of our boots.

The temple is an old apartment, windows blanked with torn newspapers, holy symbols drawn across the articles in something that may be blood or may be shit.

"Come into the chancel," he says, and opens the door to an old bathroom, toilet and bath blocked to hold stagnant water. Dead larvae swirl on the surface amongst thick detergent foam and I realise that the water has been carried up, bucket by bucket, from the last floods. Somewhere behind me a supplicant chants, each phrase heavy with phlegm and infection. The priest lights a candle. Shadows weep across the walls. The flame dances and the darkness does not. The shadows are thick layers of black mould, weeping and toxic. Sheets of spores cultured as a devotion.

"You are in the presence of our Lord. Take his communion."

I turn around. The priest has stripped, each fold of flesh blackened with the same mould darkening the walls. He drags his finger down the wallpaper and pushes his hand in between my lips. I bite through his finger clean to the knuckle, dragging teeth along the bone. His blood mixes on my tongue with the bitterness of the mould. I push him backward into the undisturbed reliquary.

There is no clean water in the city to wash the taste of the priest's veins from my mouth. Even that from the tap is heavy with flakes of sewerage. Filters clog before I have a cupful, and I clean it as best I can under dirty water before trying again. I swill my mouth. The mixture of iron and fungus remain. The city taints everything.

When I return to the library the doors are wedged shut, and it takes effort to force my way in, scraping the backs of my hands on warped timber. I hear someone moving around deep inside the building. There is a stillness I do not want to disturb. I stay silent and step over the shelves dragged across the atrium. They slow my entrance, but do not prevent it.

I see the Librarian's creation before I see her. It rises toward the ceiling dome, a cluster of globular filaments erupting from a single stem, top heavy and vast. The whole made out of page after page after page. Cemented together with river water, condensation or spit.

"I found it. I found what I was looking for."

She kneels, clothes torn against the frayed hardbacks covering the floor. Her skin underneath the same. I take the page she holds. A mycology illustration. The fruiting bodies of some wood-consuming mould magnified many times.

"I found the gaze of God. Come worship with me." She tries to grab my hand. I stare at her face. Nothing is visible on the surface, but the skin deforms and undulates as if something presses out. Narrowing to try and slide through her pores. Above our heads the sculpture flexes on its base and for a moment I expect it to kill us both.

Crowds line the river bank holding hands. I do not recognise anyone apart from the boy and girl I saw selling brand new religious relics. They stand at the head of the line, fingers intertwined, though their skin is not visible. Something else clasps them together.

They hum as if their voices will raise the white skinned dead from the water. Then I realise, they are not praying for. They are praying to. Intoning. Waiting for God to manifest. They notice me. Know that I am not yet one of them, split their holds and disperse after me through the streets like a cloud.

I make it home before they cut me off and barricade the door against the crowd. They stop outside. A whole city silent and poised, but only for a moment. The frail glass windows and paper thin doors do not last long.

Marylyn's apartment soon fills with people. They find a chair from somewhere and press me into it. Bandages sodden with river water are used to tie me in place. Pin my head back, mouth open. Jaw held. I try to struggle free. There is nowhere to go. The room is so full of people. So many silent people. Someone forces their fingers into my mouth. Presses down my tongue.

I feel every crack in the crumbling rubber hose as it is forced down my throat. It tastes of sewerage and silt. They brace me for the next stage. I feel someone's knee on my lap as they struggle to hold my head still. Something is poured down the hose. I gag.

The spores settle in my lungs, finding purchase in the damp and phlegm. Corrupting each breath.

They have been waiting. Waiting for a very long time. They needed my breath. Needed my words. Needed my voice. Deep inside the folds, the heat and moisture culture them. Nurture them. Help the spores find expression. My speech is no longer mine. Each cycle of breath helps them expand. Increases the volume of my lungs. Rots down my liver and kidneys to make way for their growth. Turns each heave for air holy. A sacrament. A ritual. The expansion of their kingdom. God lives in the city now. God lives in us all. We are all part of God. The black rot that coats each wall and corpse. The crowd is the body of God.

I? I am the Metatron. My voice grates and shatters. Maybe Marylyn can hear me, wherever she is. My voice, the words of God, go everywhere. I have no way to hear any reply. With each syllable the air around me erupts with spores. The crowd of the holy do not speak. They pass cotton and rusted needle between them. One by one they start to stitch their mouths shut. They have no need of their voices anymore. I will bring the word of God to all unbelievers and they will all be transformed.

Flow to the Sea

MAJA STEPPED OVER the line of salt around the Leviathan's corpse. She had just finished laying the circle to keep out Trojans. Her mother had always insisted on establishing a security perimeter before beginning an installation and Maja had kept up the practice. Crystals glittered her hands. She wiped them clean into the sea breeze.

The sperm whale was three days dead and already several holes had opened up around the torso, exposing blubber and ribs beneath. Maja set her programming kit down by the dorsal fin and opened the bag, releasing a hit of wet fur that lingered in the air.

Several areas of skin bulged with the gas build up inside. Ignored, they could corrupt the programming, lead to data loss and ultimately system failure. From her thigh pocket she took out a hollow steel pole, the tip scalpel sharp. Using all her weight she forced the point through the flesh, moving away as the gasses vented away from the bloating.

From her programming kit she took out the fox corpse and stroked its fur. Centring the road-kill on a rubber mat to protect it from the sand, she arranged the limbs in the correct configuration. The snails undulated the pelt giving the impression of breath. A second bag contained rolled algae. She wedged the last strip into the fox's mouth and waited.

The snails sensed the food, opening the fox's jaws, spiralled shells scraping against yellowed teeth. There was nothing for Maja to do but wait.

For the next few hours the snails were concerned with nothing but consumption, replacing food with thick mucus trails, a fine dust of copper visible in the slime. Maja ran a finger along the edge of the circuitry, held it up in the air and watched metal particles glisten in the early evening light. There was beauty here, even amongst so much death.

The snails knew their job. They had been trained to seek out the correct nodes in the rotting meat. Make the necessary connections. It took time. At different moments the chemical composition of their mucus changed, attracting microbes and insects to reroute their networks. She tasted the changes on the air. Subtle shifts in the combination that hinted at thyme, or old brake blocks, mingled with the brackish stench of nearby rock-pools.

After a two day vigil, barely sleeping, Maja saw the fox's fur flash bright blue for a moment before settling back down to a dirty russet colour. She knelt in the sand, peering into the dead creature's eyes, an imprint of the whale's corpse just visible in the milky white pupil. The connections were in place, the network live, the server up and running.

Finishing her cup of lukewarm tea, she walked across to the whale and placed an ear against the flank. The movement was slight, but there. A twitch of electricity along the skeleton as marrow caramelised into high density memory storage.

Satisfied the installation process was underway she picked up her phone and dialled the client.

The cars pulled up at the limit of the dunes, not risking the shifting beach beyond. Maja looked up from the fox then back down. Checked the connections were holding, the right parasites gathering along the snail's connections to carry the data, then strode across the sand to meet Mr. Hither.

"Thank you for coming out to see me personally," she said. "I know you're very busy with the wider project at the moment."

He shook her hand and shoved his fingers back into his jacket pocket as if the salt in the air would scar him. He smelt of cheap aftershave and printer toner. She looked at his safety boots, the leather polished to mirrors.

"Is the server online?"

"The programme is installing as we speak. It will be another few hours before you can run the cables down to start hosting data. The location is fairly exposed. I would recommend applying a skin coating to preserve the integrity of the storage. A non-invasive surface material won't disturb the internal processes."

On the horizon she saw more suited men, some observing her through blank-lensed binoculars. They always travelled in packs, like cards. She heard the saying in her mother's voice.

"They can come closer," she said, gesturing to the observers. "I know the server is a bit ripe, but they would only be here for moments before boredom and technical language scared them away."

Mr. Hither sighed and ran a hand through his over-perfect hair.

"They have not come to see your handiwork. They have come to recruit you."

She lifted the fox's head to check the installation process. Programming was installed over 56% of the whale's skeleton. Already storage locations were starting to become active.

"Colleagues of yours?"

"Of a sort," he said. "Please, Miss Benfield. This way."

Though they wore the same dark suits as Mr. Hither, the cluster of men were vastly different from her client. They were dressed in sweat and scowls. The reek of damp rooms and questions clung to them like lichen.

"We hear that you are a very gifted programmer, Miss Benfield."

They were interchangeable, but the one who spoke was older, his hands covered in fine white scars.

"Software Engineer is my job title." she said, leaving a gap for him to respond. He stayed silent. "Though the boundaries between the different roles are more fluid these days, Mr.?"

"Gunnerside. Mr. Gunnerside. You specialise in bio-servers?"

"My job is to establish the circuitry and install the bio-software which allows animal corpses to be used for the storage of data, yes."

She glanced toward the sea. Without her noticing, the men in suits had circled around to enclose her. Her hand went inside the pouch on her thigh and grasped the drainage bar.

"We have a job for you. A repair job," Gunnerside said.

"A job offer? That's very generous, but I'm fully booked for the next few months. Once I've finished here I have several projects lined up."

"It wasn't an offer."

They gave her time to check the installation process, ensure everything was progressing well enough that she could detach the fox corpse.

Opening the door, they waited for her to climb in and then two of the unnamed suits sat either side of her, Gunnerside sliding into the front passenger seat beside the driver.

"What's that smell?" said the suit to her left. Maja opened her bag. The fox's lifeless head flopped backwards.

"That will have to go in the boot," Gunnerside said, pointing to the half-rotten creature. Two maggots fell from its ear. She scooped them up and pressed them down its throat.

"Only if you want to show me your insurance policy to cover the re-acquisition and programming of a new monitoring console."

Several looks went around the car that did not involve her.

"Just keep your bag sealed, and don't let any rot fall onto the upholstery."

"Any rot from this is worth far more than your upholstery."

This wasn't her first security contract and she had learnt that hidden government installations were either in the middle of the moors or the middle of the woods. This one did not disappoint. They drove for three hours, most of the trip surrounded by a vast deciduous forest. Maja pictured the different connections. Mycelium spread throughout the thick rich soil. Trees gifting chemical signals to each other through barely touching roots. Vast untapped computing, but they were living systems and forbidden. She sat back and waited for the inevitable barbed-wire and guard posts to appear.

Driving through the gate, a concrete slab of building appeared with no visible entrance. The car paused, engine running while Gunnerside spoke in a language she did not recognise and the wall faded with a gelatinous dissolve. A ramp disappeared into the depths underneath the block of architecture.

The room reeked of oil-heavy recycled air. Light came from bioluminescent algae behind a thin strip of stained glass running around the walls.

"Please, take a seat," Gunnerside said, pointing to the head of a horseshoe table.

"Do I have a choice?"

"You can stay standing," he said, pulling out the chair.

The wall shimmered and resolved into viscous pixels, shimmered again showing a rotting carcass surrounded by a swirl of waterborne dust.

"A crypto-server?"

The man nodded.

"A bathyal organic crypto knowledge management server, to give it the full correct title."

"What programme does it use?"

"Osteopelta."

"Mirabilis?"

"Ceticola."

Reaching under the table, he placed a large box on the table. Maja lifted off the lid, the brackish stench cloying in the small room. Fifteen sea snails clung to the Perspex side, cone-shaped and unmoving.

"I don't know this OS. I know nothing about the software architecture, and I've never worked with this programme. I can't help you."

"Your mother built it."

"My mother has been missing for five years."

"The data storage is deteriorating. We need it stabilised."

She held her head in her hands.

"What data storage system are you using?"

The man pressed his fingers together and the screen zoomed in.

"Osedax?" Maja said.

Using osedax to manage bone data storage was her mother's signature development. She remembered the bone worms in her laboratory aquaria, their root structures spreading through the host material. Each sector of data stored as a male hidden within the female's harem.

"I'm not my mother," she said, looking toward what she could see of the steel door beyond two more suited men blocking the way.

"Well, you're not a criminal for a start, so you have that in your favour. The data has started to deteriorate and we need an update installing to halt the decay."

"Deteriorate in what way?"

"There is evidence of the information moving into a bacterial mat filing system and we do not have anything in place to recover it. We suspect it's either built in obsolescence or a time bomb hack."

"I don't know this system," she repeated.

"No-one does. It's a prototype."

"Then get someone else to repair it for you."

"You might not be your mother, but she did train you. She was very reluctant to do that for anyone else."

"And if I don't agree?"

There was a pause. He pressed his fingers together once more. The screen changed showing a charge sheet, her name at the top, underneath written in perfect copperplate an extensive description of biohacking a live human into a living terminal.

"This never happened," she said, picking up the tank of sea snails, and lifting it into the air until bleached light shone through.

"It has happened somewhere, but it might take months to establish your innocence. Years."

"You're blackmailing me?"

"Persuading, and please put down the operating system. They are valuable enough that depriving you of your life is cheap by comparison."

"I'll need a new monitoring console," she said, opening her bag to stroke the fox fur. "Reynard won't work at such depths. A mammal. Natural death."

"Natural death?"

"For some reason an anthropogenic death corrupts the ability to hold data. Also there is a moral aspect."

Gunnerside laughed.

"We're far beyond moral aspects here. Anything else?"

"A mammal. The architecture of other classes is not compatible. Fresh. Within the last twenty four hours. It can be preserved to bring it to me from the death site. Then I will need time to install the programme."

"That will be possible. We'll keep you in accommodation here."

"Keep. Like a pet? Or a prisoner?"

"Like a recruit. Anything else?"

"Where is the server?" she said, taking the seat once more.

"Not here," the man said, laughing at his own joke.

Maja sighed and pulled the tank of snails toward her once more.

Sea spray chapped Maja's skin as she stood at the prow of the research boat. The ocean was rough enough that her stomach did not want to settle, the company in the cabin poor enough that she did not want to go and lie down. The bathypelagic suit under her clothes was already bonding with the keratin in her skin, a process with the sensation of hot wax. She scratched at her arms, but it did nothing to ease the discomfort.

"We'll soon be at the storage site. Are you ready?" Gunnerside lifted her arm and drew back her sleeve, staring at the slowly spreading scaling.

She snatched away from him.

"I'm doing a job for you, not your property."

A smile flickered across his face.

"Make sure you're familiar with the task at hand."

"I'm as familiar as I can be for someone who has never even seen this operating system actually working."

"We won't be able to intervene in any way."

She pulled her sleeve back down.

"You're actually starting to sell this to me."

The dive-master pressed a clump of macro-algae into her hand.

"Am I supposed to smoke it?"

"Shove it into your cheeks. We've tweaked the structure to store and release oxygen over a protracted period. There might be some discomfort as the strands bond with the skin inside your mouth, but it's preferable to the alternative systems."

"The alternative systems?"

He took a diving knife from a sheaf on his ankle.

"The alternative system is that we cut in gills and use an accelerated process of DNA damage to alter your oxygen processing system. This at least is temporary."

She pressed the mass of foliage between her gums and cheek-skin, wincing as strands forced their way into saliva glands.

The boat shrugged the waves above the dive site. Maja stood in the middle of the deck and went through the safety checks. The dive-master helped slide the bag containing the dead seal onto her back.

"Don't think that you can just swim away," Gunnerside said. "The macro-algae won't keep you alive forever."

"That's a reassuring thought," she said, hooking her legs over the railing. "I'll bear that in mind."

The water enclosed her, sweeping over her head. She let herself sink. Watched the ship disappear first, the light go next. Cold seeped through the scales' second skin. Her vision split then settled as the small implants of bioluminescence began to illuminate her descent.

There was no way to communicate with her controllers above and she was grateful for the silence. The chance to concentrate and ready herself for the coming task.

Descent was fast, the weight of her bathypelagic suit dropping her through the mesopelagic to the data storage zone below.

There were predators in the water, but they ignored her, the armoured skin she wore masking any scent as she descended. Waves of plankton and fish swarms brushed against her as if she herself was a mammal fall.

The macro-algae tasted bitter against her tongue, and pressed up against the roof of her mouth as it filtered oxygen down her throat.

The whale was vast, a humpback turned belly up by the descent through the water. Most of the skin had been gnawed away by scavengers, leaving the inside exposed. She kicked over to the corpse and peered inside.

The architecture was beautiful, each osedax sector established to be locked away from the next, passing through a series of cryptographed bacterial patches that allowed a unique code to be generated far beyond any encryption Maja had ever seen before. She recognised her mother's handiwork. The delicacy in the location of the data clusters, the specific complexity of the data gateways at the juncture of the bones. Around her, marine snow fell, coating her in the decaying white of the dead.

The cause of the data loss was obvious. Near the head of the server a vast bacterial mat had already started to develop, leaching data from the main clusters. All organic servers had a shelf life. Another thing her mother had taught her.

"Always transfer out valuable data before you think you need to, Maja. Don't get caught out."

But this was not natural. It was too early, and the backup systems should have kicked in already.

She laid the seal on a nearby rock and opened its eyes. Already scavengers were latching onto its exposed cold skin. Until she connected to the system there was no way of establishing what the cause of the deterioration was. She felt for the snails under the skin and pressed them forward towards the snout, then laid trails across to the whale.

It took three hours for the connection to go live, then three more for the monitoring device to decode the first level of cryptography. The seal skin flashed blue then settled back. She tilted the head and gazed into the dead eyes, searching for the fault.

There was no fault. There was no error. There was intent and sabotage built into the system. A cluster of osedax set to decay at a faster rate and release enzymes to accelerate the data loss. She rerouted one of the snails to connect directly to the vast bacterial mat. Nothing. The mass of data was so scrambled the bacteria had broken down the data into an unreadable mess. The sectors were not just disassociated but fractured and split.

She scraped away at the bacterial mat. The data leached into the mass of cells was unrecoverable, as her mother always intended it to be. Underneath, thick silt held the ulna and radius together. She dug away until the wrist joint was exposed. A little further away Maja found a spread of finger bones part obscured by wafting fronds of macro algae. She imagined her mother ripping the life saving plant from her throat, gasping as the water overwhelmed her lungs and she killed the knowledge she held.

Maja disconnected from the bacterial mat and turned her attention back to the server, knowing what she was going to find. The control cluster was still intact. A small knot of 17 osedax, her mother's favourite prime number, each containing a doomsday programme to decay other sectors.

There was no way to save the data. She looked at the cluster as the water swayed the bone worms on their anchor points. The evidence of her mother's intent.

⁓⁓⁓⁓⁓

The snail laid the circuitry along the top of Maja's mouth and down her throat. She felt the copper draw electricity from her, route down along the mucus. The snail reached her chest and wore through her skin to her ribcage. She screamed, but the algae took her voice.

Lifting the scales around her torso free of her skin, she exposed her ribs with a single cut of her diving knife. She had only moments until the suit spread into place once more. Holding the bone worms in one hand she opened the wound, forced them in and waited.

They spread their roots across her bone, acid breaking down the protein. The data started to transfer into her. Shifting across in a series of broken images. Her mother had encoded everything. The threats. The blackmail. The torture. The designs and the deceit. How to return to the site when the scavengers, both human and not, had moved on. How to recover the data.

There was no need for a server now. For a monitoring device. Maja was the computer. Maja was the program. Maja was the data and the system. Maja was the memory her mother was unable to become and Maja had plenty of time to wait beneath the sea until they forgot. And when they forgot? Maja would reboot and remind them all.

Mask

THEY FITTED THE DEATH-MASK over Farmer Campbell's still breathing face. Loose shards of bark scraped his cheeks as the carved bracket fungus was tied to his head. Pinning him down, the villagers forced his arms into the mould-stained donkey jacket. Fastened the buttons over the tattered trousers. Down his collar they rammed a hazel rod, thick as a man's arm. Another along the seams of the sleeves. Then, using bailing twine, they raised him into the air, the foot of the post deep in the plough furrows.

He had scared his wife. Scared his children. Left marks on them the colour of December skies. Now he could scare crows, but they did not frighten like children. The seed was deep in the ground, or rotting in the storms. The birds were hungry. Farmer Campbell's eyes were very easy to reach through the gaps in the mask. His flesh through rips in the jacket. This winter the crows would not starve.

Split Chain Stitch

To cast on make sure you have a slip knot on the left hand needle. Place the point of the right hand needle into the slip knot and make a knit stitch. Whatever you do, do not slip it off the left.

Rachael found small towns had a gravity to them like some dense star lay hidden under the marketplace cobbles. Held people in place. Held time in place. She passed through like a comet. There was a skill to prizing herself away from the weight of these little communities. For now though she needed to collapse into the centre and let it consume her. Burn everything else away. She opened the café door, waiting for her eyes to adjust.

Six women sat around on comfy chairs, each headrest protected by a fine lace antimacassar. The only light came from old lamps balanced on rustic wooden shelves, a small constellation of spotlights above the café's kitchen and single mobile phone. Under the low hum of conversation the sound of needles sounded like claws clattering on tiles.

They all looked up, hands still dancing.

"Can we help you?"

The café air reeked of stewed tea and furniture polish. Rachael looked for the woman who had asked the question. She sat close to the door, lap obscured with a half-finished cable knit jumper in thick peacock coloured wool.

"I'm here for the Knit and Natter group," Rachael said, brandishing her sewing bag like a membership card.

"Knit and Natter? Plenty of both here. Apart from Sally. Always on that phone of hers."

Sally looked up from the screen and scowled, dropping her glasses back around her neck on their purple cord.

"I'm trying to find that pattern I mentioned, but the internet keeps fading in and out."

"Get it for next week," one of the other knitters said, reaching behind her for a cup of tea.

"I wanted to start tonight. Otherwise I've got nothing else to work on. I'll go outside and pick up a signal there."

Rachael watched her stand up and stride across the room.

"Sorry, can I just get past," she said.

"Sorry," Rachael echoed, moving over to let her through, shivering in the draught from the open door.

"Don't stand there letting the cold in. Some of us have arthritis. Come and get yourself a cup of tea. Sit down. I'm Joan, this is Liz, and this is Mags. Over there is Jan. Charlotte is in the corner. By the radiator. You've already met Sally."

"I'm Rachael," she said taking a seat next to Joan.

"Hello, Rachael. Now show us what you're working on."

Opening her bag, she took out her needles and the ball of wool.

"I'm not really working on anything, but I want to make something with stars on," she said, putting them down on the chair arm.

Joan smiled.

"Let's start at the beginning then."

By the end of the night Rachael knew how to cast on, cast off, how everyone drank their tea, which ring on the cooker took ages to light, whose husband had been seen with the wrong person, whose son had been arrested for fighting, and the exact place in the near deserted café to get a good Wi-Fi signal. At home she opened the door and shut out the town again.

When attaching the sleeve, match the notches as you pin it in place. When starting the round ensure the stitches of the under-arm are put on hold.

Joan was making a sweater for her son, though he never really appreciated them. Jan crocheted toys for the local charity shop. Rabbits and mice. That sort of thing. Liz knitted scarves for anyone who sat still long enough. Charlotte owned the café and knitted jumpers for penguins. She'd been making them for years to send out to the Falkland Islands. Mags mainly did cross-stitch, but they let her come along anyway. Sally was always starting the next thing. The next project. The next idea. None of them lasted until the following meeting. And Rachael?

"I just want to knit a scarf. Maybe a hat?"

"With stars?"

"With stars," she said.

Joan nodded, and smiled, her hands never stopping. Needles always clacking.

"Good place to start, a scarf. We all started with scarves didn't we?"

No-one looked up from their projects, but they all nodded. Sally clicked her phone off.

"I think I saw yours in the museum, Joan."

The older woman smiled and put her jumper to one side, taking Rachael's work to check the tension of her stitches.

"Sally likes to make fun of old people. Sally likes a lot of things that aren't normally polite in civilised society, but we overlook that. Probably better to stick to crafts though. Might prove useful one day that," she said, handing the five completed rows back to Rachael. "You're almost there. Might be an idea to use smaller needles until you get a bit more practiced. Don't you think Mags?"

Mags leant across, peered through her glasses and nodded her head.

"If you want the scarf to keep winter out, needs to look a lot less like a dog's chewed it."

"Did you hear about Michael? Jenny Morgan's son? The one caught shoplifting?" Charlotte said.

Mags shook her head and leant back in her chair, staring at the ceiling.

"More than one place too. A few burglaries as well."

Joan nodded, though she didn't lift her gaze from the ball of yarn down the side of the chair.

"More than a few. Well, they gave him bail."

"And he disappeared?" Rachael made it a question even though she already knew the answer. "I read it on the sandwich board outside the newsagents."

"Good riddance," said Liz. Holding her latest scarf up to the light, she tugged the edges to check the tension. "Town could do without him."

"That's not very Christian, Elizabeth."

"He broke into our Arthur's shed and stole his tools. My Christian charity only goes so far."

Rachael stared down at her knitting and concentrated on her stitches.

"So you've never knitted before, Rachael?" Charlotte said

Rachael shook her head. Tried not to lose count.

"What brings you to a knitting group if you can't knit?" Charlotte continued.

"Let the girl alone," Jan said.

"I'm just curious. She doesn't mind, do you Rachael?"

Rachael looked around the room. Everyone was waiting for her to answer.

"When I move to a new place I like to get a handle on the local gossip." She'd known the question was coming and had rehearsed the answer. Even with her preparation it still felt stilted in the dryness of her mouth.

"And where better than a gathering of old fogeys, who sit

around knitting jumpers for the underprivileged," Jan said.

"Helps me get my bearings," Rachael said, Jan nodding at her answer.

Some of the basic stitches you should master are;
> Knit into the back of the stitch
> The Purl stitch
> To purl into the back of the stitch
> The garter stitch
> Stocking stitch
> Reverse stitch
> Ribbing

Locking the door, Rachael dropped her knitting bag in the corner. Her notebook was still open on the dining table. She flicked on the overhead lamp and started writing.

"Most recent disappearance. Personal connection? Anger from Liz..."

She signed the bottom of the page, writing the date. Out of the window the clouds blew away, leaving stars spattered across the sky.

Make sure you have a set of stitch markers to hand. They make life so much easier.

The next few weeks went by in a bit of a blur. Her days consisted of nothing beyond staring out of the window or staring into the computer screen. Every Wednesday she took the short walk into town with her latest project, sat on the comfy chair in the corner and found her way around the latest pattern while listening to the other women talking.

In no time at all Rachael's scarf was wearable, and soon after she completed the set with matching hat, gloves, and fingerless gloves. She wore all of them, often. As time went on she sometimes met the other women for coffee during the day. Listened to them talk about their families and neighbours. Those who went missing. The needles moved in her hands without any effort. She held people's gaze and still looped the wool around itself. This did not go unnoticed. Now her constellations were flecks of colour in balls of wool.

"You've been coming on well, Rachael," Jan said, holding up the back of the jumper Rachael was working on.

"Thank you," she answered, taking the piece back and settling into her chair. "Where's Sally tonight?"

"That's sort of what we wanted to talk about," Liz said. "You know that we have another knitting group. A little more formal."

Rachael nodded.

"The Yarnbombardiers. How could I miss your work? It's all over town."

It was true. Half the town centre was wrapped in wool. Cartoon characters and scenes from local life. Local personalities.

"Your knitting has come on so much. We wanted to invite you for a while, but there are only so many places. We had to wait for Sally to go."

"To make up her mind," Jan said.

"To make up her mind," Liz repeated, correcting herself. "Very indecisive. We're not. We needed to ensure you were ready to take her place."

Rachael smiled at every woman in the room.

"I'm ready," she said.

To start the balaclava cast on 130 stitches using a circular needle and join up to work in the round.

"The Yarnbombardiers work in a completely different location than the Knit and Natter group. An isolated hut on property belonging to Margaret Travis. The building is approximately one mile from the road with no easy public access. The phone signal is nonexistent. Any communication will be before and after sessions."

Rachael closed the notebook and shivered. She walked to the car and sat staring out of the window at the newspaper posters in the shop opposite. Sally's husband was quoted as saying the children were missing their mother. Rachael closed her eyes. Started the engine.

"You found the place OK then?"

Rachael nodded. Mags wore old stained tweeds, wellington boots, and a housecoat, pockets stuffed with lengths of wool and unfinished embroidery.

"Bit of a walk, but makes sure we have privacy. Top secret this work."

Rachael tapped her foot to shift adrenaline rippling under her skin.

"Top secret?"

"We can't have people seeing the designs before they're installed. Ruins the surprise," Mags said smiling. "You like your stars. You'll love it out here."

They walked in silence through the farmyard, out past the barns and a small wood. In the distance the hut stood by itself, electric light leaking from each window to rob Rachael of her night vision.

Mags kicked her boots against the wooden plank wall and opened the door. Inside, the women sat in a circle, each with the side of a large panel of wool. Loops of yarn ran around the wall, tied into angled patterns, held in place by long carpenter nails. Taut as guitar strings.

"Welcome to the Yarnbombardiers," Jan said, "You're just in time to make the tea."

Rachael made the tea, and she got the biscuits, and picked up the short lengths of wool, and helped Joan to the small outside toilet. Most of all she listened. Listened to the gossip.

Cast on 25 stitches onto the first needle, then distribute those stitches onto three needles.

By the third week Mags no longer met Rachael at the road and she could walk through the farm by herself. Knowing that the Yarnbombardiers might time how long it took her, she ran for a stretch, giving herself time to examine the small stand of trees.

The covert was only ten silver birch, branches intertwined above her head. She ran a hand over the trunks. Small lengths of wool were caught in the bark. Kneeling, she sorted through the mass of leaves around her feet. The diamonds were knitted from different colours. Some red and some purple. She pocketed two to get them tested for any residues and carried on walking the rest of the way to the hut.

At significant points in the creation use more pins than you expect.

"We'll start you on flowers this week," Charlotte said, passing Rachael several balls of wool and two needles. "So much like the stars you love."

"You know that there's a small astronomy club in town. Did you not think about joining them?" Liz said, sipping her tea, pouring a spill from the saucer into the cup.

Rachael dropped a stitch and swore.

"Can you help me with this?" she said, holding the knitting to Joan.

"Surely you can sort that out?"

"Hands a bit cold tonight."

"Rubbish excuse, but give it here."

The best way to fix a dropped stitch is to use a crochet hook.

Sat in her car Rachael turned on the inside light and rubbed her eyes. She scribbled down everything she remembered before the memory faded with fatigue from tracking stitches. No-one had given much away. They were too careful, even now she was taken into their confidence, but she could track friendships. Rivalries. Add to the cascade of inter-relationships, leaving space to write in spouses and siblings. Children and cousins. Time consuming. Necessary. She signed the last page, dating her evidence and dropped it into the door pocket.

Begin by turning the jumper inside out. If the pulled thread has caused the fabric to bunch, as carefully as possible stretch it back into the original form.

"Not something we can do anything about," Mags said, tapping cigarette ash into a small foil ashtray "It's my hut. I'll do what I like," she said to the disapproving looks of the other women.

"What about this spate of windows getting smashed? Cars.

Shops," Charlotte said, standing to stretch out her back.

"Do we have a name?" Jan paused to look up, then carried on knitting a cartoon mouse dressed as a cricketer while waiting for an answer.

"We have a suspicion."

"Need more than a suspicion," Jan said, standing up and walking across to the door. She dropped the lock. Metal against metal too loud in the small hut. "For example if I only had suspicions about Rachael I couldn't do anything. Finding the notes she's been keeping on us? That's not just suspicion anymore. That's evidence."

The two knitting needles went through Rachael's upper arms, points far sharper than she expected. She started to fall forward across the room and Jan guided her to topple onto the large panel of knitting still lying in the centre of the room.

To make this item you can use three different stitches. Either garter stitch, moss stitch, or twisted rib stitch.

Rachael woke. She was outside but not cold. Her arms were strapped to her sides, held in place by the woollen strips wrapped around her torso. Needles pinned through the palms of her hands. She opened her eyes. Saw other figures around her. At least three. Each one bound to a tree and cocooned in wool. Faces obscured by multicoloured balaclavas. Their heads all tipped forward. Flies crawled between the tightly knitted rows.

Rachael tried to shift her weight. Every other stitch of the blanket enveloping her passed through her skin. The movement re-opened a hundred raw wounds, fine fibres of wool dragged away from scabbed skin.

"It's the lanolin. Wool fat. Delays the healing. Helps the wool slide through the wounds as you move. Very delicate work."

Jan walked into Rachael's eye-line and pointed at the other bodies amongst the trees. In the distance Rachael saw others. Older. Wool rotted through and bones tipping out into the roots. She stared at the closest victim. Tried to focus. Through the sodden stitches something caught the light. A pair of shattered glasses on a purple elastic cord.

"Back in my grandma's day it was harder to make people disappear. No-one really moved out of town, but accidents happened. Drunken farmers tried to cross the moors and got lost. Young women escaped their shame. Labourers fell into fast flowing rivers, their bodies swept out to sea. These days it's much easier. People move around a lot more." She paused and inhaled a mouthful of smoke. "Deserve it more."

The knitting hut glittered in the distance, the empty farmhouse beyond. Even further away the spire of the town church visible like a dropped needle upright in the carpet.

Rachael went to speak, but the movement tugged several stitches passing through her neck and she lost her voice. Jan continued speaking.

"Sheep die and families starve. Need to keep the ewes and tups healthy."

The herd around Rachael's feet were all dirty, fleeces clagged with mud and heather.

"Sacrifices are necessary for good quality wool. It's been that way for a long time, and we are a very traditional community. A bit of meat and blood in their diet doesn't hurt either. They have sharp teeth. I'm sorry about that, but if you will come and poke your nose in to our business. Thinking you can ingratiate yourself and 'expose' us. Who to? We're respectable ladies of the community. Our families are well established. On the Chamber of Commerce and the Church Flower Committee. Even the Parish Council."

Jan walked the short distance to the tree and held Rachael's head back. With a set of short needles she knitted a panel into place across her eyes.

"Goodnight PC Lewis," Jan said. The stars disappeared from

sight and Rachael flinched as raw fleece brushed against her feet. Out of sight the sheep began to gnaw.

Skin Like Carapace

I SLEEP SHALLOW and my memories whisper in my ear, their hand on my shoulder so I cannot evade them. They speak to me of the first time I came to the market of fragrance, 16 years old and face bare apart from one age branch carved above the broken brow of my nose. I pay them no heed, but it's hard, hard to ignore the first taste of the air surrounding the market. Then and still the greatest wonder of the Land of No Light.

Here you can buy powders to stain your skin with the scent of fly agaric and birch bark, or smoke to disguise you as a freshwater pool to hide from violent and determined creditors. Every day, between the fourth and the fifth bell, dancers gather on the cobbled square. Each one is bathed since birth in a different essence. They weave their scents into epic stories of the origins of the four Royal houses, and the spectres whose tattered odour is carried on the wind. Those who brush against the dancers never clean that patch of skin and carry the story on them throughout their lives.

If I concentrate I can still smell the tang of blood from my scuffed knees and feel the sting from picking pea grit from my scabs. Those times when my voice was too cracked to keep me on my feet. But those scars were trivial. With the help of older traders I soon learnt to navigate between the stalls by the click of my tongue and the brush of fungus that grew on the worn oak boards.

That was a long time ago and now I am not a young man. I sit in the centre of the market in a patch of crumbled marsh salt and tall wild garlic. No-one can enter without a Royal Warrant and no-one can leave without being turned to silence. I can hardly smell the market now. The anise, cinnamon and sage no longer reach me, drowned out by the perfumes leaking from my body and staining my clothes.

Some time has passed since the Royal guards brought me here. How much I'm no longer sure. I've tried to keep track of the bells, of the ebb and flow of trading. Each session flows into the other and I lose track so easily. It was an accident. I think they know that, so they guided me here with gentle hands rather than dragging me in chains.

The day was hot and my hands sweated up as I poured oils and tinctures. That was why the bottle slipped from my grip. The embossed glass smashed and spilt the Queen's scent over the poor girl walking by, soaking her rags with frankincense and saffron, sandalwood and ambergris.

Sellers and buyers alike approached her, smelling the perfume of their Regent, grasping her clothes and running their fingers across her forehead, surprise overriding any sense of etiquette. Instead of the arcing inscription scars of the Royal family they felt only shallow indentations of a house with no name. Their hands found no silk threaded embroidery, no pearls warming to their touch, or Alençon lace finer than breath, only the tattered rags of a starving girl. Rumours spread of the Queen appearing in the market wearing tattered linen, and ash to grit her skin. Skin that was cold to the touch from the lack of fine robes. Seven satires were composed by street musicians and four caricatures carved into soapstone, each coated with a wash of frankincense and wood ash.

After I was taken no-one knew or asked what happened to the girl, but not an hour goes past when I don't think of her and my collusion in her fate.

There is still time for me to run, to hide. To take handfuls of river mud and scrub my skin until my scent is worn away. I could conceal myself between footstep and speech, an outlaw. But who would I be then, a perfumer with no scent? To run would mean never smelling the haze of the market again, never becoming drunk on the mix of musk and oakmoss. Instead I will wait for the judgement of the Queen and hope she is merciful. I am not a young man and I am too tired to run.

I listen as the Queen's Justice approaches, trailed by her twelve servants. First they walk across the cloister, where trinkets of lavender are sold from rough-woven blankets. Their feet crunch on sand made of a million empty seashells. Next they cross the gravel path. I can hear mumbles of conversations and their boots scuff up small sprays of grit. They pass through the cobbled square, smooth soles slipping on the rounded stones. They are talking about me, though I know any decision will have already been reached. As one creature they cross the turf to stand around me. Their breath is controlled and shallow. I can taste it on the air, pungent with alcohol and calisaya.

The Queen's Justice approaches the garlic patch, crushing the plants underfoot and leaning in close. Reaching up I run the pad of my palm across the woman's face. I feel where age and the inscriber's chisel have turned her beautiful, marking out her life. First I trace the lines of her office, the curving fronds of the royal seal, then the tree of age rising up the centre of her forehead, following the inscriptions marking journeys and lovers. Finally I bring my hand down to her mouth, touching the impressions marking each laugh and frown. The Justice returns the greeting, her long fingers reading the carvings across my face, pushing into my beard to touch the scars hidden on my cheeks. She grips my neck just under my chin.

"My mistress could have you turned to silence, your scent ground into the dirt underfoot and your marks wiped from all memory," the Justice says. "Instead she will give you a chance to redeem yourself. Succeed and you can return to your work, though you will never again serve the Royal Court. Fail and you will be turned to silence."

"And if I don't accept?" I say, although I know the answer. The Justice says nothing.

I tense my neck muscles in acknowledgement and the Justice lets her hand smile against my skin.

"Before the end of trading you must answer this question. What is everywhere yet has no scent?"

Then there is just the sound of breathing and I listen as the Justice and her twelve servants leave. There is still time to run, but I am not a young man and I have no heart for it.

Left alone I think over her words and think over the riddle. The question makes no sense. I am a master perfumer in the market of fragrance and we are taught young that everything has a scent and we learn young how to extract it. We can take tinctures from fossilised shells, from your lover's touch, from your child's amniotic-soaked first breath and your lover's regret laden last. There is nothing in the Land of No Light absent of scent, and knowing this I start to prepare myself for silence. I am not a young man and maybe it is time to no longer be.

Yet I try to ignore the hopelessness of my situation and ask those who pass my confinement. I speak to traders who gather because they have known me since I first stumbled between their bouquets of dried flowers, and I ask those who gather out of morbid curiosity. No-one has an answer for me. They drift away through guilt, though the causes of their conscience are a world apart. I find myself alone again and try to come up with an answer, but every object and creature I bring to mind has its own taint and stench. With no hope left, I sit listening to and inhaling my home for one last time.

I hear her first, shuffling at the limit of my internment. She smells of condensation and death-watch beetles.

"You must leave," I say in a whisper. I don't want another life on my conscience, even as I teeter on the edge of losing my own.

"I can answer your riddle for you," she says. Her voice sounds like the throwing of bones, desiccated and rotten.

She moves closer and takes my wrist. Her skin is as smooth as carapace. She runs my hand across her face and I find nothing. No marks of office or inscriptions of achievement, no engravings of shared jokes and private sorrows, just blank, smooth, flesh stretched across bone, taut with emptiness. Bile rises from my stomach as my hand finds her face bare of marks. I can feel the acid burn my throat and taste it age my teeth. No-one is without a past or story. Even newborns carry the scars of birth, yet her face is absent of all of this. From the set of her jaw and razor cut of her cheekbones I know she is no child. I want to take handfuls of grit and scrub my palms down to the bone in case whatever disease afflicts her, whatever curse that has wiped her skin embryo clean, infects me. Better to let flames lick and blister my skin into strands of living liquid than touch her face. I try to bury my disgust and carry on, though she cannot be ignorant of my feelings. I am not a young man and have never been good at hiding my emotions. I bring my hand over her mouth and feel no breath, only the wet, slow touch of her lips against my fingers. Trying not to flinch I take hold of her wrist and bring her hand in turn to my face, letting her read me. Her touch is slow and invasive. It takes all my will not to run as far as the entangled plants and crushed salt will let me.

"I can answer your riddle for you," she says again, her voice no warmer.

"And what do I give in return?"

"If you don't get the answer you will be reduced to silence. Surely any price I ask of you will be less than that?"

I think on this, and am not convinced she speaks the truth, but hers is the only help that has come and I have never claimed to be wise. I place her hand on my neck and tense my muscles in agreement. She clasps my hand, fingers between fingers, and moves our grip to the oath scar on my left cheek. She speaks first.

I pause, unsure if I have heard correctly, then repeat the words. "I swear that if the answer saves me from silence we will be married." I am a master perfumer and know any answer given will be wrong.

She leans in close and whispers the solution to me. I know as she speaks that this woman with no history, no inscriptions or crow's feet to bring beauty to her face, has given me the correct answer to save me from being reduced to silence. In that moment

I know if I give her answer to the Queen's Justice then I will be released from my confinement and this woman will be my wife.

"I will leave now and return as your betrothed after you have given your answer to the Queen's Justice," she says, and I listen to her go.

Do not think that I am not considering giving the wrong answer. What value are honour and oaths when I will no longer exist to care? But something stops me and instead I sit waiting for the end of the market and the Queen's Justice to return.

They come as the sound of bartering lulls. I know the traders and sellers are waiting to hear my fate. I can taste them breathing, though they still their lungs. The Queen's Justice and her servants have scorched corpse hair and animal pelts against hot stones and dressed themselves in the smoke. They mute their shoes, but to me they sound like a storm gathering.

The Justice steps onto the salt and wild garlic and we exchange greetings.

"Do you have an answer for me?" she says, and for a moment I think I detect a hint of regret in her voice as she places her hand against my neck. I tense my muscles.

"What is everywhere and has no scent? I caution you to answer carefully as only one answer can be given."

I pause. Some think I do this for effect, but I am not a young man and it takes time to gather my thoughts.

"Sound," I say.

A gasp goes through the crowd like an echo, starting with the Queen's Justice and spreading backwards to the far reaches of the market.

The next few moments feel like an anticlimax, even for me who can now go on living. The Justice takes my hand and leads me from my confinement and the inscriber is called forward to add a new mark to my face. It takes much searching to find the symbol. Many markets have occurred since anyone left the garlic alive. Certainly it has not happened in my time. The blood from my new scars reminds me of scuffed knees all those markets ago. I allow myself a moment of relief, but it is short lived.

"Where is my husband to be?" my saviour calls out from the cobbled square.

I think about ignoring her. The punishment for oath breaking is the loss of a hand. Surely that is less of a burden than a wife I do not want? A wife who is so without experience that she does not bear one mark. Then I hear her cry taken up by others.

"Where is this woman's husband to be?" and the gossips go to ask her story.

Before long the market is noxious with it. I have little choice but to approach her and acknowledge my oath.

The wedding is short and over quickly and I do not wish to dwell on it here.

She moves into my home and I feel like she's everywhere. I go to bury my clothes and boots, stained as they are with the herb of silence and brittle salt. When I leave her alone she recovers them and I resent her for it.

We bed down in separate rooms. I say my back hurts, or my hands are so soaked in tinctures that they will burn her skin if we embrace. While she sleeps I dab diluted perfume behind her ears. Too subtle for most to sense, even my new bride, but I can smell it and leave any room she enters. I do not want to convulse in her presence. I'm disgusted by her, but I am not a young man and try to hold onto some manners. This way I carry on as before, though another Perfumer dresses the Queen's skin. A small price compared to others I pay.

She asks to come to the market with me, to sell scents to the gentry, and crush spices for me.

"Imagine how many more beautiful perfumes you could make with two of us working on your stall," she says.

"Not today," I say. "I have a delivery of herbs coming and there is little enough space for me." "I am mixing today. If you knock over the tinctures our livelihood will be gone." "I have an important buyer coming and need to give him my full attention."

She does not believe these excuses and neither do I. How can I tell her that if she came to the market and someone exchanged greetings with her I would be a laughing stock. I have little enough trade as it is. Few want to buy from me in case the taint of silence has slipped into my fragrances.

Instead she stays in the house and cooks and cleans. I come home and the house reeks with the scent of balms she rubs into bruises from moving around the unfamiliar rooms. Yet I cannot deny she cares for me well and shows interest in my work. I start bringing bottles of essence home and teaching them to her. Help her learn sandalwood from saffron and rosemary from rosehip. Though my tolerance for her in my life grows I still cannot bear for that unmarked skin to touch me, and I flinch away when her hand goes to rest on my arm.

I smell tears as I walk in, a slight tang in the cold air of the house. It takes time to find her, curled up by the side of the bed. I ask what is wrong. She says nothing. Without thinking, without giving my revulsion time to overrule my instinct, I hold her hand, stroking the back of her fingers. I lean in and kiss her cheek. She still does not move, but her back is less tense. At a loss how else to help, I go into the kitchen and prepare a meal for her. I do not know what to say to take the sadness away, so instead I steam fish and mushrooms and pour a small glass of wine before leading her to the table. Still she says nothing. I place the fork in her hand, spear the scales of the fish and bring it up to her mouth. Still she says nothing, but when my hand brushes her face her cheeks are dry and I am sure she is smiling.

"It's been a while since I've prepared food," I say. "Have I removed all the bones?"

"There are no bones, but something is missing."

My heart sinks.

"The fish is a bit dry," she says. "It needs butter."

I go to the cupboard and bring the butter to the table, cutting off a slice and letting it settle on her fish. I hear her chew, then she pauses.

"Has the butter made it more palatable?" I ask.

"There is still something not quite right," she says. "This butter is unsalted. It needs a little salt."

"But I have no salt here," I say, disappointed to have let her down.

"Reach under your bed and get your old clothes."

I climb up, groping around for the shirt and trousers. Amongst the mud I find a little salt. When I come back to the kitchen she is melting butter, and I crumble in the crystals. I hear her dip in a spoon and taste the butter, then sigh.

"What's wrong?" I ask.

"There is still something missing," she says.

I wait for her to speak again. I want her to enjoy this meal. She deserves some happiness, I think to myself.

"A pinch or two of wild garlic would make it perfect."

"I don't keep garlic," I say.

"Surely there will be a few leaves stuck in the folds of your clothes."

I find the garments on the floor. The leaves are old yet still pungent, enough to stain my fingers. I find three and take them across to where she tends the pan, break them into pieces and drop them into the now salty butter.

As the cooking stones warm, the acrid mixture rises around us sticking to our face and hair. I stand behind her and put my arms around her waist.

Her fingertips change first, calluses erupting through the skin. She is a musician, left handed and her touch knows the caress of strings, shaping the air itself. Veins rise in her hand, thick and strong. I place my hand against her cheek, slick with condensation. Marks put there by the inscriber's chisel spread. Each one rises like the scent of leaves crushed between mortar and pestle, and as with the most aromatic of herbs my breath catches in my throat. The branches on her forehead are many, but less than mine. I find the scar of where she grew up, and the journeys she made to come to the market, what her trade is and how many honours she has been awarded. I want to tell her how beautiful she is, but words evade me. All I can hear is her breathing. All I can taste is her breath tinged with honeysuckle and jasmine. Lines appear around her eyes like footprints in clay. They tell me more of her life has been spent laughing than crying, though there is deep sorrow held on her face too. On her left cheek three marks for children born, on her right two for those who did not survive. My touch explores her face and the reality of my cruelty is laid before me. It is her turn to kiss away my tears. I find my tongue and speak quiet apologies. She kisses these away too.

Later, when she sleeps, I wipe the perfume from behind ears.

Ours is a marriage of things not said and things not asked, but I am not a young man and I am content, and though it is one of the things never said or asked I think she is content too.

Beneath the Forest's Wilting Leaves

THE FOREST WAS BORDERED as all forests are. Housing estates and roads bounded the trees in place as well as any fence and ditch, and even in the rotting heart of the wood the rumble of cars was as present as any birdsong.

I locked the driver's door, opened the boot and passed Ethan his coat. He pushed his arms in, the lining bunching over his fists until I helped guide his fingers back to the air.

He slid his hand into mine and we walked down the metalled path. He leaned into my leg, and I felt him shake. The fear wasn't from the trees crowding over us, but the bikes tearing past toward a destination we didn't share. I wasn't too worried. Once we got between the branches he would let go and I would struggle to call him back.

There was no pattern to where we went, choosing different cut-throughs each time we went into the woods. Making our own maps. I hung back and let him lead the way, watching his coat cut through the foliage, only stopping to check head-height thorns or the signal on my phone.

Where branches overlapped I imagined older forests as my eyes defocussed, and had to remind myself to watch Ethan's steps. His worlds shaped out of mud and sticks, and the press of bark all around us, did not include me. I checked my phone again for emails that could probably wait, but never seemed to.

"Why are those trees leaning like that?" he said, stood at the edge of my vision. I shivered and pulled my coat closer, checking he was warm enough, but the cold didn't bother him like it did me.

He stared at a small clearing with a single tree in the centre. Someone had started building a rough shelter by balancing timber against the trunk. We had seen many shelters on our walks, woven together by children we never saw, but never one so early on in its birth.

"It's a skeleton for a hut," I said, running a hand over some nearby bark, the moss grazing my hands with dew. Ethan crouched and grasped a nearby piece of timber, staining his palm black.

"Can we build it too?" he asked.

I checked my phone again, a stress reaction, then checked it again to look at the time.

"I don't think we can. We need to get back to the house."

"Just a couple of branches," he said, rooting through the leaf litter, dragging out twigs barely longer than his arm. The stench of rot erupted from the forest floor. In the distance traffic continued to scar the motorway in an unending ribbon of metal.

I relented, because I always did.

"Those aren't big enough," I said, taking the sticks from his hand. "Come with me."

It took me a few moments to get my eye in and spot good timber lying on the ground. Working together, we carried branches across to the already balanced boughs and started making a skirt to bind them together, trampling bluebells in our carelessness.

Hunger stopped our work. We walked back down the path to the car, hand in hand, with an air of contentment.

"We did OK today, didn't we Daddy?" Ethan said, words rounded off by tiredness.

"We did OK," I said, and smiled.

⁂

I had time the next day to take him out again. Sarah was on a call which needed near silence in the house. At the edge of the scrub

Ethan ran on, the bicycles' slicking colours not bothering him. His fears often evaporated when bathed in enthusiasm. I followed behind, roped on by his eagerness. Some days the energy I stole from him was the only energy I had.

Amongst the trees, beneath the green tunnel they formed, the air shimmered with birdsong, beautiful and delicate in so many ways, but I couldn't shake the feeling that every day the forest absorbed more dead, welcoming their bones and gristle below its wilting leaves. I shuddered despite the warmth of the day.

Ethan recognised the track entrance, finding familiarity in the heavy mottled ivy. Waiting for me to catch up, he bounced from one foot to another. I got to him in my own time, just for a moment, then he ran deeper into the trees along the narrow strip of mud. I followed, keeping him in sight, his red coat glistening through the undergrowth.

He sat in the dirt, dragging decaying leaf stems from underneath his feet, face hidden by his hood.

"What's wrong?" I said, squatting beside him.

He shook his head, and when I tried to comfort him, shrugged off my arm.

"I can't make it better if I don't know."

Without looking at me, he waved an arm behind him toward the stack of wood against the tree trunk.

I stood and turned, rubbing his scalp through the hood. He pushed my hand away.

"Leave me alone Dad."

What I expected to see was the partly built shelter tumbled by some other forest visitor. What I saw was not destruction but construction, new uprights added to the lean-to, woven through with flexible lengths of willow scavenged from elsewhere in the forest. The building was by no means finished, and I could still see where Ethan and I had added our bits. I studied for a moment and called him over.

"Someone's come in and carried on with the shelter, just like we did."

"But it's ours," he said. I tried to ignore the wobble in his voice.

"Maybe the person who started building here came back. Think of it this way. They've saved us some work."

With kids you don't need to see their face to know when they've changed their mind. His whole shape altered as he took on the idea that we could still add to the shelter, and now it would take us less time.

"Where should we start?" he asked, bounding off into the undergrowth to come back with an armful of windfall.

"Over here," I said. Together we threaded twigs between the larger branches. Some broke, shattering with brittleness that seemed familiar. Something I felt deep down far too often. Others were softened by recent rain, food for the unseen and microscopic.

We worked well as a team, me and Ethan. He left me to lift in the larger curving branches, while he went off on little missions, piling material by my feet like he was preparing the burning of a heretic.

Once the collected wood was exhausted, we paused for sandwiches and juice, crumbs pale against the mottled forest floor. Ethan tried to balance his cup, watching the sticky liquid spill out of sight as it tipped.

"Do you want some more?" I started unscrewing the flask lid, but he shook his head, staring at the sodden spot between his feet. "Can I go and find more sticks?"

I nodded and poured myself another drink, watching him run off between the saplings, marking his coat with moss and lichen.

"Are these sea creatures?" he shouted.

"Are what sea creatures?" I got to my feet and walked over to where Ethan crouched by the hut entrance.

This was a bit we hadn't worked on, bark stripped away from the heartwood, then used as binding. Far more solid than anything we'd built. Ethan knelt down, poking something with one of his twigs.

Half buried, it looked like the cap of a mushroom. Only when he hooked it from the dirt could I see it was a shell. He carried it over, waving from side to side on its flexing perch, and dropped it into my hand.

"Snail shell," I said, turning it over and over. "But no-one's home."

"Have the birds got it?"

Back when we had a garden, we often found shattered remains of snails lying on the path. "Not birds this time," I said, turning the spiral over in my hand and examining it.

"Do you think the snail has found another home?" Ethan asked, trying to peer inside.

"Probably," I said, distracted. Very precise scratches decorated the outer lip, stretching, following the curve out of sight. I held the fragile object up to the light, the thin lines visible as light shone through the now empty exoskeleton.

"Can I take it home? There are plenty here."

Along the forest floor they crested through the dirt like a pod of whales. We dug them out one by one. All were empty and all were scratched in the same way.

"Can I?"

"Just one," I said. "Be careful it doesn't smash in your pocket."

He smashed the shell before we even reached home, crushed between his car-seat and hip. There were tears until I suggested we just pick up another next time we visited the forest.

We visited a couple of times a week after that, each time finding more work done to the hut (as it had now become) and adding our own. On each trip, new objects were left around the entrance; sometimes snail shells, other times feathers or tiny bones left in piles on upturned leaves. I tried to get Ethan to leave them there, but each new discovery was an addition to his 'Hut Museum' a small display, complete with labels and Do Not Touch signs.

The frog though, the frog was too much.

We had arrived early, parking close and wrapping up warm against the cold. We'd brought some string to tie up the cross beams. Our weaving had lasted so far, and whoever was our unknown workmate had reinforced their sections with thin lengths of bark.

Ethan and I had a system. For the first half hour we scoured the nearby forest for supplies, then Ethan slid himself inside the hut, all the time looking for tiny gifts, while I worked outside where I could stand full height.

After about ten minutes he re-appeared, his gloved hands wrapped around something.

"Do you think they left this for us?"

He opened his hands, and without thinking I knocked the thing inside to the ground. Ethan stepped back shaking, trying not to let me see he was upset.

"I'm sorry," I said, reaching out to put my arm around his shoulders. He shrugged me off.

"You broke it," he said, crouching to stare at the creature.

Though I wasn't gentle, someone had already broken the amphibian. I crouched beside Ethan and picked it up. Each limb had been pierced with thorns, the stomach cut open and intestines dragged out. Inside something shifted. Trying to control my stomach, I held its ribs and the chest opened like a purse. Inside several slugs slithered over each other as they tried to move in the confined space.

"Will it get better, Daddy? Should we take it home?"

I shook my head and tried to keep it out of his line of sight.

"There's nothing we can do for it now. Someone's done a very cruel thing, and we should put this down somewhere we can't see it."

I tried to imagine being so calculating to inflict such pain on a creature, and had to suppress the need to be sick again. I couldn't let Ethan see how much this affected me. I couldn't let it affect him in the same way.

We carried the frog into the undergrowth and covered it with leaves. I tried to focus on weaving together the next section of the hut, but my heart was not in it, and was relieved when Ethan said he wanted to leave.

I tried to shake the sight of the slugs crushing each other, as they struggled to fit inside the frog's chest cavity, the sinuous way they moved over each other. When I closed my eyes they were still there turning into knots of muscle and slime.

We didn't get back out into the forest for another two weeks.

My time with Ethan had evaporated in homework and computer games, until I returned him to his mother at some anonymous service station. Every day I left Sarah sleeping in bed, got up without disturbing her, and went to the woods alone. I always took a different route, but found myself drifting back to the unfinished shelter.

Every time there was a little more done, a few staves woven through, or a handful of leaf-covered branches balanced on top. Never much, almost like whoever was placing them was trying to tempt me out of cover, like a trail of steak left for a dog. I did not take up the bait. It felt wrong to do anything without Ethan there. The building was something we worked on together, and I couldn't summon up any enthusiasm on my own.

I sat in the motorway services' restaurant drinking coffee that was more scorch than flavour. Ethan came in first, his mother walking behind. I watched him sit down, reached in my bag for a bottle of water and pushed it over the table to him.

"Ethan says you've been getting out to the woods with him," his mother said.

I nodded.

"Says you've been building something. A hut."

"That's right," I said.

She straightened up and glanced back to the carpark.

"Good to hear. Some fresh air will do you both good."

With a neat step, she turned away from me and walked toward the door.

"Say hello to Sarah," she said, but I ignored it.

Back at the apartment, we were barely into the door when Ethan was pulling on his boots, still coated with fine mud from his last visit.

"It's too late," I said, taking off my own shoes.

"Just for a little bit. We don't have to do much. I just want to see that it's still there."

Sarah popped her head around the corner from her office.

"Hi Ethan," she said, smiling. "Take him. I've got another couple of hours I really need to get done, and then we can order pizza when you get back."

Back in the car I spread newspaper over the footwell, then helped him climb in, buckling the child-seat belts across. Not an easy task while he refused to sit still.

"Settle down, otherwise we'll just go straight back into the house."

He let me thread his arms through the straps, and clip him in place.

At the forest I unfastened him once more, and all the stored energy erupted at once. I locked the car fast and tried to keep up. Amongst the leaves and brambles I lost sight of him more than once, panic frosting my lungs, until I glimpsed him in the gaps the forest left for us. Taking a short cut I finally caught up with him, and busied myself collecting branches too heavy for him to lift, then pausing to help him lift the ones he'd set his heart on.

Our unknown building partner had done little since the last time I checked, but enough for Ethan to notice.

"They've been very busy," Ethan said. "That wasn't made when I last visited. Neither was that." He carried on, picking out every single improvement and change since he last stayed with me.

We worked until the light faded, then walked back to the car, and after the short drive, I carried him up the stairs, still asleep, lying him on his bed and taking off his boots.

"Save his pizza until morning," I said to Sarah. "But I'll have mine now."

Ethan jumped onto the bed far too early, knee catching me in the ribs.

"Can we go now, Daddy? I'm ready to go and do more."

"It's 6 a.m., Ethan. Go back to bed."

"Nice and early. No-one else will be in the woods."

I rolled over to try and get some support from Sarah, but she was turned away, asleep or ignoring.

He grabbed my arm and pantomimed dragging me out of bed. I could have sent him away, lost my temper, but I was already awake. Instead I let myself be prised from the last of my sleep, grabbed coffee, then bundled him into the car.

The shelter had changed. Where our unknown collaborator had built their sections, the wood was now obscured by smears of what at first seemed to be white mud.

I watched Ethan run up and peer close.

"What is that?"

I ran a hand over the rippled surface.

"It's some kind of daub. A very ancient way of stopping the wind and rain getting inside," I said, and winced as something snagged my skin. At first I thought it was one of the pieces of straw binding the mud together, or the uneven surface. Then I saw the tiny bones embedded within the mixture, sharp spurs protruding out. In the forest's gloom I struggled to see what animal they came from. Some curved around like a tail or serpent. Others were grouped together like any pattern the worker had in mind had slid apart as the mixture settled between the timber.

"Can we do some?" Ethan said. He reached out to copy me, and I grabbed his wrist. A look of hurt was there for a moment then gone.

"We don't have anything we need to do this. We need water, mud, some straw," I said, trying to explain.

"OK," he said, shrugging, his coat coming half off in the process. "I'll go and find some wood instead."

He almost knocked me off my feet when he ran back up.

"I've found it," he said, the words thinned by his breathlessness. "I've found it."

Unsure what 'it' was, and worried to let him investigate further by himself, I allowed myself to be dragged away.

"Look," he said.

If the leaves hadn't been sodden there would have been no sign of the spring beneath. A few feet away someone had dug into the water-logged ground, as if carving out a shallow grave. Instead they'd scraped out wet clay, beside it a pile of blackened straw.

"Can we do some?" Ethan said.

I stared at the spring and shuddered, glancing up to see if the sun was still high.

"Someone else has started working here. We can't really change what they've started."

"But we did when we started making the shelter better. You didn't say no then. You just don't want to get dirty."

I shook my head, trying to think of another reason to discourage him.

"We don't have anything to carry the clay in, or to mix in the straw."

"You have loads of old buckets at home. Please can we go and get two. We'll only need two. You can carry one, and I can carry one. I promise not to spill anything."

I let myself be persuaded as I always did. He asked whether he could stay at the shelter until I got back, and whinged when I said no, that high pitched whinge that cuts right through.

"We can go back and stay, or go back and come out again. Your choice," I said, grabbing his wrist and starting back to the car. After the first couple of steps he fell in behind me and I let go.

We drove back to the apartment, and rummaged in the garage, Ethan finding the buckets and tipping plaster encrusted tools onto the concrete floor in his enthusiasm to haul them back to the car. I picked up the old tools and searched for a spade, throwing both in the boot, and strapping him back in his car-seat to make the short journey back.

The approach to the shelter was covered in snail shells, hundreds of them, all lying on their side, spiral up to the sky. I grabbed Ethan's shoulder to stop him crushing them and knelt to pick the nearest one up.

Bones inside the shell rattled out into my palm. I had no way to identify them, just another one of the dead buried in the woods. A frog or mouse that found a grave beneath the fungal rot.

Ethan pushed past me and picked up handfuls, dropping them into one of the buckets, more bones rattling out as they fell upon each other. A container filled with two slaughtered populations. The awareness of what that meant crept in slowly. I hid my disquiet and fed off Ethan's enthusiasm instead.

I dug, while Ethan used his bare hands to scrape balls of clay into the bucket. With dirty hands he smeared lines under his eyes and down the centre of his forehead. Using the other bucket, I collected water from the spring, not worrying how many beetle-infested leaves I caught up, then poured it over the lumps of clay. Both of us slid our fingers into the unkempt straw and dropped it into the bucket, watching as it sank below the surface leaving specks of mould floating upon the surface.

Before we started the next stage I laid out the rules to Ethan. We only work on the parts of the shelter we'd built. I'd put the daub on, and he could smear it in place. When I said it was time to stop, we stopped. Nodding so hard I thought his head might fall off, he stepped back and let me start.

I noticed him flagging before I noticed the light failing. All through the afternoon, we worked in silence carrying bucket after bucket of daub to the shelter and smearing over the timber. I knew we were only play-acting at skills we did not have, but in the silence I felt a companionship I wasn't sure I'd ever felt with him before. By the time I realised how late it was, he had no more energy to walk back to the car and I carried him in my arms, letting him fall asleep against my shoulder.

Back at the flat I went into his bedroom, walking quietly so I didn't disturb his sleep. Looked at his Hut Museum. The small snail shell scraped clean alongside the shattered frog bones and the broken snake vertebrae arranged like gaming counters.

We went back the next two days, starting after breakfast and working until teatime, until he slumped to the forest floor exhausted. Each day there were more gifts spread across the leaf litter, scraped out shells stuffed with moss, or animal bones arranged in intricate designs that broke up when we stood on them, unseen in the forest floor. I didn't draw attention to them, and neither did Ethan, though I saw him notice them, his gaze flicking over the patterns, and filing away the memory for future.

At the end of the third day, we sat down with our backs against a nearby tree and shared a small packed lunch, dividing the sandwiches between us. I knew the question was coming, in the silence between us and the expressions flickering across his face.

"Daddy? Can we camp out here? We can put a blanket across the front of the doorway, and the plaster on the wood will keep the wind out."

"I'm not sure, Ethan," I said, taking a sip of coffee from the flask cup. "It gets very cold at night."

"But you've got those really warm sleeping bags and it would only be for one night."

"I don't think it's a good idea," I said.

"I think it's a great idea," Sarah said when we got back home. "It's only for one night, and you can always sleep in the car if it gets too cold."

"I won't get any sleep if I do," I said, trying to talk her out of talking me into it.

"You won't get any peace if you don't," she said.

"Doesn't matter. He's going back to his mum soon."

Sarah's gaze flicked behind me. I didn't need to turn around to see him. Sarah's expression said it all.

"Well done," she said, and ran out of the room to find where he had hid himself.

≈≈≈≈≈

He packed too much into the car, the rear window obscured by bedding and supplies, but I wasn't allowed to say no after the previous day's upset. We drove in silence, him smiling and me not. Once parked, I grabbed as many things as I could, but not everything designated essential by him, and we walked in silence into the woods.

Someone had come during the last twenty-four hours and finished the hut, smoothing out the last of the plaster, and decorating the roof with what looked from a distance like pink garlands. Ethan ran up and dragged one down, pulling as it snagged on some bark.

"This is wet," he said, letting go.

The intestines were fresh and still full, stinking with waste and undigested food. I sent Ethan to collect firewood while I tore them away, dropping them into a bag I'd brought for rubbish.

"What are they?" he said.

I sat down and stacked the wood in front of the hut, explaining as I worked.

"Do you think the animals they came from were OK?"

I shook my head.

"I don't think so. I think they've probably been eaten now."

He went silent and stayed that way for a long time. I busied myself laying the sleeping bags out and tying torches to the ceiling, my mobile phone hidden under my pillow, to give me something to read if he ever went to sleep. As night fell we sat around the fire listening to the forest wake and watching the flames. We didn't talk much. It wasn't an uncomfortable silence, but I realised how little I knew about my son. How little I'd taken the effort to find out. It's not that information was hidden from me, I'm sure if I'd asked his mother she'd have told me who his best friend was, or which homework he struggled with, but in those moments around the fire I realised how much of a gulf there was between the two of us.

We stayed awake too late. He told me stories he thought were either funny or scary, and were neither. When I looked at my watch and saw it was nearly midnight I insisted he go and lie down, expecting him to still be awake when I too laid down.

Walking around the small clearing I tried to see between the trees. The night was another creature draped over the forest's branches, unknowable and impenetrable. I tried using the torch to see further. A slight mist in the air walled the beam in so I saw less than without it.

Not wanting to wander too far, I walked back to the shelter, climbed into the sleeping bag and turned over to go to sleep, Ethan lying turned from me, his feet just catching my bag as I settled down.

When I woke I checked my phone to see what time it was. Barely past two in the morning. The forest sounded full of more noise than during the day. Every sound was warped and twisted by the stillness and my imagination. I thought I heard crackling and I glanced outside to check the fire was out. Apart from a few glowing embers the night was cold and forgotten.

Though I tried not to, I soon fell asleep again, waking only when Ethan's knee hit me in the ribs. His eyelids undulated as if deep in dream, but something about the way his chest moved told me he was awake.

"Open your eyes," I said, reaching out to stroke his face to gently ease him back to the world.

The light changed a touch and I saw delicate fronds of moss stuck to his lashes. He grabbed my arm, thorns embedded in his palm snagging my skin. I reached up for him, but my arms did not move. I tried to untangle them from the sleeping bag, the inside damp from sweat and the forest floor. Something I could not see snagged my ankle and I felt a movement against the back of my knee. Outside, the blanket door was dragged aside, and hands damp as rotten wood reached in. The arms were endless, knotted with bindweed and mould, dripping softened bark across my sleeping bag. There was no body beyond I could see. The fingers turned upwards, sensing the air. Waiting for something to change. I tried to shake Ethan awake but sleep held him too tight.

The hands tore through my sleeping bag, the nylon stuffing looking far too white and artificial caught on the broken nails. I felt one bark covered fist press against my throat, pinning me to the ground. The second hand ran across my cheek and my lips, almost a caress, then slowly but surely prised away my left eye.

I wish I could say I blacked out then, and that the pain saved me from watching. The hands lost interest in me. I tried to get up, fight my way out of the sleeping bag. The more I struggled the more I was clutched by the soil and sticks below me. The hand was now reaching toward Ethan, clasping his fingers and gently lifting him to his feet. I watched his fingers grasp the hand back, and even through all my pain, and panic, and anger, the jealousy still appeared.

Ethan stood, his sleeping bag falling away, even as mine cocooned me to the ground. With no way to move I tried shouting, not caring who heard me as long as Ethan did. The second hand reached for my mouth then, forced fingers between my teeth and, with fingernails sharp as blackthorn, tore several holes through my tongue. My mouth filled with blood, drowning any words I still had.

There was no violence toward Ethan, barely any coercion, just the gentlest of persuasion and my son was gone, and I was alone.

When I woke, the entrance was sealed over, hazel staves woven into each other turning a door into a wall. I searched the shelter for weaknesses, for places rotten, where softened wood had been used. Places I could shatter. Slowly but surely I snapped my way out.

They don't believe me, the lawyers, the judges. Sarah. They're sure I left him amongst the dead, lying beneath the forest's wilting leaves. Search in my head for answers I don't have. I run my hands over the plastered walls of the cell, wary of snagging myself on bones. If the conditions are right I can smell the forest on the wind, and in the distance I hear the rumble of cars, as present as any birdsong.

Why the Sea Tastes of Salt and Why the Moon Always Looks Toward Us

THE WITCH OF THE RED HOUSE fell in love with the moon. With no wings to lift her through the sky, she went to the marsh and asked the stagnant waters for advice.

The drowning pools gurgled with the voices of slit-throats and of the bog-crushed.

"You must slip off your skin. Lay it by the north wall of your house at the new moon. Until the full moon scrape the fat from the inside of your hide, the hair from the outside, and shape both into a candle. When the full moon rises, light the candle, and your skin will become a carpet of honeysuckle and magnolia to carry you to your beloved."

When the new moon came, the Witch of the Red House peeled off her skin, stemming her blood with salt, the agony making her choke out the names of all Five Dead Gods.

For one month she scraped fat from the inside of her own hide, and hair from the outside, shaping both into a single candle.

When the full moon rose, and the light fell on the Red House, the Witch lit the candle. She stepped onto her cracked skin, hooking her feet into the eyeholes and grasping the now limp scalp to steady her balance. The skin rose into the air, fissures becoming petals of honeysuckle and magnolia.

Skitter-footed beetles and gnaw-toothed mites fell in mists to the garden below. The platform of flowers climbed through the clouds to orbit her beloved, the moon.

And the moon saw The Witch of the Red House without her skin. He saw her as a thing of tendons and tissue, of muscles and marrow. He saw her as a thing of gristle and gore, and slowly he turned his vast face from her.

In fury the Witch of the Red House tore out her ribs, turning the moon with the broken sherds, and pinning him to look forever at the Earth.

With nothing else for her on land, and nothing else for her in the sky, the Witch of the Red House threw herself into the sea. The currents dragged her to the ocean floor. To the hidden land of scavenged whales and the pressure of one hundred fathoms. As she fell, the salt crusting her wounds spread through the sea, so all who sipped it would remember her pain.

Every month the moon tries dragging the Witch to him, begging her to snatch out the slivers of bone, but she is too deep, feasting in the dark on sailors whose lungs hold cold oceans of their own.

Dirt Upon My Skin

SALLY NOTICED CAMPBELL had gone, and the surveying pole fell from her cramped grip to smash beyond repair upon the kerb. Moments earlier they had been alone together in the disowned housing estate. Now Campbell's hi-vis jacket was not in sight. Sally and the tripod-legged Level stood at opposite ends of the deserted street.

Shouldering the pole she unclipped the two way radio from her belt, pressing the talk button, still warm from their last exchange.

"Stop fucking around," she said. They had worked together long enough and often enough. "If you want to sneak off for a piss, let me know." She let go of the switch and waited for a reply that didn't come.

Either side, empty houses canyoned over her, walls salt-stained and windows blinded. She pressed the button again.

"Seriously, stop dicking around. We need to get this bench-mark transferred. The machines are arriving in the morning."

No answer. Campbell's bag lay on the floor beside the Level, the notebook he used to write down measurements left on top. She picked it up and shielded her eyes from the harsh sun. The page was blank. While she knelt amongst grit and used needles, he had made no attempt to take a measurement. She stared down at the tiny spirit bubble in its emerald green liquid. The thing wasn't even set up properly.

"Fuck's sake." She picked up the radio once more. "Me and you are going to have words, Campbell."

The equipment was too valuable to leave, and there was no way she was waiting for him to return.

Garstang Estate was vast, one of the biggest in Europe when it was built. Row upon row of back-to-backs fused together, sharing bricks like conjoined twins shared arteries. Long avenues and narrow back lanes. The whole lot bought up to be cleared for new development in 2006. And in 2008? Left to rot when the money markets were mined out from underneath.

Six years later and no progress. Windows and doors were shuttered to keep out the growers. No matter how many activists shouted that the houses were still good enough to live in, the buildings were caught in confusions of ownership too complex for any single entity to unravel. Silent streets. Abandoned. Forgotten.

Static bubbled from the speaker. She put the Level into its polystyrene cradle and unclipped the radio again. The red LED glowed to show someone on the paired handset speaking. The static did not clear. No words were audible.

"If you can hear me, say something," she said, cutting across the broadcast. When she finished the red light had blinked out once more. She was alone. No-one was listening.

For an hour she waited in case he returned, walking up and down the short length of street, then sitting a while on the kerb, tarmac too hot to touch. To distract herself she peered into the backyards. Rats ate dead crows now there were no binbags to rip open.

Campbell was not returning. She was not going to achieve anything by herself, and the car had aircon.

The tripod strap dug into her shoulder, prongs banging against her shins. The small car-park lay beyond the fence on the far side of the estate. She checked one pocket for the wrench to open the razor wire topped gate. Checked the other pocket for the car key.

Working alone didn't bother her. Being deserted did. She stopped every few houses to check the radio. Nothing came after that first eruption of static. She thought about turning it off to save batteries, but what if Campbell was in trouble? Wandered off and concussed himself? She caught her breath once more, hefted the equipment and walked on toward the estate's core.

The playing field was big enough to hold a football pitch and some rusted climbing frames. On one side the slight rise of earthworks they were here to survey.

At one time the Iron Age hillfort extended its embrace through the land now thronged with houses. Sally had seen the 19th century Ordnance Survey maps, the triple bank and ditch still roping the escarpment.

She remembered tracing that ribbon of ramparts with her finger during the rushed Desk Based Assessment of the site.

The rest were long gone. Scraped and scoured by the flattening plough long before the streets were planned out. The single crease of earth on the playing field was the last survivor of that once majestic structure. An artefact of ownership, preserved by chance. Now even that was to be lost, ruptured with steel to sling mobile phone signals from one part of the city to the other.

She climbed the slope and stood on top, the turf skin underfoot wearing old blackened scars of fires. Pivoted as lightly as she could. Listened for steps in the streets. Any movement would be Campbell's. No-one else was in the estate.

The house was fifty metres away and stood out from all the others only because there was no shutter across the door. The windows were still heavy grilled, gridded steel nail-gunned in place, red painted door an exposed bruise.

She hesitated. They were not out to do a building survey, though of course they could, and they were not there to investigate anything beyond the small length of surviving earthwork. But.

That word was sour wine on Sally's tongue. She checked her phone. Still no signal. Maybe Campbell had decided to get out of the sun. Not that he had the tools to unfasten one of the shutters. Maybe he just got lucky. Felt too hot and got lucky.

The stone around the door casing was smooth. No sign of any bolts. No sign any shutter had been put up at all. The only disturbance was a clumped smear of red on the doorstep. She ran a single finger through the mark. Ochre. They had found some in a burial across town earlier in the year.

Putting her ear to the wood, Sally listened. There was no electricity in the estate any more, all the power turned off eight years ago. If there was a growing operation inside they would be using generators. Generators were loud and disturbed the air like summer storms, but the house was silent. No reek of diesel or dope. She waited a moment to try the door, and turned on her phone torch.

Nothing had been touched. Sally had spent days working in abandoned houses. Hours clocked up sidestepping voids left by stolen floorboards. Avoiding piles of rotten pigeons as she sketched original architectural features. Photographed bricked-in windows. Tried to record important plaster decoration cleaved by the theft of copper wiring and central heating pipes.

Through the red door everything was in place as if the last residents were coming back from work at the end of the day. Curtains still on rails and bulbs still in their fittings. Curiosity got the better of her and she flicked the light switch. Nothing happened. Apart from the pale blue phone light she stayed in darkness.

"Campbell." Her voice trespassed through the air and came back an interloper. There was no-one else. She opened the front room door.

There had long been rumours of empty houses on the Garstang used to hide dead bodies. Why any of the city's gangsters would risk discovery during demolition was beyond her. The harbour's schools of fish were hungry and efficient.

Twin piles of soil reached walls on both sides of the lounge, tipping away from the hole in the centre. She looked back the way she'd come, then down at her signal-less phone. The Police should deal with this, she told herself, but what to say?

Dead bodies went with the job. This one would just be more recent than the usual Romano-British skeletons she excavated. More soft tissue. Fresher. She directed the torchlight down and stared into the hole.

The pit was a metre deep and about the same wide, under-cutting the floorboards. A single horse foreleg jagged across the middle. On one side a spread of Iron Age pottery sherds, inclusions glittering in the black, oxygen starved, clay like galaxies. The far end of the pit base was hidden beneath a barn owl, wings splayed and pinned with damp-softened wooden pegs. She crouched down, gripping onto the splintered floorboards, and leant over. Blood clotted along the severed limb. She directed the torch light toward the owl. In the harsh glow from her cellphone its chest feathers rose and fell.

She ignored the horse leg, and the dying bird of prey, trying to look at the room with professional eyes. The pit cut (sharp break of slope-top; irregular sides with steep gradient; gradual break of slope-base; uneven base), the texture of the soil (silty clay with occasional small limestone inclusions), and the colour (brown yellow, though the artificial light was misleading).

The stench of torn muscle reached Sally, dragging her attention back to the leg. Exposed joints twitched as tendons dried out. The owl was still. Reed-like bones collapsed against the dirt. Sally leant against the wall to catch her breath, and ran into the deserted street.

The door opposite was exposed. Frosted glass bisected by a single crack. She stared toward the sanctuary of the playing field, then remembered Campbell.

Free of brick dust, the doorstep was once more marked in ochre. A thick, red, mineral line and circle on the rough stone. She tried the door, the handle's corroded chrome against her skin. It opened, catching on the distended carpet beyond.

The broken glass let in enough light to see by. Enough for Sally to set her feet between the dead woodlice littering the floor.

"Campbell!" She shouted up the stairs. No answer came. "Campbell! Are you in here?"

Still no answer. It was possible that the teams securing the buildings had cut corners, but she hadn't noticed the unshuttered entrances on their way into the estate that morning. The house creaked contractions as it inhaled heat from the now open entrance. Wood twisted. Plaster tried to collapse in upon itself.

Kneeling, she ran a hand along the skirting board, wood softened enough to let her press through to the wall behind. She wiped her hand on her jeans.

In the kitchen the pit stretched from the laminate worktop to the cooker. Spoil heaps collapsed into the sink. Taps dripped rusting water through rotten washers, small patches of dirt turning to mud. Sally brushed against the edge of the pit cut and turned her torch on the base.

The femurs had been picked clean. Correction, she thought. The femurs had been scraped clean, heavy knife cuts around the cartilage. In the centre a rib cage, thin bones broken during splaying. Ropes of nettle fibre knotted around the remaining vertebrae. An intact bowl balanced where the head would be, the rim thinned with finger pressed decoration. Climbing down, she reached into her back pocket for her trowel and scraped out a sample of the contents. A thick rendered fat, spattered with small pieces of rotten meat congealed on the metal blade.

She stepped back, heel slipping, and collapsed the pit edge. Only then did she uncover feathers lining the hole behind a thin layer of backfill. Magpie feathers, quills packed with the same fat in the bowl. She squeezed the grease into her palm and smeared it on the wall.

Outside again she bowed her head, the taste of her own stomach on her lips, and stared at nothing apart from the pavement. Despite the scorching sun the wind had got up and banged the two open doors in their frames. The sound multiplied. Eight more houses were now open, none showing any trace of ever being shuttered.

Picking one at random, she ran over and opened the exposed entrance. The air inside was thick with the reek of dried cooking fat coating the walls. Wallpaper underneath discoloured by nicotine and mildew. She did not enter, stopping only to stare at the ochre mark on the step; three circles linked by three lines.

The next was across the road. She pulled the door toward her.

The pit was just inside the hallway, spoil tipping away into the darkness. Cattle forelegs were arranged on the base so they crossed just above the hooves, skin flayed back. Petals of uncured hide, blowflies laying their young between fat and bone. She stumbled out again. The radio crackled on her hip. She turned up the volume and held it against her ear.

The drumming was distorted by dirt ground into the speaker. The sound fibrous and thin. Fading in and out, signal not quite strong enough. She heard the echo from one of the terraces opposite. A dull rhythm, beaten out on stretched skin. The other handset was nearby. Inside one of the houses. Campbell was nearby.

The drumming got louder as she approached. Constant and complex. Repetitive. Insistent. She walked up to the unshuttered doors. Nothing came from within. The noise was elsewhere. She walked further down the street. Another opened house. Turned the handle and listened. The drumming continued. Still no closer. She stayed still. The noise came from the neighbouring building.

The house was still fastened tight against looting, no wood or glass visible behind the grills. The sound continued behind the walls. She pressed the talk button, and held the radio to her mouth.

"Campbell, can you hear me?" Her own voice came back at her from inside, muffled by the thick brick walls. Not an interloper this time, but a prisoner, trapped by the emptiness within the house. She did not speak again. Each word she heard made her want to run and keep on running.

Across the road was yet another unfastened house. Still no brick dust. The same red ochre marks scrawled on the entrance. Concentric circles rippling out to the step edge. The door was already open. She gripped either side of the frame. Stepped inside.

The downstairs rooms had been knocked together sometime in the past. The pit was the largest she'd seen so far, cut reaching all four walls. Any spoil taken upstairs, she guessed. She had no idea how deep the hole was. The whole thing was covered in severed crow wings. Hundreds of them overlapped each over, laid carefully so their extended feathers did not entwine. She fumbled with her phone and turned on the torch. The light reflected off the barb's tallowed surface. In places the stack of wings was lower in the ground, not reaching up to the floor. She stretched out her foot. Kicked them to one side.

The hi-vis waistcoat was stained where blood had pooled down Campbell's neck, the waist of the vivid green clothing riding up as she moved the severed wings. His skin hung loose in strips, petalled like the cattle limbs. Ribboned fat scraped from underneath. Sally tried to think of it as just another burial, just another body. On her radio the drumming got louder, echoing in the room. She threw the wings over her shoulder, not caring any more where they landed.

More feathers lay under him, several broken pot rims arranged around his hands. A single boar's tusk forced into his mouth. Two more through his eye sockets, pinning in place two balls of hay. His arms were severed at the wrist, hands clasped together.

There was no way to save him. There was nothing left to save. He was a collection of finds. A burial record to be written. Context sheets to be filled in. A plan to be drawn and levels to be taken. One more of millions of dead to rot in the ground, names forgotten. He was just another collection of finds. Another burial to be excavated. Another collection of finds. She repeated the words to herself like a liturgy.

The feathers left thick grease across her palms. She tried wiping it away on her jeans. Her boot slipped on the fill, and Campbell shifted as if disturbed in sleep.

Unable to stare at his skinned face any more she climbed out, ran into the street and vomited into the gutter.

The house opposite had no shutters now. All of them gone. Windows exposed and door open. She ran her hand across the pale bricks. Not a single nail scar anywhere. The sills were marked in red ochre. The door too. Inside, she heard the radio screech feedback. Drumming louder now. A single horn blown. Mournful. Hollow.

If she got the radio it was proof. Proof that Campbell had gone missing and she'd found him. No need to disturb the burial. Easy. Just enter one more empty house. Entered many empty houses in her career. All full of dead birds. These were just more houses full of dead birds. Abandoned. Vandalised. Just dead birds.

Sally went inside. Through the first door. Through the second. Within the front room, the pit was vast. Spoil heaps stacked against the chimney breast and covered the gas fire. Limestone bedrock shovelled into the open plan kitchen. The staircase. She stood on the edge of the hole and stared in. The pit was empty. No bird wings. No cattle bones. No joints of meat. No pottery. Nothing. A scoured cut sloping down to a smooth U-shaped base. She stared around the room looking for the dead. Looking for the rubbish. Looking for the corpses. Behind her the doors clicked shut.

No Sun To Guide The Way

DAGMAR WAITED FOR PHILLIP to get off his phone, and looked anywhere apart from at the retail unit they now paid rent on. The road beside the shop was shattered, tarmac cracked like old shoe leather. Plants tried to survive in the open wounds, thriving until crushed by the tyres of the traffic that did not let up.

"Sorry about that," Philip said, dropping his phone into a pocket, sliding his hand in afterwards as if the touchscreen kept blood pumping through his veins. "Urgent call."

"You expect us to run a business from here?" Dagmar said, finally turning to stare at the building. Dull metal shutters were jammed halfway up. Spray paint turned window glass opaque. Fresh piss stained the door and ran in rivulets across the pavement.

"It needs a clean-up," Phillip said, pushing the shutters up on reluctant rollers. "There's a reason it's cheap. Shall we look inside?"

The unit was industrial, but tidy. Bare concrete walls, and corrugated service pipes running across the ceiling. Through a chipboard door at the back was a small stock cupboard and little else. Dagmar ran her hand over the bare wooden counter, scraping dust together and letting it fall to the floor.

"What do you think?" Phillip said. He searched for the light switch. Above them two ancient bulbs played a harmony of insects and glowed. His hand stayed on the switch as he waited for her reaction. She kept him waiting.

"If it was in the city centre it would be perfect."

He took out his phone, fingers running over the blank screen.

"If it was in the city centre rent would cost five times as much. What about online sales?"

"Why would we need a shop if we could rely on online sales?"

"How about destination shopping?"

"Needs to be a destination worth visiting."

Phillip held his hands up and backed toward the door.

"We've signed the contract. Let's make the best of it."

Dagmar cleaned inside first. Mopping the floors with too much water and sponging down the walls. Grime scrubbed away, the concrete shone like beach pebbles, then dried to a dull grey. Outside, Phillip scrubbed the graffiti from the window. She watched him oil the roller and clean the doorway, filling bag after bag with rubbish.

"You're doing a good job," she said, standing in the door. "I knew there was a reason I asked you to be a silent partner."

"I lend you money to buy stock, I find you a shop, I clean piss off your steps, and you want me to be silent?"

"And I'm going to ask you to scrape that off too."

Old orange and red paint arced across the shop front, only interrupted where the door and window had been cut through the concrete.

"Really?"

"It's horrible. Like someone vomited a sunset up and then left it to go off."

Phillip took a step back and laid the mop down across the pavement.

"Looks like it's the original paint from when it was a shopping centre. Probably a historic monument."

"Not so much of a historic monument when they demolished the rest of the building."

Phillip shrugged. "That's why this is worth keeping. Not much left. It gives the shop some character."

"Still hideous. I'll go and get the paint scrapers. Don't worry. I won't leave you to do it on your own."

"What about the landlord?"

"He's not here, and if he doesn't like it he can keep the security deposit."

By the time they lost light, the pavement glittered with paint flakes and the shop front was back to bare concrete.

"Do you want to go for a drink?" Phillip said, holding open a rubbish bag. Dagmar shovelled in large citrus curls.

Dagmar shook her head.

"Bath and bed tonight. Still loads to do in the morning."

Dagmar knew she was in the sea by the saltwater in her mouth, crystals crusting her lips and tongue. She looked down and could not see her body. No reference points to lead her to the surface. Something flitted against her cheeks, and she flinched until she realised it was her own hair.

Dagmar was deep, and the sun did not shine to guide her. Her arms and legs goose-bumped with cold. No oxygen reached her lungs, just the tang of saline. She did not drown. She floated in the darkness.

The water battered against her. Whatever was out there in the dark circled her. More than one. Spiralling around her body. Staying distant. She tried to swim, but had no way of knowing which direction to go. Where was up or down? They kept pace. Looped over and under, then brushed her out of the way.

Her skin did not come off in sheets, but small platelets, each one incised by a single razor-sharp scale. The water filled with blood. She tasted iron, and more salt. Her own. The things outside her sight circled once more, but did not bite. Instead they ground against her again and again. Wore through her muscle, her bone, until marrow was exposed to the cold of the water and she flowed out of herself through rasped veins.

"You look like shit," Phillip said.

He sat on the step drinking overpriced coffee from a corrugated cup, one headphone in place, the other dangling down to his waist.

"Bad night's sleep," she said, leaning over him to unlock the shop. The key jammed and did not turn until she positioned it just right, lifted the door in the frame, and felt the tumblers align.

"Are we doing the shop fittings today?"

Dagmar pushed her sunglasses up into her tied back hair.

"Did you not find a shop fitting firm?"

He stood, leaving his coffee on the ground. Dagmar picked it up, sipped the dregs and walked inside.

"You wanted to do things on the cheap, remember?" he said. "I've brought my tools."

<hr />

She watched him carry in box after box of brackets, only helping him when red welts laddered his arms.

"Before you get started on any drilling you need to finish getting that paint off the front."

"I did finish. Well I thought I did."

The red and yellow decoration streaked ribbons across the front.

"Maybe you only took off the top layer. Whatever, I want it gone."

The paint came away quicker this time, curling to the ground like flowers dying in the snow. Dagmar wrenched it free. The greasy texture sent a shudder through her. She let it fall into the rubbish bags and watched Phillip climb down the ladder.

"Happy?" he said, in a voice that told her he was not.

"I'll be happier when we get a sign up. Don't tell me. You didn't pay for a sign-writer."

"I paid for some vinyl printing, which was expensive enough. It will look perfect."

"And cheap," she said.

"And cheap. I'll put it up this afternoon. Do you want to do the drilling or shall I?"

Dagmar smiled and walked inside.

"I'll add it to the long list of things I'm staying silent about," he said.

"Are you sure you want the cabinet here?" Phillip let the tape measure retract.

Dagmar pointed to the blade of sun's glow across the floor and wall.

"The light will help show off the jewellery. Catch the colours in the stones and chains. Otherwise I'm looking at more expense, unless you have some very cheap, good quality track lighting to install."

He shook his head, clipped the tape to his belt and picked up a drill.

"You might want to clear out while I do this."

"Got another dust mask?"

He pointed at a moss green bag by the door. Dagmar fitted on the paper mask, pinching the metal clip. Her breath misted her face.

The screech of drilling filled the small shop, followed by dust that hung in the sunlight. She watched Phillip lean into the drill, driving the hardened bit through the floor, his weight pressing down against any resistance. The drill gave way, accelerating through the floor and the air filled with the stench of burning hair. Phillip stumbled as he lost grip. Dagmar hooked his arms to lift him up.

"You OK?"

He nodded, resting against the wall to catch his breath.

"Must have hit an air pocket or something. Can you check that's turned off?"

Dagmar lifted the drill and nodded.

"What's that stench though?"

"Very old air."

"There's something stuck to the drill bit."

She was sure it was skin. Rough and dry. Overlapping plates, ridged and sharp. She tasted saltwater on her lips.

"Well, it's not human," Phillip said.

"And that's better?"

He unhooked the rest from the drill and held it up in the light.

"Human would mean contacting the police. Detectives digging up the floor. Never good for a new business." He put something else in her hand. "Looks like some kind of bone."

Dagmar closed her hands around the remains.

The water is deep and there is no surface to swim to.

"Drill another hole, but go slowly."

He shrugged and started again, half a metre from the first.

He took his time. The concrete plumed up and then didn't, only the scent of more burning.

"Can you make the hole bigger?"

"Not with the tools I've got here."

"Let's call it a day. I need to make some more stock anyway."

Phillip carried his tools back to the car while Dagmar locked up

"I don't know what they painted this place with," he said. "But it's hanging on."

She stepped back and looked at the shopfront. The sunset colours were still there, pale and faint against the rough texture of the concrete.

"Another job for tomorrow."

The wounds on her arms and legs were not deep. She felt saltwater seep into the scabs. In the distance the murmur of conversation. Music. Saw faint electric lights through the water. Beneath her, something brushed against the soles of her feet and her heels came away in single sheets, hanging loose and shifting in the current. She tried to spot the creatures. They moved too fast and she was not a natural under the water. Too buoyant. One dragged against her back, abrading down to her spine. She felt the chill of the water seep in behind her bones and splash around her organs. Something bumped her face, searing away her eyelids. Now she could not help but see.

Dagmar woke lying face first on her workbench, unfinished necklaces spread out amongst semi-precious stones and unused clasps. The stench of her own blood stayed with her. She checked herself over, but couldn't find any injuries. Her bed was too far away. She walked over to the sofa. Curled up under a blanket. Sleep did not come.

"What the hell did they paint this place with?"

She watched Phillip haul the stepladders over to the front of the shop.

"They wanted it to last. Maybe we should just give up."

"Maybe we should just do it properly."

"You're the boss."

"And you're the silent partner. Less talking more partnering."

"I've brought a sander this time," he said, running the cable through the door. "That should get it away once and for all." He fitted a new belt and turned it on, peering along the edge to see if the sandpaper was spinning right.

"Did I ever tell you about this place?" he asked, "What it used to be?"

"Some kind of shopping centre?"

"With sharks."

When he found her she was sat at the back of the unit, arms wrapped around her knees.

"What did I do?"

"Winding me up like that."

He sat down beside her and held out a bottle of water. She shook her head.

"Winding you up like what? They had huge tanks with different species of sharks. Thirty in total. Must have looked like some kind of Bond lair."

"Did you plant that skin yesterday?"

"The stuff we found in the floor? Of course not."

She dragged over his bag and pointed to the two drill holes.

"Did you bring your tools?"

"A hole saw, but I'm not sure the landlord will be happy."

Dagmar handed him the drill and stared, trying to see if he was lying.

"We can plug them with fresh cement."

If you're sure," he said.

The hollow drill bit was the size of her hand. A cylinder edged in serrated teeth.

"I'm going to go slow, so this will be loud," Phillip said nodding toward the door. "Maybe have another go at that paint."

"Let me know when you're done."

The drill sounded like a living animal caught in a trap. She waited and watched the traffic passing by.

"Torch," she said.

He put a heavy rubber flashlight into her hand and she peered down into the small tunnel. The gap was only six inches wide but big enough to see the creature's skin, and the cartilage underneath where the saw had worn through.

"They never got rid of the sharks," she said. "They put them here and poured concrete onto them."

They both stared at the hole and the column of concrete beside it. The air was thick with dust and a slight hint of friction.

"I need to get out of here," Phillip said.

Dagmar nodded.

"I'll get my tools later," he continued.

She watched him go. The air turned her grey as it settled.

The drill wasn't as heavy as she thought. By balancing it on the vast circular cutting edge she could press down with all her weight.

There was no pattern to the holes she made, only stopping when the blade cut into hidden tissue. The dust choked her mouth and she could barely see what she was doing, but still she drilled into the floor again and again and again until the plug wrenched free of the socket.

Sitting down, she loosened the last column from the drill bit and turned it over. A shrunken, milk-coloured eye stared back, still held in place by taut, preserved ligaments. The cylinders balanced around the holes like unlit candles at a grave. She kicked them all over until they rolled against the wall.

The music was louder now. Close to the small portholes Dagmar saw drinkers sat at tables, cocktails balanced in front of them. People dancing. She banged on the glass, but no-one looked. They sipped their Manhattans and Singapore Slings, ignoring the hammering.

She pivoted in the water, her lungs full of salt. Felt it settling inside. Something bumped her forward, sending her flailing into the Perspex wall. She tried to balance herself. Scrabbled to stay upright. A second shark came at her from behind. She saw their eyes now. Nightclub lights glistened their pupils. They pushed her back and forth. Breaking her ribs. Puncturing her lungs. As she lay on the bottom of the tank they swam over her. Ground away her flesh until she was powder. A sodden dust swirling in the currents of their paths through the water. In the nightclub a phone rang but no-one was answering.

Tangled in her blankets, she struggled to free herself and answer her mobile before it stopped ringing.

"Yes?"

"What did you do? What the fuck did you do?"

"Phillip? Where are you?"

"At the shop. You drilled through the floor how many times?"

"I'll explain. Wait until I get there."

She put the phone on speaker and started to get dressed.

"And that paint is back. I'm going to have to sand it again, because you're insisting on getting rid of the fucking stuff."

"Just hang on."

"I'd love to, but the landlord is coming by to see how we're getting on."

She did not eat, just grabbed her coat and keys, and a swill of water to clear the taste of salt from her mouth.

The door was open when she parked, a stepladder open in front of the window. A pool of something slopped over the doorstep, clouds of flies landing to feed. She stepped over the mess. The sander lay just inside, power cable wrapped around the handle.

Phillip was spread-eagled in the middle of the room, his clothes frayed. Every exposed piece of skin was worn through, bones underneath ground away. Knuckle bones fell from his skin-less hands, ligaments snapped. She turned him over. What little remained of his face was bruised, everything else ground down.

His work bag was in the corner. She found the torch and peered into the holes in the floor. The cavities were empty of bone and skin. Nothing but more concrete. Walking outside, Dagmar vomited and waited for her head to clear. The sun caught the shop front, and the orange and yellow paint glistened.

Atelier

MUNICH DROWNED.

Rainwater collected on the gallery floor, each room heavy with the scent of sweat and damp wool. I tried to concentrate on the Franz Marc in front of me but the showers hitting the window glass took my thoughts away.

I noticed her for two reasons. Firstly, like me, she was alone, and secondly she only stopped before the paintings by Gabriele Münter and Elizabeth Epstein, not moving, examining every single detail. Not caring if other visitors became impatient behind her. I still admire her for that, though I only knew her for a few hours. Though I was attracted by the new ideas within the exhibition, the controversy and rivalry, I did not possess that single mindedness to put myself between men and the art they coveted.

I carried on watching her as people walked past, their clothes heavy with cigarette smoke and winter, and when she moved to the next canvas I stopped beside her.

"It's the use of colour I admire most," I said.

"It's the choice. The ability to make the decision to paint what they want," she said.

While she spoke she did not turn to face me, but kept her head turned toward the artwork.

"Sophie," I said, holding out my hand. She did not take it straight away, and when she did it was barely a moment.

"Frau Weber. Katherina," she said.

"Are you here just to see the exhibition?" Above us the December rain continued to clatter the glass dome of the Arco Palais.

She shook her head, though it was hard to tell if it was in annoyance with me or as an answer.

"I've come to study at the Künstlerinnen-Verein," I continued, though I felt I was just talking to myself. "When I found out this exhibition was on I had to come and see what the fuss was about."

"You're English?" she asked, her hand in the air, tracing each brush-stroke on the still life in front of us.

"I am."

"You speak good German."

"My father was from Regensburg."

She nodded.

"I used to be a student at the Künstlerinnen-Verein."

"And now?"

Behind us someone opened a door and all the heat left the room.

"And now I paint portraits in styles I detest and stand in front of paintings by artists I envy more than admire."

Even then there was something haunted about her. Distracted, as if she was crowded by people I could not see. In the gallery I thought it was just the disappointment of not being recognised for her talent. Later I would learn different.

"You are a former student of the Künstlerinnen-Verein?" I said, not really worrying about hiding my enthusiasm. "Would you have time to go for a drink. Maybe talk more about your experiences?"

It was then that she really seemed to notice me. Turned to me and looked me straight in the eye, something glittering deep inside her pupil that might have been mockery or might have been fear.

"I'll tell you about my experiences. Let's finish viewing the paintings, then yes I will tell you about my experiences."

We walked around the rest of the exhibition in silence. I left her staring at the deformed houses of Gabriele Münter's

Reiflandschaft, while I lost myself in Franz Marc's animals and Kandinsky's swirls of colour. She found me.

"Let's go," she said. I still had one room to view, but something about her insistence made me decide to return to the gallery another day.

Outside, we sheltered in the doorway watching rain overflow the gutters and tramlines.

"Shall we walk up through the Englischer Garten?" I asked, adjusting my hat. "I know it's wet, but the trees will shelter us from the worst of the weather."

That was the first time I saw her show true fear. Her whole body seemed to compress at the thought, and I saw her hands claw in her gloves as if the nails would rip through the thin leather.

"I prefer to stay to the lit streets," she said.

I nodded and followed her out onto the pavement. A tram went past, sending up a spray of rainwater that seemed to pause for a moment before falling back to the road. I looked up and she was already several paces ahead. I rushed to catch up, and ignored the rain that did not end.

The walk took twenty minutes and by the time we arrived at Simpl we were both soaked.

On the way conversation had been stilted. She asked me where I was from in England. When I answered, she had not heard of it. I asked what style she painted in, and she did not speak, though I felt she was saving the answer for later.

Inside the small cramped Wirtshaus we hung our sodden coats beside the door and sat down at a nearby table. It was only when we were settled I noticed how much her hand shook.

"You're wondering how I can paint when I can barely keep my arm still?"

I said nothing, not wanting to seem impolite.

"It wasn't always like this, but I can barely hold my nerves since I started my last commission."

The waitress came over and I paused to order us both a keller-bier, lit a cigarette and let the smoke warm my lungs.

"Your last commission? You mean your most recent?"

She shook her head.

"I mean my final. I will never paint again. I do not expect to survive the night."

The fatalism hung in the air like the smoke. I did not speak straight away, instead stubbing out my cigarette and taking a mouthful of beer.

"Is someone threatening you?"

She looked at the table and spoke, and I did not interrupt.

"It is not easy to make a living as an artist in this city, and it is not easy to be revolutionary or experimental, especially if you graduated from the Künstlerinnen-Verein with no inheritance behind you. As you may have guessed I do not have rich dead relatives.

"I live in a modest room on the outskirts of town, and I paint portraits for patrons who always haggle over the price or change their mind when the artwork is finished. They know I have no choice but to accept their lower pay, or starve. What am I going to do with an unsold portrait of an overfed family that their own relatives barely want to look at?"

I did not answer, though she stared at me as if expecting some response. Instead I pushed my cigarette case across the table, waited while she took one and lit it with a single match.

"Three months ago I went back to the Künstlerinnen-Verein to pick up some of my materials. Stood on the pavement outside was a man leaning on a walking stick. I did not think this unusual. Many times men hang around outside the building to try and dis-tract the artists from their pursuits and tempt them into the local drinking houses. Transform them from artists to models.

"When I finished my errands, I returned to the street and found him still standing there. As I walked away he followed me. I did not quicken my pace or call for help. Little men do not frighten me.

"I paused to let him pass by. Instead he stopped in front of me and held out a card. I remember he smelt strongly of bergamot and violet, as if he had bathed in them to conceal some rot that was not visible. The marks on his cheeks suggested duelling scars, but his clothing was ragged, and I had no reason to believe he was anything other than a servant sent out to harass people by his bored employer.

"'Frau Weber,' he said. 'I apologise for the intrusion into your routine. My employer wishes me to engage your services as an artist to paint a series of portraits for them.' I tried to walk away, but the man kept pace. 'They require discretion and certain conditions, but their money is good and for the duration of the contract they will pay the rent on an atelier for you, which will remain yours to use for six months after the paintings are finished.'"

She looked up, and stared straight at me. For the first time I noticed the tiny scars around her eyes. Much more precise than marks left by aging.

"They knew exactly what to say. I have no spare money to pay for a studio. I can barely pay my rent. I stopped to listen to what he had to say.

"'Frau Weber, I realise that the street is not the place to make such a decision, but if you are willing to meet with me, in a public place of course, two days from now, I will give you the full details and conditions, as well as the contract for the atelier.'

"I took the card from him, with the address of a small Wirtshaus written on in smudged ink. 'And the patron? When will I meet them?' I said.

'My patron has certain conditions which mean that the time they can spend away from home is limited. You will meet them at the first sitting,' he replied.

"It was hard to place his accent. Though there were hints of Bayerisch, there was something else in his pronunciation. I asked him if he was from the city. 'Not originally,' he said. 'But then who of us is?'

"Of course I met him. You would too," she said. I did not answer, because we both knew she spoke the truth. She reached over for my cigarettes and took another. I did not object. Around us Simpl had begun to fill up, artists and writers arguing and drinking together. No-one paid us attention.

"I made myself familiar with our meeting place. In the end we only stayed there long enough for him to give me the agreement and contract for the atelier."

She reached into her pocket and handed me a much-folded piece of paper. I opened it carefully and read the agreement. I would like to say, especially after what she told me later on, that I would have walked away, but I doubt if I would. The contract was simple. She would make herself available twice a week for portrait sittings with the unnamed patron. Always at night, and always for a total of twelve hours. In return she would have full use of the atelier at all other times and also be paid a retainer, as well as a final fee for her time. The patron would expect her to be well rested and able to paint for the full time. At no point did the document mention who the patron was.

"They remained completely anonymous," she said as if reading my mind. "Even the agreement was signed by their representative on the patron's behalf.

"Once I'd read the conditions, added my signature and shook his hand, we left the bar and walked up LeopoldStrasse in the direction of the atelier. The representative barely spoke, just walking in front of me, and moving at such a pace I could hardly keep up.

"The old palace was down a narrow side street and much decrepit, though the walls and heavily spiked fences were in good repair. He opened the wooden gate and waited for me to enter. The lawn reeked of autumnal rot. As we crossed the grounds I thought I saw figures moving through the undergrowth. On turning my head I saw nothing but the shadows of leaves unsettled by the breeze. The representative seemed to tire of my distraction and placed his hand on my arm to lead me into the building itself.

"The atelier was painted in dark colours and hard to navigate around with the shutters tightly fastened against the late summer sun. I went to undo the latch and found the wood nailed tight. Several buckets were placed around the floor to catch the rain that must have lingered in the roof and still dripped through the floor above.

"I walked around examining my new place of work so lost in my own thoughts that I almost forgot about the presence of the other.

"'You can of course set up the room how you see fit', he said. 'But during the patron's sittings the shutters will be kept closed, and the lighting at a minimum. Just enough for you to work by.'

Of course I agreed, distracted by all the other work I could do in the vast room.

"'The patron's first sitting will be in two days' time at ten pm. You will be required to vacate the atelier for one hour before that so that my patron can be in place.'"

"And none of this struck you as strange?" I said to her.

"Of course, but all work for hire is strange. All has conditions that seem odd. The farmer that insists his cattle is included in the portrait. The husband who insists on changing his outfit fourteen times, and then makes you repaint his gaze, or he won't pay you.

"For the rest of the week I worked on moving my materials into the atelier, and setting up the room so it fitted my work, informing my existing clients of the change in venue, and preparing myself for my first sitting with the mysterious patron.

"I arrived just before ten pm, walking through the open gate into the grounds and into the main building itself. Outside I heard a noise. Through the staircase window I saw a figure of an old woman cross toward the street, a large white bundle over her shoulder. Something about that bundle unsettled me. The way it seemed to twitch and move in her grip. I put it from my mind and knocked on the door to my atelier.

"'Come', the representative said, and I let myself in.

"The smell hit me first. Not just the bergamot of the representative, which seemed more intense than ever in the enclosed, shuttered room, but something else. A mixture of decaying lilies and spoilt beef. Next the gloom. The room had been rearranged to create the most shade possible. In the centre was a single chair with screens on three sides, and in the chair the patron, their head turned away from me.

"My easel had already been positioned, leaving me no options of choosing the angle or form of the painting. I gestured toward the representative and moved toward the door. He followed me into the corridor.

"'Do you not wish me to have a say in the best position to paint the portrait? The best angle? Also the light makes it incredibly difficult to capture the detail necessary.'

"The representative held my arm, his fingers digging in until the muscle went numb. 'You will complete the portrait as requested and you will not question the requirements of the patron. Do you understand?'

"I nodded and once he let go I returned to the room. The Patron had not moved. They still stared in a different direction, their face totally turned from me. Thick rat-tails of hair hung down their back, hard to distinguish from the collar of their jacket. Barely able to make out the colours I was using in the poor light, I began to work."

The tremor that until then only affected Katherina's hand spread to her voice, and she paused for a moment.

"For twelve hours the patron did not move. I left the room several times throughout the sitting, but not once did they change position or stretch to relieve the cramps that affect all who most sit unmoving while an artist works.

"At six in the morning I sat on the window sill in the stairwell and watched the sun rise over the palace's outside wall, shadowing through the hooked steel fence. Several figures dressed all in black moved across the lawn, at the back the same woman I saw earlier, the bundle still on her shoulder.

"While I watched she paused as if to catch her breath, the gap between her and the other figures becoming greater. It was then I saw a face stretched against the fabric of her bundle from the inside. Her fingers reached out and pressed the features back in and she continued on her way.

"Returning to the atelier I found the patron still hadn't moved, and I returned to my shadowed work, the only sound in the room the laboured breathing of the seated figure.

"Somewhere in the distance a clock struck ten am, and the door opened, the representative letting himself in. Without being invited he lifted the still wet canvas from the easel and moved it around.

"'A good start. I think this will be a very productive arrangement.'

"'I must insist you don't move my pieces until they are ready.'

"He turned and smiled at me with what I can only describe as disgust. 'You and I both know that you cannot insist. Your artwork belongs to my patron, and your time belongs to my patron. You are in no position to object to anything.'

"I should have left then and not come back. Maybe if I had decided to walk away that first night the dreams would not have started."

"So you did not walk away?" I'd lost track of how long we were sat in Simpl. The tables around us had filled and emptied several times. I lit another cigarette.

"I did not walk away. Once I had the space of my own atelier I could not give it up, so later that week I made sure I returned to the studio at 10 in the evening.

"The second sitting was notable for the representative's absence. When I entered, the patron was already sat, shutters closed and screens arranged in such a way that there was only one angle from which to work.

"This time I was once more limited to a view of the back of the patron's head."

"Did that not strike you as absurd?" I interrupted.

"Of course. How could it not? With the reek of rotten vegetation and the low lights in the room, and the constant nagging thought of returning to trying to find places to carry out my work, I soon pushed all thoughts of absurdity to the back of my mind.

"Once more the distant clock struck ten, and I left to return to my lodgings and sleep. I did not sleep for long.

"My accommodation is on the middle floor of a very modest

boarding house near the edge of the city. Most of the other residents work during the day, so resting during daylight is not difficult, yet on this occasion I could not settle. Footsteps up and down the staircase, the rattling of door-handles, and mutterings upon the landing. All conspired to prevent me getting my rest, so much so that when the evening came I did not wake, instead dropping into a half sleep, haunted by candlelight and something rotting just out of sight.

"In the early hours a church clock woke me, though there is not one nearby, and I walked to the window. It was raining heavily that night, the gutters barely able to cope. In the street outside several figures dressed in black, like those I had seen in the grounds of the castle, paraded past the Pension. Each one seemed slightly too long in the limbs as if they had been stretched in some way. Afterward I could not remember seeing any hands or feet.

"Then at the rear of the line once more came the old woman. She shuffled along with the white sack over her shoulder, her hands gripping it tightly shut even as whatever was inside struggled to loose itself from the confinement in which it found itself.

"I stepped back behind the curtain, but not fast enough and the woman turned her head in my direction."

"She must have heard you. Noise carries further at night."

Katherina nodded and continued with her story.

"She turned her head to me and I saw she had no eyes, just empty cavities bare and exposed. Rainwater collected in the hollows and spilled out over her cheeks.

"Every night until the next sitting I woke in the early hours to find the black parade walking past my pension."

"And you asked others in the building if they too had been disturbed?"

"Of course, but sleep kept them protected from seeing the visitors walking up the street, the old woman carrying the struggling bundle upon her shoulder."

I lit another cigarette, adding to the tobacco fog around us.

"Did you not think to confront them?"

"It crossed my mind, but there was something in that expression when the woman with the sack looked up toward my room that filled my mouth with the taste of dried flowers every time I considered venturing into the street."

"And the sittings?"

"The sittings continued, always in the same way. I arrived at ten pm. The patron was always in place, the room reeking of rot. Each time the room was arranged so I could not see their face, and each time I worked in silence, apart from the creaking breath coming from the sitter, until," she paused.

"Until?"

"Until last week. Sleep has been a distant friend for many weeks now. Last week I arrived at the atelier ready for the latest sitting. Walking through the grounds of the Palace I saw figures lingering beside the walls, staying as far from the path as they could. Inside, the building felt too warm, and as I opened the door to my studio a wave of heat hit me.

"It took me a few moments to realise that the screens had been set up differently, the chair moved to the side to where my easel waited.

"The patron looked to the side and as my eyes adjusted to the low light I saw their face for the first time."

She stopped then and said nothing for five minutes, sipping her beer and taking another cigarette. I glanced toward the window and thought I saw someone dressed in black and white move up Türkenstraße. When Katherina started to speak her voice was barely a whisper.

"Their hair was swept back and across their eyes was fixed a bronze grill, laminated by thick accretions of verdigris. Around the edge rusted screws sunk into the flesh of the patron's face, the holes scabbed and infected. Where the grill ended so did any hint of features. Rotted strands of flesh hung down, draping over the patron's neck. As I watched, the ribbons of skin rose and fell, knotting together and untangling. Channels like fine chisel marks shifted around the visible skin, weeping a clotted liquid that evaporated as it dripped into the air. Something about those patterns started an itch in my pupils that spread beyond where I could reach. Only when I picked up my palette did I notice skin from around my eyes underneath my fingernails."

As she described the Patron I felt something squirm deep in my bones and it did not stop for the rest of our time together.

"How did you concentrate?" I asked.

"There was no difficulty in studying the patron, the subject. The twisting designs did not let me look away. I barely glanced at the canvas, the brush smearing colours into each other almost by itself, until it rendered everything into black.

"That night I took no breaks. Time seemed to stretch and compress on its own. When the clock struck ten I had no idea how the painting came to be finished.

"Packing away my materials I heard the patron shift in their seat, and the desire to turn and see them scraped my resolve raw, but still I did not turn.

"Stepping out of the atelier, I closed the door. The woman with the white sack stood directly in front of me upon the landing. On the staircases running above and below waited the black-dressed figures, their overlong limbs draped across the banisters. I went to walk past them. The woman laid the white, twitching bundle on the floor and let the fabric fall open. I did not look, but smelt the stench of decaying lilies and spoilt beef. Whatever rested upon that white sheet mewled and struggled to free itself. In the unlit stairwell I saw a tangle of too many limbs and knew that if it touched me I would be lost there and then.

"I have not slept in a week. Every time struggling to rest became too much, I rose and walked around my room. Every time I gazed outside the woman with the white bundle was there as if carrying a gift I had forgotten to take."

Somewhere in Schwabing church bells rang the half hour. Katherina stood and pulled her coat around her shoulders.

"You need to leave?"

She nodded.

"Tonight is the last sitting. I will not see the morning."

"At least let me walk you."

She thought about it for a moment while I settled our drinks with the waitress.

We walked in silence up Ludwigstraße, past Siegestor and off the main road into the streets that would lead us up to the old palace. As we got closer I felt Katherina become more nervous, her footsteps smaller, and her voice constantly muttering as if the words would keep the night away. Several times I heard a noise behind me and turned, thinking I saw figures stepping just out of view.

The palace was on the corner of a junction, the vast yellow wall visible from a distance away. Once in sight Katherina sped up, as if rushing toward something she could not avoid. The main gates stood open, heavy metal spikes upon the fence scraping the air like unfurled claws. She stepped inside and I tried to think of something to say, but the rain took my voice.

A light flickered in a single window of the building. She closed the gate and fastened the chain. In the far corner of the shadowed grounds I thought I saw a black shape with a white bundle over its shoulder, something inside twitching and straining against the cloth. I watched Katherina walk up the path and into the building. She did not turn.

Discarded Skins

THE SCENT OF AFTERSHAVE stopped at the sea edge, no oak-leaves or moss able to survive the drenched cloying rot of the sea. Margaret kicked through the sand, disturbing a freshly cleaved crab leg.

Eight tides had scrubbed the beach since Spiri left. No trace of his footprints to show where he walked into the fret. Whatever called him back was not the sea.

Their romance had not been larceny. Margaret had not stolen his skin from chalk rocks like some washing line thief. He had folded his foam encrusted pelt, dried over paint-flaked radiators, then vacuum-packed and slid below the bed they shared. Stowed like cargo beside her dry-suit. Claimed residence of the house. Claimed residence in her arms.

Of course, he went back to the waves once a year for the gathering, when barks echoed like the cries of drowned fishermen. But they were creatures of two worlds, Spiri and his kin, and for him the call of the Marram grass and cliffs pulled stronger than the tide.

He had been gone four days and the gathering was still six months away.

Moving old paint tins and gardening tools Margaret rooted about in the back of the shed for her scuba tanks. Back in the house she reached under the bed for her own swimming skin, the neoprene padding dry for too long. Her hand brushed the empty vacuum pack and a gasp of wet fur erupted. She stopped for a moment and rested her head against the mattress.

Spiri's scent was even gone from the beach now. He could have returned to the sea out of choice, of course. Felt the call of pressure against his skin. The taste of salt and krill upon his tongue.

"I have swam into coves on distant beaches, and danced with blind fish far below the hulls of boats. I have eaten the finest urchins from amongst forests of coral, and I have no desire to live under the surface any more. I want to see the seasons change, and dance through the leaves in Autumn. Taste snow and whisky to the sound of songs played on instruments older than the hands holding them. I am sick of the cloying cold of the water and the silt that hides the dead."

Margaret walked into the waves as if she had left her own clothes in a pile for a loved one to find. Even through the dry-suit, the cold lapped up her skin, kelp and bladder-wrack creasing past in the waltz of the currents.

Four more nights she searched the bay, the harbour, each day driving to the dive shop in town to fill the tanks once more. On the fifth night she swam the water below the cliffs where the vast fibre optic tentacle slid under the surface, bringing conversations and porn through the ocean.

Spiri's kin fringed the cable, teeth clasped into the insulation. Their pelts were threadbare and scorched, tails swaying silt from the sea floor, splinters of seashells rising in plumes. She needed to see his eyes. Look into his face to know him. Mud filmed her diving mask, and she saw nothing but the dirt of the sea.

Margaret ran a finger across the glass. Her skin was old and slack on her bones. Not for the first time she wished she could detach it as Spiri did. Shed her flesh to start again and walk under different skies.

The fishermen knew her. They'd known her husband, Karl. Shouldered his coffin into the chapel. Made sure the cheques arrived from the widow fund every month. Some had tried to tempt her into drunkenness, and into bed, but she could out drink them, and out think them. After the first turned up with shattered knees, and no way to feed his family anymore, none of the other predators hunted her affections. They knew Spiri, and though they did not speak to him in case his kin sung them down through the waves, they did not disapprove.

Margaret walked into the bar and shrugged off her coat, beads of rain staining the uneven wooden floorboards. No-one looked up.

She pulled a chair toward her, sat down and pushed the envelope across the table. Bill looked up, sipped the last of his whisky, and held the glass out to her. By the time she returned from the bar the envelope had gone.

"What makes you think I can get this for you?" He turned the glass around. She tried not to stare at the tattoo on his arm, and the ragged cut where the surgeon's knife had taken his hand.

"Karl crewed your boat for ten years. I know you weren't just netting fish out there, and with Larne across the sea I know what you were hiding under the packing ice wasn't just Lebanese red."

"You know, do you?"

"If I was going to let slip, I would have done it by now."

Bill sipped his whisky and closed his eyes.

"I don't need to know what you want this for."

Margaret stood up.

"That's good, because I'm not going to tell you."

Three days later the crate was in her shed, planks reeking of salt and dead cod. She cleaved off the top and lifted out a satchel, the olive green of the sky. Undoing the buckle, she checked each black plastic-wrapped block, letters printed on in yellow telling her things she did not need to know. Fastening the bag once more, she sat on the crate and wept.

When the doorbell rang she thought it was Spiri returned to climb into her bed. Then the police to bury her in granite far from the coast.

"Can I come in?"

Bill stood on the doorstep, wrist cupped in hand.

She nodded and stood aside as he ducked to avoid the lintel. While the kettle boiled she watched him stare at the photo on the mantelpiece. All five of the crew stood in front of the boat, his arm still intact.

She passed him the cup and he nodded thanks.

"Can I help?" he said after a pause, steam smearing his glasses.

Margaret shook her head.

"Whatever it is, it can't be that bad."

She pictured Spiri's kin welded to the undersea cable, they're canine teeth sheered through the insulation, eyes rolled back in their heads.

"It can."

Bill drained the scorching tea and put the cup down on the hearth. Standing up, he wrapped his arms around her.

"They'll come after you, you know."

He smelt of fish and sweat. Of a husband under the soil and a lover under the tide.

"I know."

That night she went under the sea for one last time. They still clung to the cable, eating nothing but ones and zeroes. Ragged fur stretched over ribs. She swam between them. None paid her any attention, their skin buckled with limpets grinding in sores.

This time she spotted him, his brindled fur moulting with each brush of water. She tried to catch his gaze. Swim so she could gaze into his eyes. The cable blocked her. In desperation, she grasped his waist. Tried to haul him away from his addiction.

With a lazy twitch he flicked her loose, sending her tumbling across the seabed, silt and dead scales rising around her.

The hut was brick built, double-skinned and barely bigger than her shed. Triple locks bolted across the metal door. She soon wrenched those free, not caring if hidden cameras transmitted her vandalism back to some control room in a landlocked city.

She worked quickly, placing the satchel underneath the vast cable, wedged against the concrete floor. Trailing the detonating cord, she walked backwards out of the door, and sat in the long grass. She sat for a long time. Watched the tide wrap in upon itself. Then, when it started to turn, she switched the detonator.

The hut unfurled. Splinters of fibre-optic sleeted through the air. Bricks pushed outwards. Several chips cut her skin to ribbons and she ran her fingers along the wounds, sucking her fingers to taste the truth of the sea in her blood.

The waves bubbled and the first seals broke the surface, jaws open, eyes closed and spines to the sea. They did not dive or grasp for the beach. Instead the tide rucked their lifeless bodies back and forth. From the cliffs, she could not gauge which ones wore different souls under their skin. Could not see if one of them wore brindled fur. Her eyesight was tired. She was tired.

The vehicle sirens sounded like a flock of geese in full voice, until they parked behind her. Margaret's hand went down to the second satchel tucked under her legs, her fingers playing with the thin cable coming out of the corner. They would lock her away from the coast. Box her in granite far from the sea. She knew that. Maybe she deserved it. On the beach the waves tipped one corpse after another onto the sand. She would always have the salted water in her blood.

Letting the bag strap go, she stood, raised her hands and put them behind her head.

Verwelktag

Blumen, Blumen selbst pflücken
Kommt mit mir nach Hause
Du bist süß und sehr, sehr schön
Drinnen oder Draußen
Eine ist weiß, eine ist gelb
Einige begann sich zu röten
Ob im Boden
Auf dem Tisch
Immer für die Toten

COMPETING HONEYSUCKLE and magnolia wafted in from the castle grounds as Angela opened the small apartment's windows.

"Don't they smell beautiful?"

"Hmmm?" Joe didn't look up from his laptop, attention held by cascading columns of figures.

"The flowers in the gardens. Don't they smell beautiful?"

He put the laptop on the rented sofa. Angela stood aside, resting against the thick, cool walls. Joe leaned out of the casement.

"Do you think they'll mind? If I pick some to brighten up this place?" Angela asked, putting her hand on his.

"As long as you don't go overboard. Don't strip out every last bloom. I'm sure they'll be fine."

~~~~~

She knelt on the grass, leaning into the border with a pair of scissors as a substitute for the secateurs she didn't own, beside her a pile of already cut hyacinths and marigolds.

"Entschuldigung. Das ist leider nicht ordnung. Diese Blumen dürfen Sie nicht pflücken."

Angela turned, noticed the grass stains on her skin and tried to see the person speaking to her. The sun was behind them and their face hidden.

"Es tut mir leid. Mein Deutsch ist nicht so gut," she said, unable to hide her English accent in her rehearsed German.

"Sie sprechen Englisch?" the figure said.

Angela stood. It was the gardener she'd seen maintaining the grounds over the past couple of weeks. He rested on his leaf rake as if he had trouble standing.

"Ja, Englisch," she said. "Angela Bay. We've only just moved in. The corner apartment on the second floor of the castle."

He nodded and looked down at the pile of flowers by her feet.

"Residents are not allowed to cut flowers from these gardens."

"Sorry." She held out her hand and he ignored it. "I didn't think you'd miss a handful."

"And if everyone did that? Then replenished their vases when the flowers died? How many would be left?"

"I said I was sorry."

"On the outskirts of the town there are patches of Selbst Pflücken Blumen. 'Pick them yourself flowers.' There is a small charge, but you must get them from there, not damage these plants."

Angela nodded and glanced up toward her apartment. The window was shut, Joe out of sight.

"I will do in future."

The gardener pointed at the severed plants. Sliced from their soil-bound roots the flowers were already wilting to sepia in the sun.

"Those will have to stay."

"I understand, and I'm sorry."

"Please don't do it again, Frau Bay."

"I won't."

She tucked the scissors into her back pocket and, hands empty, walked toward the vast gates leading to the town beyond.

The flower patch wasn't hard to find. An eruption of colour on the edge of a rattling maize field. By the roadside stood a concrete-filled barrel with a small coinbox. A neon-handled kitchen knife hung from a piece of green nylon string.

The flowers were arranged by type. Dahlias to the left of the field, sunflowers rising in the centre, and gladioli on the right-hand side. Tucking her trouser cuffs into her socks, Angela walked down a plough furrow into the midst of the flowers, stumbling on uncleared stones in the soil.

The scents pulled her in, dragging her from one stalk to the next. Blue and purple petals stained with yellow. Reds more vivid than any forest fire. She ran them through her fingers, feeling their velvet skin and the slight bulge of veins under the surface.

Sunflower heads drooped as if embarrassed to be so tall. Stalks like sharkskin. Then dahlias. Globes of dead planets reborn in nested florets. She cupped one after another in her hands. Let them settle in her palms. Lowered her face and allowed the fragrance to rise into her. Lost to herself she wandered from row to row to row. Deeper into the centre, far from the road, to the middle of the small field, she spotted something tight to the worn dirt and her breath caught in her throat

Sunlight reflected off the metal staples holding the limbs in place, fur flayed back to show yellowed bones. The chest cavity was empty of organs, instead stuffed with petals and seed-heads.

Angela stepped back, losing her footing on the loose soil. The skull had been separated from the body and placed a few feet away, delicate bottom jaw still in place. She had no way to tell what the animal had been. In between the picked-clean head and the body grew three rows of the most beautiful flowers she had ever seen. Each stalk inclined to the floor with the weight of blooms, barely any open. Hints of colour far more vibrant than those in the plough furrows around her. She only meant to pick two or three. By the time she finished Angela balanced over a dozen stalks in the crook of her arm.

"Why do you think the colours are so bright?"

The flowers lay on the table in front of her, spread out on old newspaper. Four vases stood around the edge, the blades of her scissors to one side smeared in green.

"Nutrients from the body? What did you say it was again?" Joe said, picking up one of the severed stems.

"Couldn't tell. Rabbit maybe?"

"Probably some kind of bio-dynamic farming thing. Burying cow horns full of manure under the third crescent moon and all that nonsense."

He gathered up the other offcuts and dumped them in the bin.

"What do you know about bio-dynamic farming?"

"I read about it in a magazine once. On a plane. As far as possible from any fields and cow shit," he said, kissing her neck and carrying one of the vases over to the window.

"Brings a bit of colour to the place."

In the grounds the gardener was de-heading espalier roses. Several flowers in full bloom fell into the soil. Instead of leaning down to pick them up, he ground the petals under his boot, and turned to look back at the house. Angela shuddered. Walking back to the dining table, she folded the severed foliage into the newspaper and dumped it into the bin.

"Did you replace these?"

Sunlight shone through the vase's green water, several drowned flies trapped between the stems. Where the petals had started to curl the night before, they were now plump and fleshy again. Joe looked up from his suitcase, piles of clothes fanned out around him. Shook his head.

"Did you top up the water? Pour in some more plant food?" he asked, compressing two jumpers into the suitcase.

Angela replaced the vase on the windowsill, lining the base up with the circular water stain.

"I didn't feed them. The colours have changed too. I'm sure I put the reds and the blues together, and the yellows and oranges over in the kitchen. Now they're all mixed."

She watched Joe pick up three shirts, try to choose one, then stuff all of them in.

"Maybe they change pigment as they age."

Kneeling, she folded a suit jacket in half and passed it to him.

"Are you sure you're not playing a little prank on me before you go? Did you sneak out last night and pick some fresh ones?"

"Because that's the sort of thing I do the night before a conference. Go traipsing around the fields in the dark picking flowers."

She handed him a stack of vests and waited while he found space for them.

"Well, you certainly weren't packing."

"Funny. Check my shoes. I didn't go out last night. It's not like there's anywhere to go around here."

"You do like it here though, don't you? It is beautiful."

He encased her hands in his.

"It is that. And I do get regular work trips away to civilized places, with shops that open on Sundays, and bars with more than one type of beer."

"How are you getting to the airport? Driving yourself?"

"Taxi."

"Ernst?"

"Are there any other taxis in town?"

"Ernst it is then."

She watched Ernst's pale grey Audi make its way down the castle drive, Joe's suitcase visible on the back seat. Alone, she looked again at the flowers. Several petals had already fallen. She picked one up and held it between two fingers, squeezing the silken flesh until it smeared her fingertips with colour. She brushed the remains into her hand, dumped them into the bin and went to bed alone.

Saturday morning, and the small town centre was full. Everyone trying to get their shopping done before midday closing. Angela let the tide of people carry her through the square, past the small shrine to a saint whose name she never remembered. Small bouquets tied with red ribbons were stacked against the statue's marble feet.

She went into each shop, coming out to find herself beside the statue once more, the flowers still stacked up.

"Are those normally there?" she said to the baker, filling her shopping bag with fresh Brez'n and Semmel.

"The flowers? They're for tomorrow."

At home Angela unpacked and sat down at the table sipping her coffee, phone in front of her. She pressed her finger against the screen and checked again for an SMS. Still nothing. Turning on messenger, she brought up the thread she shared with Joe and stared at the last three unanswered messages.

I know you get distracted by the bright lights of the city. A reply once in a while would be nice. X

Throwing the phone out of reach she stared out the window. In the grounds the gardener was burning a pile of waste branches and leaves. Smoke drifted back toward the building. Half-scorched leaves glittered in the fumes. She closed the windows. The smell of ash still found its way inside, around the old wooden window frames.

Church bells rattled her awake. Putting on her dressing gown she watched the other residents parade from the castle's main entrance down to the gate. Most wore their Sunday best, children holding gloved hands. The gardener waited by a vat of hot liquid atop a worn wooden table. He handed each new person a glass and Angela watched each one take a sip, faces obscured by steam. She closed the curtains and got dressed.

Each door on her floor held a different coloured rose, broken stem laced into the lock. She turned to look back at her own apartment. The flower was pale yellow, already wilted. She pulled it free and forced it into her pocket.

Angela took the cup, the decoration of gold-edged blooms glistening with the heated wine inside. She took a mouthful, trying to identify the herbs.

"Frohe Verwelktag, Frau Bay," the gardener said, wiping his hands on his smock.

"Verwelktag?"

"Wilting Day. A time to remember that all things must rot into the soil so others can grow."

She tried to join in. Sipped the drink until the bitter flavour tainted her tongue. Bought a bouquet from the children stood at the entrance to the market place. Took photos of the traditional costumes, all lace and velvet and animal fur. The young girls wore white dresses and carried bunches of daisies tied together with parcel string. Garlands of fuchsias, foxgloves and asters hung between lampposts, low enough to brush pollen on the heads of those passing beneath. Dray horses with bridles decked in blooms the colour of the local Brauerei dragged a barrel-stacked cart in endless circles, mouths foaming with the effort.

Angela held her phone up to take a photo, and attached it to a message for Joe. Show him what he was missing out on. When she saw there was still no reply any enthusiasm left her. She threw her bouquet of already dying flowers into the bin. It landed on half-empty beer bottles, sending up a cloud of drunk wasps, and she set off back to the apartment.

In the corridor the mixture of summer fragrances and rotting vegetation was overpowering. She opened the door and the stench intensified.

Angela walked the short distance to the bedroom and threw her coat on the chair-back. The figure was barely visible in the gloom, curled up under the sheets as if in pain.

She looked around for Joe's suitcase, gripping the collar of her coat.

"Joe? Are you okay? I didn't think you were due back yet. You should have called ahead. I was in town."

The bedside lamp pushed shadows against the walls but did not disperse them.

"Are you ill? Do you want me to get you something?"

She pulled the sheet back.

The legs were shaped from twisted lengths of ivy, each leafed strand woven into the next. Where the chest should have been hundreds of flowers had been placed on top of each other. Roses, lilies, pansies and foxgloves, all arranged into the form of a sleeping man. Lupins as knuckles. Daisies as vertebrae. Where the head should be, a crush of the same flowers dying in vases around the apartment.

"Joe? Are you under there?"

The last drop of hope left her as she tore through the dying flower heads to the sheets underneath. The mattress was sodden, stems already rooting themselves amongst the springs. Searching for nutrients. She wrenched a handful free and flung them to the carpet. There was nothing but petals and seeds and stems.

She tried to clear the bed, filling bin bag after bin bag with dead plants, stopping every few minutes to catch her breath. Instead she sat on the floor and tried her phone again and again until the battery ran out and she was alone with the stench of death.

The singing woke her. Out of habit she reached for her phone to check the time, but the battery had not charged itself while she slept.

Standing, she looked out the window. The townspeople stood around the perimeter wall. Each wore a mask of wilting blossoms. In their disguises it was hard to recognize anyone, not that she knew her neighbours well enough. Children stood between their parents. Priests from the local church next to uniformed police, and farmers. They did not move. In their hands were lanterns. Those held by adults were cylinders of light, the children's shaped like ships, trains and horses. They swung them in low arcs leaving trails in the dark. The flowers danced in the flames.

One figure separated himself from the cordon and walked up the path. His flower mask was old and complex. Layer upon layer of roses and gladioli woven in until the weight bent his neck toward the ground. He rested on a leaf rake, a large knife in his other hand.

While he walked the others began to sing. She recognized some of the words from her basic German. Others were too heavy in dialect for her to make out. All the time the gardener made his slow progress toward the castle.

There was nowhere to go. Only one door out of the apartment, and then what? Run through the crowd into the countryside? She listened to him climb the stairs, each step marked with the clatter of rake tines on stone, the knife scraping the wall as if he couldn't quite hold the blade's weight. He stopped outside the door and knocked. Waited. Knocked again.

"Frau Bay. Bitte öffnen Sie die Tür. Please open the door. There is nowhere you can run."

Looking out of the window, Angela searched for a ledge to get as far from the old man as possible. Where was Joe? Why wasn't he here? All she could see outside was the ring of flames illuminating the floral masks. In the stillness she recognized more of the song they were singing.

Blumen, Blumen selbst pflücken
Kommt mit mir nach Hause
Du bist süß und sehr, sehr schön
Drinnen oder Draußen
Eine ist weiß, eine ist gelb
Einige begann sich zu röten
Ob im Boden
Auf dem Tisch
Immer für die Toten

A key slid into her lock and turned. The door opened toward her, letting light into the living-room. The gardener blocked the way. He panted from the effort of climbing the stairs.

"Frau Bay, there really isn't anywhere to go."

Angela ran. She was taller than the old man and he fell easily, the rake wedging itself against the wall so he couldn't turn. In the hallway she hit the light-switch and ran toward the staircase. There was no-one else in the castle. Every other apartment was silent.

She took the stairs two at a time, hesitating in the hallway. One door led to the drive, straight into the waiting arms of the singers. Behind her was another, small and wooden, that led into the courtyard and beyond to the service part of the complex.

She opened the latch and ran. The paths were overgrown, strawberry runners creeping over the gravel. Brambles and rosebushes erupted from the beds. Ignoring the scratches, she ran toward the old glasshouses at the far end of the grounds. Her plan wasn't complicated. Through the nurseries. Over the wall.

The door hung loose on its hinges. She pulled it toward her and dried putty fell onto her arm. Inside the air was heavy with the sweet scent of compost. On either side of her wooden tables held soil and bedding plants. Seedlings not mature enough to endure the cold outside. Spindly tomato plants knotted around thin canes.

She looked back at her footsteps in the dirt, then forward to make sure no-one was cutting off her escape.

The scream was out of her mouth before she could quiet herself. Joe's body lay in one of the vast seedling trays, naked, arms and legs held down with metal brackets. His face was intact, eyes open, torso split from neck to groin, organs emptied out and the space filled with rich, dark topsoil. Skin blackened with rot around the broken tips of his ribs. In the cavity that once held his heart and lungs, seedlings now grew. She pictured the gardener mulching down Joe's liver for plant-food. Crushing bones as meal to sprinkle in the beds.

Reaching out she touched the tips of his fingers, feeling where roots thin as worms prised apart his skin. Remembering for a moment when his hand last held hers.

Behind her the door opened. The gardener stood with his knife hanging toward one side.

"Please don't flee, Frau Bay. I'm getting old and get tired these days."

Joe's fingers tightened around hers.

"Go, Angela. Just go."

She shook, wanting to scream out all the air in her lungs. Give it to her husband. Stitch him back together and repair him. Scoop out the dirt with her bare hands and hold him until he faded. Instead she ran.

The back of the glasshouse was mildewed and she soon kicked through the wooden panels, glass shattering into foot-long splinters. Behind the building a forgotten pile of rotting kitchen waste rose against the boundary wall. She climbed up, ignoring insects skittering over her legs.

Straddling the wall she checked the drop and lowered herself into the woodland beyond. She heard the townspeople singing. Too many people. She ran deeper. Amongst the trees. Away from the lights. Away from the singing voices. On the other side of the wall she heard the gardener follow her route.

"Sie flieht. Sie ist zu schnell. Ich kann nicht verfolgen. Durch den Wald."

Angela allowed herself a moment of relief. Ducked into the undergrowth. Away from her pursuers. Couldn't remember where she would come out. As long as she kept heading away. From the castle. From her home. She would be okay. Get to the next village. She would be okay. She would be okay.

She spotted them by their lanterns. A line of lights drifting through the dark. Sweeping up the hill. She watched them getting closer. Knew they would be around the wood in moments. The far side was still clear. She took off her coat. Threw it to one side. Ran through the shrubs. Kept low.

The woodland ended at a ditch. She scrambled through. Grass and mud against her skin. Reminded her of Joe's broken hand. Her fingers grasped. She emptied her stomach into the brambles.

Ran for cover. Knelt down.

The sunflowers loomed over her. Behind them the rows of gladioli and dahlias. She tried to see a way out. The townspeople just stood. All along the edge of the flower patch. Lanterns held still. They were not singing now. Just waiting. Angela did not move. Stayed hidden in the flowers. Sunflower stalks rasped her skin.

As one their voices rose and they moved forward. Angela waited to see if they would stop again, but they did not, instead trampling the flowers into the dirt and stones. She waited until the last moment and ran deeper, not caring about the streaks of pollen on her clothes or scratches across her face. Nothing at all, apart from getting as far away from the lanterns as possible. She pictured Joe, holding onto life through some cruel trick of nature. Waiting to say her name. She drew strength from it.

Just before the middle of the flower patch the ground rose slightly, crowned with four large rhododendron bushes, all the flowers removed. She stood beside them and looked out into the night.

The lanterns were on all sides now, the petal-masked shoulder to shoulder. There was no way to break through. Their voices rose again. Not singing. Raucous with joy. She stumbled down the far side of the hill. Tripped over something embedded in the soil. Cold. Metal. The first of four tethers. Each hammered into the furrows.

She pulled herself up. Scanned the villagers. Tried to spot the children in the crowd. Saw one. Lowered her shoulder. Ran forward. Ready to break through.

There was no impact. The child stepped to one side and something sharp slid across the back of her ankle. Angela fell face down into the dirt. Adult hands turned her over. Held her in place as they wrapped her wrists in garlands and placed a crown of honeysuckle on her head. Slowly, they put their lanterns aside and carried her back to where the tethers waited to hold her to the soil.

Under the Banner of the Black Stamen

SABINE CANNOT SEE the archipelago. It is hidden as all islands of the dead should be. A bank of fog runs down the middle of The Channel, the white cliffs beyond hidden for a generation. The stories say it is held in place by the spirits of the dead, their buttoned fingers pinning the strands of fret to the sea floor. She does not know if that is true, but every time the ferry passes through the fog the cold gets into her bones like un-exorcised spirits.

She was born on the islands before they became so isolated, though her feet never touched that land. Her mother and father carried her away on one of the last boats out before the ports closed to the living. She knows none of street names or what the ancient cities are called. Now she only sees her birthplace when leaning against the rail as the corpses are unloaded. Now the dead are the only ones who touch soil on both lands.

Her hands are blue against the bare steel of the handle. There is no shelter on the coast and the wind is full of spray that corrodes skin and metal alike. She pushes the gurney from the storage building, down the stone of the quay toward the ferry. It is the twentieth she has loaded today and her arms ache from the effort. She sweats under the heavy waterproof jacket she wears, once worn by staff of the ferry company, now used only by the Psychopomps.

The contraption is loaded with five corpses and difficult to manoeuvre. Small plastic wheels catch on the lip of the ramp. The gurney skews to the side and for a moment she thinks the shroud wrapped dead will topple to split open on the concrete, but she has done this before many times and wrenches it in the other direction, before they fall.

The ferry wraps her in sound as she moves from the dull glow of the hidden sun to the harsh electrical lights strung up inside the body of the ship. At one time the vast compartments were used to move cars between the island and the continent. Move tourists on their holidays. No-one makes the journey now apart from the Psychopomps and the dead. The hull sings around her, like it is keening for its cargo. She shudders and moves the trolley into place, hooking the tie downs to the rings on the floor. The sound of metal against metal is too loud and sounds like a clattering bell in the confined space of the deck.

The weather has closed in. They gather in the old club lounge. Out of the window she can see the ensign, stamens heavy and black against the pale blue background.

The chairs and tables in the lounge are old. At one time they would have been replaced as they became worn. Now they wear chips and tears from rough crossings like scars.

No-one sits. The Psychopomps stand in a circle around the Captain. Sabine stands between Joe, a few years older than her, but only recently trained for the daily transporting of the dead, and Mary, her skin whitened by the harsh erosion of the sea. Most keep the waterproof hoods up. Sabine is still cold in her bones and keeps glancing outside to the bank of fog that waits for them.

"In age order," the captain says, holding out a handful of paper slips. He still wears the uniform he wore when taking the living across the sea, the ferry companies logo on the cap faded and tarnished with age.

Sabine is the youngest. She steps forward and takes a slip of paper, turning it over to read what is written on the hidden side.

"Corpse deck One."

She steps back and watches her colleagues choose their duties. Joe will spend the crossing guarding cremation urns crammed into the old passenger cabins. Mary will make the journey on the deck, carrying out the rituals that are necessary, though all the Psychopomps know they make no difference to the passage. Once the last piece of paper is chosen they all leave. No-one but the Captain speaks.

Sabine does not mind guarding the dead on their gurneys. They do not smell of rot, but the chemicals pumped into their collapsed veins. Formaldehyde soaks out and into the brass pinned shrouds that cover them. She leans against the wall and bows her head as a colleague seals the door from the outside. Alone she reaches into her pocket and takes out the small bottle of whisky, lifting it in toast to the dead. The Psychopomps all have their own rituals of respect. Somewhere high above her the fog horn sounds, a single dull note that does not end. Sabine folds her hands over each other. The room is warm and sweat pools against her back. The dead smell astringent. A scent that catches in the back of her throat, but is comforting in its familiarity. She closes her eyes.

At one time, when the ferries brought the living back and forth, the goal was to move as fast as possible. Be the quickest on the water. Now that the only cargo is those that do not breathe, and those that do not have a choice, the ferries go slow and mournful.

There is little for Sabine to do but walk between the gurneys, keeping the blood flowing to her limbs. Whisper rhymes to herself. Sometimes she pauses beside a bundle that looks too small to deserve to be there. At one time she would have wept at a life finished too early. Now that it is her job to care she no longer does.

The ferry creaks as it pulls away into The Channel, waves ebbing and flowing against the hull as if they're trying to get to the dead inside. Sabine sits in the corner and waits.

Though she cannot see their faces, she tells herself stories about the dead that surround her to pass the time. That body is a sailor from Calais who hung himself on the rigging of his fishing boat. The corpse below is a fireman who choked to death on the soot and toxic fumes as he got the last family members out of a burning building on the German border. Three rows away she imagines a gurney carries all the members of a same family. The short-sighted mother harvested the wrong mushrooms from deep inside the forest, slowly killing her family in her error with mushroom fricassée. None of these are true. The dead have already been mourned and are now anonymous. No more remembered than clay or stone. In this way she passes the first hour at sea.

The scent is sweet, but not that of preservation. Sometimes the grieving hide white lilies upon the dead and these rot before the muscle of their loved ones. This is not fragrance but decay. Though they only transport preserved corpses, all Psychopomps spend time working in the mortuary. Sabine is familiar with the stench.

She stands and stretches cramp from her limbs. The crossing is smooth today, the waves not pitching the ferry as it sometimes does. She has no need to cling to the guide ropes around the edges of the deck and moves in between the stacks of bodies, searching for the smell. The Island of the Dead will not take rotten meat, and she does not understand how the corpse has passed through all the stages of checks and certificates to make it onboard. The stench seems everywhere and nowhere at once. She cannot pin it down.

The shroud hangs loose down the side of the gurney. She sees it from several rows away, and pauses. It is not unusual for gases in untreated remains to swell the dead and burst them like a child's overinflated balloon. She has seen the photos from when they tried transporting the deceased in lead coffins. Every day they pass the skeletons of those ferries, hulls breached from the exploding dead.

Her nails pick at the skin of her knuckles. She moves backwards and around to avoid coming to the exposed corpse directly. It takes her time to pluck up the courage. To steel herself for confronting death.

The shape is that of a person, though that is where any similarity ends. The arms, legs and head are all made from the same hard crust. She runs a hand above the surface, but not touching. It is mineralised and fibrous, like metal feathered against cloth.

Strands grasp as her fingers pass over and she snatches her hand away. Liquid coats the inside, streaking across the fissure where the thing that is not a corpse has split. She leans over. The substance pools in the bottom reflecting the halogen light above. The scent is overpowering, meadow-sweet and cloying. She steps back, knocking into a gurney, scraping the skin from her arm, blood pooling in the sleeve of her waterproof. She hears something gouge across the metal floor, ricochet into several gurneys then change direction. From far across the compartment she hears a similar sound. Whatever crawled out of the nest hidden within the torn shroud was not singular.

Her breathing is too loud and nothing she can do will quieten it. She tries to keep her limbs steady while she walks. Trying not to clatter into the corpses lying silent around her. The door is not far away. A single metal portal between her and the rest of the ship. She does not speed up. She does not want to panic whatever else is in there with her. The door is only a few feet. The rest of the Psychopomps will be in quiet contemplation. Remembering the dead. They will hear her when she calls for them. There is no protocol for this. She will have to invent her own. Standing beside the door she hammers with her fist as hard as she can against the metal. No-one answers and the sound echoes around the deck.

"Open the door," she shouts, but her voice returns to her, and hidden within it is a mimic of her words. Still no-one comes.

Leaning back against the door, Sabine stares around the deck. Somewhere far out of sight water drips. She does not move from her place of rest. The sickly sweet smell surrounds her now. She lifts her arm and sniffs it as if it was a bouquet. The scent is on her as well.

The corrosion on the metal walls was not there before. She has spent many hours in this metal box with only the dead for company. At one time or another she has gazed upon every steel plate and rivet, and she knows enough to know corrosion comes on slow. The patches of rust are fresh and fibrous. They run from the floor up to the wall. In their outline she sees the vague shape of arms and legs, and as she approaches the aberrations they begin to scream.

Once more she hammers on the door, this time until her knuckles bruise, then crack, then bleed. No-one comes, but she knows that the ferry moves on. Even above the screeching of the rusted figures she hears the engines deeper in the ferry, and the mourning of the fog horn above.

There are seventeen of them, some grouped together like a family waiting for a photo. Others solitary. Her mouth is dry and she can hardly keep her balance, though the ferry is steady beneath her. Walking around the room she stands in front of each in turn. There is no point hiding from them. They will not mistake her for the dead as she did them.

Their mouths are broken steel shaped from layer upon layer of rust. Between the flaking sheets of corrosion the same thick liquid drips, pooling on the floor. She backs away to avoid stepping in it because of an overwhelming feeling that if she does she will never move again. Across the deck something cracks, a slow opening, then the tearing of fabric that was intended to never be opened, never mind rent apart, again. Sabine looks over toward the sound. It is several rows away, from the middle of a gurney. She sees something corroded and knotted streak across the surrounding shrouds then burrow along the floor as if the halogen glow disgusts it. For a moment she feels an affinity, then a shuddering, creeping uncertainty. How many more of the corpses are not dead, but incubators for these living stains that are grasping for life in the metal of the ferry's hull?

She tries the door once more, splitting the skin on her other hand, watching her blood collect on the floor. The lock holds tight, the seal around the edge too compressed to let her get her damaged fingers in. There are more figures on the wall now, rusted patches thinning and buckling the metal of the ship. She does not want to think what will happen if they find their way through the inner skin to the outer hull. Breach their way to the sea.

They are still screaming, though she doubts they have lungs. She walks toward the nearest stain, planting her feet solid. She wants nothing more than to run. Air rushes out of the corrosion that seems to be a mouth. There are no words, just sound and breath.

She looks at the creature, because she has no doubt now that it is living, despite being shaped from the lamination of rotten metal. Thinned and curled, crumbling as it vibrates with each smeared syllable.

Backing up she reaches behind her to the nearest gurney. To the nearest shrouded dead. The brass pins are easy to find, and barely make a sound as they tumble to the floor, though it takes some manoeuvring of the body to remove the cloth. The material tears into strips easily and Sabine wraps her hand until no skin is visible, ignoring the blood soaking through from her injuries.

On the first punch the metal holds, scales flaking and fluttering to the ground, even as the patch of rust carries on screaming. The second and third punch forces through the skin of the deck, light coming through from the corridor on the other side. Pausing to wrap her other hand, Sabine braces her feet against the wall and widens the rent in the metal, folding back the sharp edges until the rust goes silent. She pulls her hood down over her face, and ties the pull cords tight.

The hole is barely wide enough for her to squeeze through sideways and even then the metal snags at her waterproof, ripping through the plastic, but not reaching her skin.

Out in the corridor she crouches and catches her breath. Beneath her the engines still thrum like everything above is a war between ticks upon its body. Standing, Sabine unfastens her hood. The fabric around her hands is soaked red now and she strips it off, letting it fall to the ground. From far away she hears more screaming, the same noise of air whistling through corrosion and damage. She needs to get above deck. Raise the alarm. Warn the rest of the Psychopomps. Warn the Captain.

Joe is standing in the middle of the corridor, head turned down toward the worn carpet.

"Why aren't you with the cremations?" Sabine says. Her voice sounds too loud as it always does after not speaking to anyone for a while. She does not know why she questions him about being out of place before warning him about the things of rust and sound.

He looks up but does not speak. His arms are stiff in his coat, and his neck is held at the wrong angle. She needs to get past him, to get to the deck and then the bridge.

"Are you OK?"

It is not unusual for Psychopomps to get overwhelmed by the death they are surrounded by. The training they receive is meant to inoculate them against the shock, teach them meditations and black humour to cope. For some even that is not enough. The screaming is incessant. Sabine wonders if Joe thinks it is only in his head. That the corpses are trying to talk to him from their rest. She knows that her main priority is to get to the Captain and warn him, but she cannot leave her colleague like this. Cannot leave her friend like this.

She approaches slowly, speaking all the time.

"It's OK. It's just me, Sabine. Something strange is going on with the bodies. While that's bad, and it is very bad, it's not you. Please don't worry. It's not you. It's the ferry."

Joe raises his head, his neck creaking like a vessel at harbour. Sabine is close enough to stare directly into his face, despite the faint glow of the lights above. She notices his eyes first. They are coated with a thin layer of rust, veins of minerals running through as if all the calcium and iron in his body has leached out of his bones and blood to coat his sight. His breath reeks of mown grass fermenting in the sun. Sabine covers her mouth so she does not inhale the fumes.

The split starts at his chin, running up his face, slightly off centre, both halves pulling apart like cheap fabric. Underneath he is solid, like iron ore, or a meteor that has melted to human shape through the friction of the atmosphere.

Sabine can no longer watch this thing that was her friend. There is nothing there anymore. She wipes her eyes to keep her vision clear. Runs past the corroded statue that is no longer Joe, and makes for the stairs that will lead her to the deck.

Out in the open the sea fret obscures everything. It veils itself over her, turning the deck to a ghost and scrubbing anything beyond to a pale grey. The screaming is here too, and by her feet she can see human figures in the checker-plate, vague arms and legs shaped in rust, each one part of a choir that will not stop. Occasionally through the fog she sees the vague figure of a colleague standing by the rail. She thinks about shouting at them, warning them to get to safety. Telling one person at a time will take too long. She focuses on getting to the bridge. Getting to the Captain. The deck is wet underfoot and several times she loses her balance.

Mary stands on the gangway, head slumped forward over the edge. Her waterproof hangs in tatters, strands fluttering in the breeze, a parody of the flags above them on the mast. Even before Sabine reaches her she knows that her colleague is gone. Her skin is little more than a smear over the rough geology of the ore that has replaced her.

There is no way past without touching the metal. Mary's hands grasp the rail, her fingers corroded into the hollow steel. Sabine strips off her own coat, the cold and damp seizing its chance. She wraps her hands once more and walks toward the frozen figure. Gripping the waist she tips it forward. The arms snap in two with the extra weight and the body topples forward to shatter on the deck below. Shadows separate from the fragments, leaving a trail of rust behind them as they embed into the ship. Sabine cannot let herself mourn for her friends. She runs on.

The bridge is empty and open, the door creaking backward and forward with the roll of the sea. She runs in and slams it shut. Two of the marks have embedded themselves in the wall, their screams too intense in the small space, drilling into Sabine's head as if that too was oxidised steel.

She stands in front of the console. There is no way to steer the ship, automatic route followed again and again programmed into the navigation system. To one side the radio hangs loose. She picks up the handset and pushes the talk button.

"SOS. SOS. We need assistance. We will be coming into dock and we need assistance."

She does not know what to do. What the people of the Island of the Dead will do. If they will come in launches to take her off the doomed vessel or hole it beneath the waterline to become another skeleton littering the narrow band of water between continent and archipelago.

The rusted shadows behind her are still screaming. She ignores them, puts on a set of headphones and plugs them into the radio.

The navigation system is showing they are not far from the coast. Within range of the radio towers that line the hills. She repeats her message, waiting for an answer, hearing nothing in reply but static. The sea fret clothing the ferry muffles the fog horn and sound of engines, but coddles the screams closer. Trying to ignore them she concentrates on where the ferry will arrive. Normally the Captain would bring it into the harbour. Now there is only her. She pulls over the chair and perches on the seat, allowing herself a moment to mourn her friends, her colleagues, while she waits.

The radar system howls, a proximity alarm alerting her to another ship nearby. She looks out to the port side and sees one of the skeletons that litter The Channel, switching side to side in the waves. She tries the radio again, but there is no reply. The static dense and unending. Around her the mist is clearing. The ferry is nearing the coast. She has no control but to watch and wait. Behind her the rust screams with no lungs. She peers through the Perspex windows, watching for the coast to emerge. They are close now. She turns the radio off. She waits.

There is no-one to hear her. The scent is the first thing to hit. A wave of sweet rotting vegetation rolling down the cliffs to greet her. It overwhelms the ferry until Sabine can no longer even smell her own skin.

At first she thinks they are crowds lining the quay, waiting to unload the corpses below. Then statues. Maybe tributes to the un-named dead. It is only as the ferry enters the stone arms of the harbour she realises that they are people, occupied and hollowed. Turned to mineral by creatures that are paper thin and still scream their rage.

The ferry is not infecting the Island of the Dead. The ferry is taking the creatures home.

This is the time when the Captain earns his position, guiding the ferry into rest. There is no sign of him, and without his guiding hand the ferry turns in the calmer water, the back swinging around, scraping along the stone walls. Opening holes in the steel skin that do not scream. Smearing paint along the harbour.

The collision topples Sabine from her seat, throwing her across the bridge. She collides with the crowd of rust crumbling the far wall, her arms cut and bleeding.

Pushing herself up on her arms, Sabine tries to rise from the floor and fails, muscles locked solid. She opens her eyes and tries to focus on the ceiling. Already crumbs of rust are floating across her vision, collecting to obscure the outside world. Under her skin her muscles turn to metal, absorbing her blood first, then her bones. Deep inside something starts to scream, though it is not her, no matter how much she wishes she could.

Our Lady of the Tarpaulin

FROM THE BALCONY we heard sirens announcing the boat's arrival. Deep undulating notes echoing against worn stonework lining the river.

The Goddess was toward the stern, sitting or crouching. It was hard to tell. She was wrapped in green tarpaulins, held in place by salt-stained ratchet straps.

Sarah sipped her wine, and passed me my vodka. The ice rattled against my teeth and started to melt with the warmth of my breath.

"Where will they unveil her?" Sarah asked.

Along the riverbank devotees stripped to the waist, backs rib-boned with welts.

"Where the three rivers meet," I said. "At the apex of the town."

The siren called more people out of their houses. On the boat a single priest wound the handle, deforming the air. Meant to be as close as possible to her voice. He glanced up and I shuddered. Dark liquid seeped out from the tarpaulin, collecting in pools on the deck. Blood, oil or ink. Hard to tell in the gloom.

"Let's go downstairs," I said. "Get into the street."

Sarah grabbed the wine, running the bottle's condensation against my bare skin. We walked through the apartment, stopping only to grab a couple of glasses. She slid my arm around her waist and I hooked my hand into the belt of her summer dress. The light turned itself off behind us.

Outside, the streets were crowded with worshippers. Many times we could only hold on by fingertip and risked getting swept apart. At the corner of Hafen Straße and Tiere Gasse she paid five Euros for a bag of powder paint and glitter. I watched her unfasten the wire tie then throw colours into the night sky. The dust hung in the air for a moment before falling, coating us with vivid greens and teal. We smeared the pigments into swirls and spirals as we hugged.

Carried along by dancing we traded wine for whisky and whisky for kisses until the press of people left us with nowhere to go apart from the harbour side. We sat, feet dangling above the river.

"I want to see what she looks like," Sarah said. Her words were threadbare with too much alcohol and other people's lipstick.

"The Goddess? We will. When they unveil her."

"Do you think she's beautiful or withered skin over shattered bones?" She hooked her ankle strap away and let the yellow shoe fall into the water below. It floated for a moment before sinking out of sight.

"I don't think anyone will care about her appearance when they gaze on her and she gazes on them."

The other shoe followed, carried out a little by the current before that too shuddered away to the riverbed.

"I want to see before everybody else. Before the priests suck her dry."

She pivoted, bare feet on bare stone, and lifted her dress over her head.

I followed her into the water, swimming toward the boat on the far shore. No-one guarded the Goddess. No-one was going to steal her away. In the streets the songs, chants and drunkenness continued. Silt heavy water filled our ears and mouths.

The ladder onto the boat was wet and worn, chafing our skin to grazes that did not stop bleeding.

The Goddess still waited at the boat's stern, still encased in the same vast green tarpaulins. Our feet left wet footprints across the deck, stains of our trespass that would go with the coming day's heat.

I gripped the covering and hesitated, staring across the river toward town. Toward all the devotees too messed up on praise or cheap weed to notice our transgression.

Sarah grabbed the tarpaulin from my hand, lifted the corner and climbed underneath. Too cold and too exposed I followed her.

The Goddess was vast, sitting cross-legged, hands resting in her lap. In between her wooden muscles were all the coins pushed into trees throughout the world in devotion and desperation. Euros, dollars, baht and rubles. Some of the offerings were from countries that no longer existed, their borders rewritten or scrubbed out.

Her limbs were feathered with ribbons tied to thorn trees. Ribbons left to rot with prayers and confessions. Sarah reached out and ran her fingers across the fronds of cheap man-made fibres, inhaling the Goddess's wild garlic scented breath. The air was brackish, heavy with the reek of the salt pans where they'd found her.

We fucked right there, Sarah leant forward across the Goddess's limbs, rounded edges of coins digging into her arms and back. Her arms stained grey and green with lichen as she lay upon the splintered, writhing bark.

We whispered words to each other in languages neither of us spoke. Glitter slid from me to her and back again, grinding miniscule ruts into our exposed skin. Our alcohol soaked sweat and spit dripped into the ancient timber that creaked when the Goddess shifted position. We got closer to coming. I felt the Goddess reach down and stroke our skin. Thorns embedded in her palms drew blood. Under those tarpaulins that scent of forest floor soaked by a distant sea was narcotic. Shuddered away anything apart from each other. The Goddess breathed onto us, gilding each exposed pore of us with her name while we worshipped.

Sarah pulled me toward her, kissing me. Forcing me deeper inside her. Held my arms tight until I felt bruises unfurl against my bones like May blossom. Her muscles tightened. Pushed me out of her as she came.

She slid the condom into a crevice below the Goddess's knee. Sarah and I lay beneath the tarpaulin in each other's arms until just before dawn, then walked barefooted across the plank between boat and shore.

The unveiling was timed for moonrise that evening. We slept most of the day. When we woke our bed was scented with rotting ferns and estuary silt. The crowds flowed past the apartment building. We slid in behind, green powder paint and glitter still in our hair. Thorn scratches scabbing on our skin.

No-one paid us any attention and we forced our way close to the front of the crowd as the procession arrived at the town's apex.

Still covered with her shroud of tarpaulins they carried her in on a funeral bier of railway sleepers, the priests bent double with the weight. Resting her in the middle of the grass they pressed back the crowds, lighting fires of old newspapers and discarded clothes. The smoke stung our eyes and sludged our lungs, but we saw coins glisten and ribbons flutter as they unbuckled the ratchet straps.

The crowd fell upon her, pushing the priests out of the way, searching for the oldest coins or the highest denominations. Prising them from her skin with knives and needle-nose pliers.

They turned their tools on each other too. Stabbing, cleaving and tearing until gobbets of flesh coated her limbs like an infection. They did not care about the prayers or her beauty, her power or her ability to fulfil their dreams and ambitions. All they cared about were the coins hammered into her flesh.

When they left we walked over to her, running our hands across her arms and face. There was no enchantment left. They had stripped away the offerings, and with them any magic. Mould was already rotting the timber. Beetles drilling through to the heartwood. She no longer exhaled leaf litter scented breath. She no longer exhaled at all.

In the following days we saw them paying for rounds with 19th century rubles. Buying the weekly shopping with Marks from the DDR. Across the river we watched the Goddess collapse in upon herself with dry rot and infestation until nothing was left but mulch.

Dancing Sober in the Dust

THE INSIDE OF THE MASKS are rough with nails and wire. I push my hand inside. Raw metal snags my skin, adding new blood to old. I place the head-mask to one side and take the leg piece out of the wooden trunk. Built from cardboard and skin, it has been made heavy with plaster of Paris and encased bandages that healed no-one. I lay it in position, followed by the arms and body piece. The gauzed eyes stare at me, daring me to try on the outfit. I ignore its challenge and continue to empty the crate.

~~~~~~

1. Der Schlaffman (The Sleeping Man) *Outfit, 1923, Gypsum, Cardboard, House Paint.*

Der Schlaffman is a costume made to be worn during the dance The Dream of the Still Sea. *While the dancer appeared on stage wearing the costume, the first act is for him to be sewn into the outfit. The stitches run up the back, across the slash representing the mouth, and through the eyes reducing visibility to very narrow slits. The dance is then performed purely in response to the location of sounds performed by the second dancer representing* The Still Sea.

~~~~~~

By the time I have finished, ten costumes are laid out, radiating from where I sit in the museum attic. I count three times just to check. Six are too small for me to wear. The others would fit, but not comfortably. Comfort was never intended to be part of the performance. At the bottom of the empty crate I find three files of papers bound with cheap red string. I do not open them in case the words within animate the masks and they prevent me from leaving this room of grey light and dust. Cradling the documents to my chest I climb back down the metal ladder, leaving the costumes prone upon the wooden floor like sacrifices around a king. It doesn't feel right to crate them once more.

The curator walks up to the desk, where I sit with choreography plans and costume designs spread out around me. He is a small unkempt man who hovers before he speaks. He reminds me of a bird who waits until the killing is done.

My first instinct is to shuffle the papers away. To hide them from sight, but they are obscure enough in their language. By the time I make my decision it is too late. He picks up a piece of yellowed paper and turns it over to better see in the light of the archive's high windows.

"Die Schiedler Tanzen," he says, putting the document down and picking up another.

"You know of this?" I say. I shuffle the papers as if looking for something and conceal two pages. He picks up another, adjusts his glasses and sighs.

"Of course, Frau Armstrong. We have records of all that is held within the archive. These were donated by the police when they finished their investigation. Of little value apart from morbid curiosity. No artistic merit."

"Morbid curiosity?"

"The Schiedler Tanzen were husband and wife. Their approaches were unconventional and not to everyone's taste. Not to anyone's taste, even in the febrile atmosphere of the Expressionist movement."

In my head I see the costumes still laid out on the wooden floor several storeys above us. Smell the painted cardboard dulled by dust. Feel the iron scratch against my skin. My hand goes to the scab on my wrist and I resist the temptation to scrape it off.

"Do you know where I can find out more?"

The curator looks toward the floor then back up at me and nods toward the door.

"Not here," he says and turns his back on me.

I slide the papers into my rucksack, and leave. The curator will not interfere with the costumes. They will stay where they are until I return for them.

2. Der Tod Von Tieren (The Death of Animals), *Outfit, 1927, Gypsum, Roofing Nails, Fur From Unknown Animals, Mummified Meat From Unknown Animals, Papier-mâché*

Der Tod Von Tieren was only used for one performance, offending even the decadent tastes of the audiences at the time. Little detail remains of the choreography, (the diagrams are highly stylised), but they seem to suggest that a live animal was used during the course of the show.

The microfiche reader is rarely used anymore and it takes time for the librarian to find first the machine itself and then the roll of newspaper records.

"We have a project to digitise our archives," the librarian says, leading me through the corridors of paper. "We haven't got that far back yet. Are you sure you cannot be more precise about the year?"

I cannot. My only guide is the date of the last document in the files. I do not remove them from my bag until she leaves me alone.

It takes all afternoon to find the notice of their deaths, searching through year after year until I find the column hidden within a morning edition of the city's main paper, removed by the time of the evening edition. Once I have the date I visit the police station to find out the address.

The police are still housed in the same building they were in the 1920s, a vast arc of windows and wall painted the same green as their officer's uniforms. The entrance smells of vomit and regret, and I step around two recently released drinkers who are only suffering their hangovers until they have enough energy to drink once more.

Inside, I hand the receptionist my print-off and wait while they disappear to return with a police officer whose rank I do not know. He holds my piece of paper in his hand, low to his side like a knife.

"What's your interest in finding this building?" he says, without introducing himself.

"I'm a theatre historian. Dance mainly. I saw a photograph of one of their costumes online, and I was intrigued."

"We've had people trying to find the address before," he says, then goes silent.

I lean on the counter, my rucksack heavy on my back as if its weight is pushing me to ask the next question.

"And did you give it to them?"

"They were ghouls. Wanting to do murder tours. We don't need that kind of tourism."

"That's not my interest," I say, and hand him my university ID hoping he does not look at the date. He hands it back, writes something on a piece of paper and pushes it across to me. His handwriting is neater than I was expecting.

3. *'Das Tier Unter der Erde* (The Beast Under The Soil), *Outfit, 1921, Wire, Clay, Glass, Stones, Concrete*

There is no evidence Das Tier Durch Unterseite was ever used in a performance. Although the files found contain both choreography and sheet music for a short piece involving the 'mask' no contemporary accounts exist of a dance involving the outfit. The costume is incredibly heavy (weighing in at 13 stone) and would have been far too restricting to perform in for very long.

Apart from graffiti on the outside walls, the house looks like it has been untouched since the 1920s. It stands alone on the outskirts of the city, hidden within a copse of overgrown blackthorn trees. The river runs beside the fence, water shattering against the tumbled stones of a broken weir. In its shudder and shift I hear music and pause to make notes, before returning to the task in hand.

Although the shutters are rotten and askew I can see no signs of entry, so make one, wrenching damp wood away from soft plaster. There is no glass in the windows.

Inside is dark. I think about widening the gap in the window to allow in more light, but something about the house suggests that it does not want to be lit by the sun. Instead I find my lighter in my pocket and let that guide me through the broken rooms.

There is no floor. I am tempted to blame that on thieves following the abandonment of the house, but everything else is in place. I say that as if the rooms are crammed with furniture and crockery. This is not the case. Stepping along the exposed beams, I walk into the second ground floor room. The two hammocks hang from the ceiling, swinging from the breeze caused by my movement through the door. For a moment I expect Jochan and Sabine to sit up, annoyed to be disturbed, but there is nothing in the hammocks except dust and dried blood. I walk over and push the nearest one, letting it swing back and forth. The dirt of eighty-years slips through the bullet hole like sand through an hourglass.

✺✺✺✺✺✺

4. *Lawine* (Avalanche), *Outfit, 1920, Gypsum, Copper Wire, Lime Paint, Razorblades*

Lawine is the earliest of the eleven known costumes attributed to Die Schiedler Tanzen. The attention to detail is exquisite, with finishing touches that are lacking from their later outfits. For example the stitching on the gloves, and the detailing on the face show a degree of care that seems to be missing from subsequent costumes. It is noticeable too that Lawine is much lighter than their later outfits and that the interior is not as raw, with padding in place to cushion against any sharp edges left by the production process. The razorblades have all had their edges dulled, though it is noticeable that when the costume was repaired (possibly for the brief reprisal of the dance for the disastrous 1926 retrospective), that the lost razorblades were all replaced with sharp ones. Examination during recording found many rusted due to the presence of blood.

✺✺✺✺✺✺

The upstairs of the building is barely used, with dead pigeons covering most of the floor, mummified and still. I step my way through the corpses to reach the single cabinet on the other side of the room. I'm not surprised to find it is older than the 1920s, and broken. Poverty meant that even the one piece of furniture they allowed themselves would have been scavenged from the streets. I open the doors, just to make sure, even though I know that nothing will be inside, and then tip the whole thing over onto the carpet of dead birds, turning my face from the rising cloud of dust. I reach into the cavity beneath the floor, until moments before hidden by the cabinet. The box is heavier than I expect and it takes all my effort to lift it out and carry it back down the broken stairs. It smells of rotten meat and sealing wax. I resist the temptation to open it straightaway and leave the house to its ghosts.

⟋⟋⟋⟋⟋⟋⟋

5. *Der Wartende Mann An Der Kreuzung* (The Waiting Man at the Crossroads), *Outfit, 1925, Sackcloth, Iron Nails, Iron Barrel Hoops, Wooden Splinters, Bottle Glass, Tar*

At the time of the performance Der Wartende Mann An Der Kreuzung (worn during the dance by Sabine) was interpreted as taking its inspiration from Voodoo, and particularly the rituals surrounding Baron Samedi. When this was suggested in a local newspaper, Sabine is supposed to have flown into one of her characteristic rages, threatening to burn down the printing press responsible for producing the publication. No other clues to the inspiration were left by the couple, so only supposition is available to us. However, the most fitting interpretation has recently been put forward by Dr. Helen Canterbury, during the conference that preceded this exhibition. Dr Cantebury pointed out Sabine's grandmother was born in the North of England and would almost certainly have been familiar with folklore surrounding criminals gibbeted at crossroads. This seems far more in line with the other themes in Sabine and Jochan's work.

⟋⟋⟋⟋⟋⟋⟋

I leave the box unopened in my room and return to the museum, ignoring the temptation to stay and just open the lid a touch. To reach inside and feel the texture of the costume. I control myself like all good dancers should, and leave.

The curator looks up as I knock on his open door. He carries on reading for a moment and puts his book to one side.

"Come with me," I say and do not wait to see if he follows. I hear him shuffle in his chair as he rises, then smell the reek of aftershave as he falls in step behind me. We climb through the museum in silence until we reach the ladder up into the attic.

"After you," I say and wait until he climbs, placing each foot with care as if preparing himself for a betrayal. He is not looking in the right place for treachery.

Once he is inside, I follow him up and stand aside as he turns on the overhead bulb. The light glares down, the dull costumes waiting upon the wooden floor like skinned clowns.

♋♋♋♋♋

6. *Die Frau Der Weiden* (The Woman Of The Willows), *Outfit, 1929, Copper Wire, Stones, Gauze, Velvet Curtains*

One of the last costumes Sabine and Jochan made, Die Frau Der Weiden is also one of the most elaborate. Each length of copper wire has been knotted to create some kind of approximation of willow branches. The detailed choreography found in the archive accompanying the costumes shows the complex performance was designed to create sound and not just movement. As with all the later costumes designed by Die Schiedler Tanzen the interior provides no padding or protection for the dancer, and the sharp copper wire would have been incredibly uncomfortable for the performer. Indeed, one contemporary report describes visiting the backstage area after the performance to find Jochan's body covered in slashes, blood seeping down to collect on the floor.

♋♋♋♋♋

I can tell by his posture, by the way his shoulders slump, that the curator has no interest in my find. He turns to face me and shrugs.

"You found the costumes then?"

"You knew these were here?" I say. He looks me up and down as if searching for some glitch or error that might explain me.

"Of course. I told you before. We have records of all material we hold within the museum. We just choose to—" he pauses while searching for the right word. "Emphasise some of our collection over others. No-one is interested in this amateurish fancy dress."

I nod, because I know that what he says is true for himself. Unless it is chipped marble or dusty oil paint, then it will find no place within his exhibitions.

"I will ask you to please pack them away, and in future not enter areas of the museum that are off limits to visitors."

"I'm not a visitor," I say. "I'm a researcher."

He pauses halfway down the steps, just his head and shoulders above the hatch, looking like he is emerging from the earth.

"You are a visitor. You are not accredited by an academic institution recognised by our organisation, and you will do well to remember that I only allowed you to have a certain amount of freedom as a favour to an old friend. An old friend, I might add, who only had the vaguest of recollections of you."

He disappears out of sight and leaves me with the ten costumes of Die Schiedler Tanzen, but all I can think about is the eleventh waiting for me.

∽∽∽∽∽

7. *Hügelgrab* (Burial Mound), *Outfit, 1924, Soil, Clay, Moss, Grasses, Stones, Sacking*

Hügelgrab seems to represent a changing point in the approach of Die Schiedler Tanzen. Here is where we first see seams left raw enough to raise welts on skin, due to the movement of the ill-fitting costume during the marathon 5 hour performance. In some ways the chronology of Die Schiedler Tanzen's costumes represent an abandonment of skill through time, as if the shedding of detailing was part of the intention.

Although known about in private circles for a long time previously, it's believed that the performance of Hügelgrab was the first time that Sabine Schiedler's violent rages played out in such a public forum.

In the attic I cannot resist the temptation and strip, leaving my clothes beside me in an untidy pile. I take my time. There are many decisions to be made. The costume must be big enough to fit, and it must be in good enough condition that I do not have to worry about damaging the fabric. These narrow my options and I choose Der Tod Von Tieren.

Even though the meat has mummified over the decades I still feel I can smell a hint of rotten flesh as I pull the sleeves onto my arms, and step into the leggings. There is no flexibility. No allowance for knees and elbows. I pause, remove the arm pieces and slide the mask over my head.

The weight sits on my shoulders, grinding welts into my collarbones. Slipping on the arm pieces once more I pick up the fur covered gloves and flex my hands until my fingers are in place. The points of roofing nails scratch their way into my palms, and through the discomfort I wonder if they reroute the destiny hidden in the lines there.

I have no urge to dance or to move. I can barely keep standing in the outfit. Inside the mask is raw, the gauze used to carry the gypsum roughly cut and inward facing. If I turn my head to see better out of the narrow eye slits my cheeks are cut many times and blood collects in my mouth. I cannot tell if the iron taste is from the wounds or the rusted metal. I am so engrossed in my own discomfort I do not notice the curator behind me until it is too late.

8. *Waagen (Weighing Scales), Outfit, 1923, Metal strips, Heavy weights increasing up to 14lbs, Meat hooks (rusted), Leather straps, Buckles, Wine bottles, Rough hemp sacking.*

Waagen was most certainly one of the most extreme performances by Die Schiedler Tanzen and may reflect the deteriorating mental

*state of both Sabine and Jochan. In contrast to many other perform-
ances, the choreography involved the dancer (in this case Jochan)
dressing in the outfit on stage. First the basic clothing is worn and
strapped up at the back, then the iron strips are affixed to the arms,
preventing them moving from a crucifixion pose. On the end of the
metal strips were rings through which the meat hooks were threaded. Once this was done Sabine placed the mask over her husband's
head. Many witnesses recorded that this was the most disturbing
part of the performance. Extending from the mouth and each eye
was a single glass wine bottle. Apart from this the mask was feature-
less. It did not take a leap of imagination to imagine what would
happen to Jochan if he fell, unable to use his hands to break his
descent.*

*Then, over the next ten minutes Sabine suspended increasing-
ly heavy weights from each side of his outstretched arms. There
seemed to be no pattern and no attempt to 'balance' the distri-
bution. Waagen was performed three times and on each occasion
was halted by worried members of the audience, concerned for the
wellbeing of Jochan. Sabine's rage at these interruptions was only
matched by her husband's.*

"Whatever my personal feelings about these particular items of
our collection, that does not give you licence to wear them, like,
like..." he stumbles, his anger overcoming him. "Some toddler
rummaging through a dress-up box."

I am still stood as Der Tod Von Tieren. He seems unsettled
by my appearance, as if I am the dead animated by cardboard and
Papier-mâché. My face hidden, I smile at his discomfort.

"Outfits such as this are made to be worn, not locked away.
Die Schiedler Tanzen did not put so much work into their costumes for them to be forgotten."

He looks me up and down. I notice his hands are clenched
into fists by his sides. I smile again.

"You will take the costume off, and you will leave the premises."

"And if I say no?" My voice sounds muffled.

"Then I will bring the authorities to eject you from the premises," he says, but there is uncertainty, as if in that sentence he is acknowledging he is no longer an authority. He is used to compliance. From artefacts. From visitors. From colleagues. My resistance unnerves him. Only the pain stops me laughing at his growing awareness that he is a fallen king. I undress in front of him, taking my time to put on my own clothes. This time he sees my smile, and turns away to stare into the darkness of packing crates and forgotten artefacts.

9. *Der König der Küste* (The King of the Coast), *Outfit, 1928, Sacking, Metal Funnels, Papier-mâché, Sand, Rubber Tubing*

This late costume was very simple and eyewitnesses reported that at first they thought it represented a new direction for Die Schiedler Tanzen. Jochan appeared on stage in what appeared to be a comical outfit. Light and loose the sacking juxtapositioned with the regal name suggested some kind of comment on poverty and wealth. However, as the performance progressed, the audience became more and more disturbed.

Sabine joined her husband on stage, carrying a large bag of sand. With no other music or real choreography she began to use the funnels to pour the sand into the clothing, until the weight was so great that Jochan was no longer able to move. Then, using the tube and funnel affixed to the mask, she poured in dirty seawater, presumably into the mouth of her immobilised husband until his stomach held no more and the water and vomit fountained onto the stage.

Back in my accommodation I sit on the edge of the bed and stare at the box for half an hour before lifting the lid. I wish I was more versed in the rituals of saints. The Church must have liturgies for exposing holy relics, but having never taken holy orders I do not know such words. Instead I sit in silence, and when the moment feels right I open the lid.

The mask is on the top. I lift it out and hold it up to the light. It is obvious straight away that it is far too small for me to wear. I cannot deny I am a little disappointed, but as long as it is worn then everything will go as it should.

There is little decoration. The eyes are gauzed, so that the performer can see the reactions of the audience. I reach inside, and catch my hand, blood collecting in my sleeve. I am not the performer for the dance to come. Yet it is fitting that I, the one who brings this performance back to the waiting world, is the one who it takes a price from first.

Next, I remove the tunic and hold it in one hand, gauging the weight. Again, the beauty of the costume is in the lack of adornment. The simplicity. All the detail is hidden on the inside, away from the gaze of the audience. The only way for those who watch to know what is hidden is in the movements of the dancer. The interpretation.

I lay out the whole outfit on the floor. Each piece as well made as the last. Sitting beside it, I run my hands over the plain fabric and sigh. It's hard not to be disappointed that someone else will bring life back to such an exquisite piece of tailoring. I pick up my bag and leave to visit the museum for the last time.

10. Moderne (Modernity), *1922, Outfit, Papier-mâché, Cement, Rubble, Glass*

Although Die Schiedler Tanzen later themes veered more toward the esoteric, their earlier work suggested a tension between the emergence of a modern world and their discomfort with those changes. In Moderne, one of their earliest known performances, Die Schiedler Tanzen expressed this in the discordant orchestration and awkward movements. Moderne was responsible for the initial interest from audiences in their work, an interest that seemed to fade over the decade.

If I hadn't left a note with the address of my accommodation I doubt the curator would have ever found me. Though he knows I have stolen Lawine, he is surprised when I open the door wearing the costume. He walks past me, into the room and waits for me to shut the door, holding his hands behind his back, face toward the floor.

He is lost for words, but only for a moment.

"As soon as I leave here, I will be contacting the police."

"And yet you didn't bring them with you," I say. I like the sound of my voice inside the costume. I imagine that my words rustle the metal stitched to the outside.

"We have matters to discuss first."

"The eleventh costume. The one believed to have never been made, or worn," I say. I point to the floor, the rusted razorblades rattling along my sleeves.

"Take off that outfit, donate this one," he says, sweeping his hand toward the mask. "And we'll call an end to the matter."

"I thought you weren't interested in amateurish fancy dress."

"I'm not," he admits, and I admire his candour. "But hidden things and lost things will bring attention to the museum and attention brings funding."

"And that's all you care about? Funding?"

"All I care about is the museum. And what do you care about?"

I pause for a moment, and really think about the answer. Give it some time and consideration. He kneels down and runs a hand over the front of the mask.

"The performance," I say.

The sleeves of Lawine are baggy enough that he does not know about the presence of the iron bar until it makes contact with the back of his skull. I try not to break the skin, but there is a small cut and for a moment I have a few nerves that it might ruin the performance.

Carefully I slide him into the costume. It is not easy. He is a dead weight. Soon though he is ready and I wait for him to wake up.

It is hard to tell at exactly what point he realises he is the star of the show. There was no chance for him to rehearse so all his choreography is improvised. The buckles that hold the sleeves to the thighs make it difficult for him to stand and as he does the razorblades and nails inside the mask press down into his skin. I listen to them grind rather than cut through his skin and muscle, and for a moment I imagine I can smell scorched bone from the friction. As he sings, the blood soaks through the plain white fabric. Die Schiedler Tanzen never named the outfit, but I think I shall call it Die Blumen.

By now he is upright and his full weight is on the blades in the feet of the tights. He stumbles, trying to reach the door, but every gesture increases the intensity of the performance. Die Schiedler Tanzen designed the costume perfectly. None of the blades cut his tongue, so he is able to provide his own accompaniment through-out. Eventually he is tired out from all the work he has put into the choreography and collapses to the ground. When I lift the mask from his face he wears the marks of his strenuous performance. I am saddened that the costume is only suitable for one show, but now I have seen the dance as Die Schiedler Tanzen intended, I'm sure that I will be able to recreate it many, many times.

11. Unknown, 1930?

It is rumoured that at the time of their deaths Sabine and Jochan had been working on a costume that was to be the culmination of their performances throughout the decade. However, though their notes, diaries and sketchbooks have been very thoroughly re-searched, there are only hints of such a costume.

Soon after their final public show, the bodies of Jochan and Sabine were found. The conclusion of the police at the time was that Jochan was shot first while he slept and Sabine then drowned herself in the river beside the house. The final costume was never found.

Grenzen

Once across the border we will have four hours to reach West Berlin.

I fidget with my wedding ring. The guard runs a finger across the framed map, smearing the glass.

"Take this exit. It is extremely important. Do not stay on the Autobahn. If you do, we will not be able to guarantee your safety, and remember, do not interact with any officials or citizens of East Germany."

I add the rules to the list of all the others, and nod, just desperate to get back to the car and crawl the next two hundred yards to the East German border control.

The room is too hot, air heavy with the smell of sweat, tobacco, and woollen uniforms. I glance past the other travellers toward the door. Kathleen is sat in the car, Heather in the back, already bored and restless after the two hour long stop-start journey from Hanover.

"I realise that this isn't the most thrilling information, but if you don't pay attention you and your family can find yourselves in real trouble," he says, handing me back our passports. "The sort of trouble we can't get you out of."

I nod.

"No need to overdo it. I know the drill."

He adjusts his jacket, and I notice the skin rubbed red raw by his collar.

"And don't speed. Don't give them an excuse to fine you, or detain you."

"I just want to get back to Berlin, and have a beer," I say and the guard looks into the middle distance as if he could drink the word and taste a nice cold Helles.

Outside he checks the fuel, and I open the trunk so he can see the spare tyre, toolkit, and bottle of water for the radiator. He nods, bored already, and moves onto the next person who wants to cut through the hostile countryside to the isolated city of West Berlin. We do not exchange any more pleasantries. It's too hot and I've still got a long way to go.

I open the car door, and climb into the driver's seat. Inside smells of crayons and arguments.

"Everything OK?" Kathleen says.

"That was the easy part. Now we've got the East German border to negotiate," I say, and glance in the back at Heather, colouring books spread out over her lap, plasticine flattened into the paper. "And here?"

Kathleen opens her handbag, takes out a packet of cigarettes and winds down the window.

"Don't ask."

"I know you didn't want to come," I say. The car crawls forward and stops again as the queue moves toward the second set of huts. The silence grows. Even Heather doesn't speak. Kathleen finishes her cigarette and lets the smoking filter drop to the tarmac.

"It's not that I didn't want to come. It's nice to get to spend some time with you. For you to see Heather. It's just I'm not quite sure why we couldn't fly. Avoid all this."

I can't tell her, of course, so instead I say nothing.

"Do you want to see my picture Daddy?"

I turn around. Heather is kneeling, the white ribbon Kathleen put in her hair for the trip half untied. She holds up her drawing book. In shaky blue wax she's copied the watchtowers that over-look the route between the two borders, stick-figures of guards leaning out to see who is in the cars below.

The line creeps forward a couple of hundred yards until we're level with another hut. A soldier in Russian uniform walks out and meets us, leads us forward to a second barrier, now inside East Germany.

"When are we going to be there?"

Heather is leaning forward in her seat, trying to see the man alongside the car. Kathleen reaches in her bag for a sandwich and passes it back. Heather takes it, and eats the bread and cheese with her mouth open, crumbs dropping all over her toys.

I park and get out, go into the second hut and feed my paper-work through the slot in the window, focussing on the tiny details to ignore the fact that I'm almost certainly being watched. The worn baize on the small shelf behind me. The peeling veneer sur-rounding the white painted glass. I don't know how long I wait there. There are no clocks, just the golden hammer and compass surrounded by tarnished sheaves of corn.

Outside I hear other vehicles waved through and move toward the door. Two Soviet soldiers are looking under the car with angled mirrors. Kathleen sits rod straight in the front, looking ahead. Heather is clinging to the window trying to see what the guards are doing. She catches my eye. I signal for her to sit back down, but she thinks I'm waving and waves back. I turn and go back in before the Russians notice.

A hand opens the window and holds out my pass. I take it outside and hand it over as I climb back in to the car. The engine is already starting to overheat, steam coming from under the hood. I hope once we are moving things will settle down. We wait for the guards to open the barrier. They're in no rush. I stare at the weeds growing in the cracked concrete alongside the lane, stretching back into West Germany. Some things don't have to respect borders.

We creep forward to the final barrier. Beside the road an East German policeman holds out his hand. I give him the pass, and he continues to wait, just in case I break protocol by handing him the rest of the paperwork. Heather is singing in the back, lying down across the back seat, her feet up against the door. The officer wanders off without letting us through and I stare at the temperature gauge.

Have they guessed, but why would they? I'm just some Ami heading back after leave in Hanover. I stare at Kathleen and smile. She turns to check on our daughter and ignores me.

"You OK in the back there?"

"Too warm," Heather says, sitting up and crossing her arms. Kathleen feels around under her seat and passes back the flask of juice. Heather takes a mouthful and pulls a face. For a moment I think she's going to spit it out.

"It's too warm," she says, and passes the flask back. Kathleen gives it to me and I take a sip. It is too warm, and gritty, the chemical orange flavour burning my mouth.

The policeman comes back and taps on the window. I take the pass from him.

"Danke," I say, but he ignores me and lifts the barrier for us to go through.

We reach the Autobahn later than I hoped, and the earth is starting to consume the sun once more. I glance back at Heather. She has slipped down into the footwell behind her mother and is using the backseats as a desk, making small figures from the modelling clay.

"She'll sleep soon," I say, glancing in the rear-view to see if we're being followed. It is unlikely, but I can't help checking.

"I don't think so," Kathleen says. It has been a couple of months since we saw each other, and the last five days have not been the easiest.

"The apartment is big enough for all of us," I say, filling the space in the car with words. "Jimmy is on leave, and I made sure I stocked up so that we don't need to go out as soon as we get back."

She does not answer me. I think about trying again, but don't. Let the conversation die. The road curves away.

The East Germans get money from the West to maintain the road, but I can't help feeling it goes elsewhere. Forests line the hard-shoulder, and I wonder if it is their roots pressing up the tarmac.

Steam hangs in front of the windscreen. I have to stop myself cheering as I see the circled R on a pole and turn off the Autobahn into the transitraststätte, pulling the car to a halt alongside several Trabants. The western cars, BMWs and Volkswagens, stand out like whales washed up on a beach of dead fish. This is a twilight place. Somewhere the meeting of two worlds is permitted, as long as they don't truly meet.

"Take Heather for a walk," I say to Kathleen, who doesn't move. "I'm going to have to wait for this to cool down. You can stretch your legs."

A family walks past, heads down so we don't catch their eye. I know it isn't us they are afraid of, but the Staatssicherheitsdienst that lurk behind cameras hidden around the service area, and behind the eyes of their fellow DDR citizens.

Kathleen wraps her arms around herself, Heather following at her heels as she walks across to the small grass verge, toward the rundown playground beyond. I watch them go, and cut across the carpark to the intershop, noticing that the DDR family come nowhere near. Inside I grab more snacks and drinks for the journey, show my passport to the assistant while trying not to notice the camera in the corner of the room.

Branches are caught in the windscreen wipers, thorns cutting into the perished rubber strips. I drag them free and throw them into the gutter.

"Did Heather do this?" I shout across the carpark. Kathleen looks up while everyone else looks away. I've managed to scratch myself and blood bubbles up across my knuckles.

"We've been over here all the time," she says. "Are we ready to go?"

I put my hand on the hood. The engine underneath has cooled and I feel happier making the next stage of the journey. Kathleen settles Heather into the back seat, and climbs back in next to me.

"I don't like it here. That mother over there dragged her daughter away when Heather tried to play."

I watch the woman sitting on the grass, arms around her knees, watching her daughter go up and down the slope in a constant loop of time. I wonder how many people are watching the woman after her daughter was seen so close to Heather. If they will be pulled to one side and questioned before she leaves the service area. If she is Staatssichereitsdienst herself.

I pull onto the Autobahn and the transitraststätte diminishes behind us to nothing.

"They're very spiky people," I say, looking at Heather in the rear-view. A Transportpolizei car overtakes us. For a moment my foot hovers over the brake, but they carry on.

"They're people that live in the forests," Heather says. "They need to hide in the trees. They wear thorns."

"Are they from a TV programme? The people who live in the forests?"

"No Daddy," she says. "They're from my head."

She is dancing the figures across the top of the back seat and something about their blank faces makes me shudder.

We've been on the road for an hour when the radiator finally boils low and the temperature gauge flickers into the red. I switch the turn signal and pull in, sitting in the driver's seat and resting my eyes for a moment.

"Aren't you going to do anything?" Kathleen says. I open my eyes and stare at her.

"I need to give the radiator a moment to cool. Otherwise I'm going to scald myself."

She nods, shoulders hunched away from me as she climbs out. Behind me, Heather is trying to open the door.

"You need to stay here. It's not safe so close to the road."

She shakes her head.

"I need to wee, Daddy," she says, wrenching the door handle so hard I think it's going to break.

"Can you not wait?"

"I'm going to have an accident," she says, shaking her head.

I tap on the window. Kathleen comes back, and opens the door. Heather almost falls out, gathers herself and runs toward the trees.

"Go with her," I say. "She needs the toilet."

Kathleen looks to the sky and follows our daughter up the grass bank.

I step out and get the water container from the trunk. The air smells of pine and the temperature is already dropping. I cannot see the sun behind the trees anymore.

Using a rag, I take off the radiator cap and step back from the steam. It hangs there like a ghost. I told them we should have hidden the parcel in the exhaust, not the radiator. That the reduced capacity would cause problems. I wait until the mist has gone, and start pouring in fresh cold water. Job done, I stand the bottle by the wheel and drop the hood. Kathleen stumbles down the bank, almost falling as she gets closer.

"Heather's run off," she shouts, and, under my breath I swear, though I know it will do no good.

I meet Kathleen halfway up the bank. She turns and we walk side by side toward the trees.

"What do you mean she ran off? She can't run off here. We need to go."

"She was going to the toilet, and then I looked around, and she wasn't there."

Kathleen's trying to catch her breath. She holds onto my arm, I go to pull away from her, then don't.

"And?"

"I shout at her. I shout and say, 'Where are you?' and she shouts back, 'Hide and Seek.' We've been playing it in the local park, but nowhere like this."

I don't know how often the Transportpolizei patrol this stretch of the route, but it won't be long. Then we'll have to explain to them, and I'll have other people to answer to.

We're in amongst the trees now. The bark is thick with moss and lichen. Rotten pine needles sink under our feet letting out gasps of air.

"Where did you last see her?"

Kathleen points to a tree. It smells of plasticine. I can see bits of blue pressed into the bark.

"You left her here by herself?"

She shakes her head, and opens her bag to take out her cigarettes. I knock the packet out of her hand, and they scatter across the forest floor.

"Stop fucking smoking," I say, then regret it, pick one up and hand it to her. "Which way did she go?"

She carries on shaking her head.

"I don't know, I don't know."

I turn and look, trying to keep myself even. Remember my basic training. Keeping calm, but that was about holding it together under fire not losing my kid.

"She can't have run back past you," I say. "So she must have gone that way."

Kathleen nods, though at that moment I think she would agree to anything to help get rid of the guilt. If we're too long. If a patrol find us. If they take the car apart. I try not to think about it.

The thimble is half buried in the pine needles and I nearly miss it. It is slightly crushed as if stepped upon, distorting the patterns decorating the outside. Inside someone has forced vivid blue plasticine. I press the tiny metal cup into Kathleen's hand. She takes it from me and starts shaking. I can feel myself crying.

"We have to find her," I say to no-one in particular. "We have to find her."

There are no further clues as to where Heather has gone so we follow the most obvious route; an overgrown animal path between the trees. The light is fading and temperature dropping, and I do not have any idea how long it will take to search the undergrowth. Children can get into the smallest of places.

Kathleen shouts her name and I rest my hand on her arm, shaking my head.

"What? We need to try and get her attention."

"It's not her attention I'm worried about." I don't know for sure if the woodland has regular patrols, but it is close enough to the road that I expect to see soldiers at any moment. I do not know what I will say. Constructing a lie distracts me as we continue to search. The light has almost totally gone now. Kathleen is holding a lighter in one hand to help us see, the thimble tight in her fist.

I dismiss the flash of white as berries, then it moves, fluttering in the breeze. I run, not caring that branches are slashing my skin.

The ribbon is Heather's, blonde hairs snagged in the final tiny knot, but it is longer, and I see it going into the distance. Into the darkness. The trees are changing, the forest here is older. Oaks and elms. Floor stacked with hundreds of years of decayed leaves. My feet sink into the skeletons and it is difficult to keep going. Kathleen is behind me.

"Is it hers?" she says, and I nod. I try to dislodge it, this final sign of my daughter, and now I do not care about patrols, I do not care about some illicit cargo a suited superior convinced me to carry back to West Berlin. I do not even care about being picked up by the Staatssicherheitsdienst. All I care about is finding Heather. I shout her name until my throat is lacerated and swollen, and there is still no answer.

Unhooking the ribbon, I let it lead me further into the stand of trees, into the silence which Heather is now part of.

The ribbon ends and then starts again. There are other things too. Strands of wool and animal fur. Every tree is covered in fungus I don't recognise that scrapes like shark skin. Looking down at my arms I see blood pooling through my shirt sleeves, but I cannot feel pain, just picture my girl curling up against the cold.

Kathleen is beside me. I put my arm around her shoulders.

"If we don't find her soon, she won't make it through the night."

She does not reply, and I do not want her to.

"You brought something back didn't you? That's why we had to come by car."

"I needed the extra money. It's official," I say, because it doesn't matter now.

"But unofficial. What would the East Germans do if they found it? Or the Russians?"

I say nothing. I can't see her face in the dark, but I know she's blaming me. I'm blaming me, even though I know it's doing no good.

I almost walk into the thorns and at first I think they're barbed wire, run at head height to catch out people sneaking through the trees. I run my hand across the branches. They've been woven together from several strands. I reach behind me and Kathleen passes me her lighter. There are fragments of scalp caught on the spikes. For a moment I think they belong to Heather, but the hair is grey and short. Someone older than me. The skin is partially mummified.

I wrap my fingers in my sleeve and try and lift the thorns out of the way. Find a path through. It's delicate work. Even with my skin protected I still tear my hand to shreds.

The sound Kathleen makes as she's dragged into the darkness is small, like she's slumped and deflated. Her body snags on roots and I only just hear her be taken, before my mouth is covered, the hand smelling of mould-covered bark and softened timber. Fingernails hook into my eyelids, cutting them. I'm dragged after Kathleen, my body finally giving up on staying awake.

∽∽∽∽∽

I am in a net suspended in the air. Somewhere below me and off to one side is a fire. Heavy smoke blowing into my face makes my eyes stream.

I'm face down. Underneath me on the forest floor I see metal badges glinting in the shifting light, the hammer and compass just visible. The net's trammels are woven from sandthorn and black-thorn, the spikes cutting into me. Held in place by my own weight. I see my blood running in rivulets to land in the leaf litter below.

By the fire are two figures. One crouches over the flames, poking something in the embers with a metal rod. Their hair is long, running down their back, plaited into a complex pattern of knots. The smoke and blood in my eyes makes it hard for me to watch for very long and I try to blink my sight back. I cannot make out the second smaller figure.

I hear a whimpering from nearby. Kathleen is lying in a similar net, the thorns threaded through her arms to hold her in place. She is on her back and cannot turn her head.

"Are you OK?" I say, because I can't think of anything else, and of course she isn't.

My head starts to clear, and though I can't see well I can still smell. The smoke is dense with pine sap, and meat is cooking in the fire, and somewhere amongst all the fumes I smell the chemical tang of plasticine.

"Heather!" I shout, my throat still raw and cut.

"Yes Daddy?"

The smaller figure is looking at me. Her hair is no longer up since she lost the ribbon, but it's Heather. The wind changes direction taking the smoke away, and I see her mouth and chin are covered in blood. I shout something but it doesn't come out as words, then I realise the blood is not hers, and I do not know if this is better.

The larger figure stands up and moves around the fire. Their skin, what I can see of it, doesn't look right. Rough and channelled. They glance my way and their eyes are blank. Thorns blur their mouth and cheeks. With their metal rod they poke the fire and pierce the meat lying in the embers. Pulling a knife from their pocket, they slice off a piece and hand it to Heather. She takes the food and gnaws it.

"You're right," she says. Not to me though. "It does taste better cooked."

I watch the other figure lift the joint of meat to their mouth. Something glints in the firelight as they chew. The heat has softened the edge of the silver ring, sinking it into the scorched skin. I look down toward my hand. The tourniquet is made of the same woven thorns. I stare at where my arm now ends.

"Don't worry Daddy," Heather says, the larger figure sitting her on their knee and feeding her some more cooked meat. "I don't have a very big appetite, so we're going to be able to spend a lot more time together before you're all used up."

The Jaws of Ouroboros

BROKEN FEATHERS SLID OUT of pinioned songbirds in the hawthorn hedge above me, falling as rotted grey rain. The ditch was not the dirtiest place I'd hidden myself in my life, but it was by far the most unpleasant. I knelt on sun-faded crisp packets, crushing down festering fur and hollow bones that snapped as I shuffled around and tried to get comfortable.

Pasha rested forward on the ditch edge, staring through a set of night vision goggles into the field beyond. Grains of silt and clay clods smeared across his cheeks as they forced their way past, dragged upward and out of sight. Out of habit I reached down and checked the drab coloured climbing rope around my waist, fingers tracing the knots like a rosary.

"Four other teams around the edge, and one in the fox covert on the far side of the stone circle," he said, not bothering to quieten his voice. Over the sound of sandstone grinding against sandstone we barely heard each other speak.

"Are you going for all of them?" I asked, leaning close.

He grinned, rubbing his face to smudge more dirt across his skin, and pulled out the machete from inside his jacket.

"Every single one."

He pushed himself out of the back of the hedge, using his rope to help him gain a solid footing on the convulsing soil.

The standing stones had always been teeth. We did not see

the jaws until they started chewing the earth from under our feet and tyres. From underneath our towns. All across the country the landscape was eating itself, the topsoil itself digested. If you stilled yourself and watched the fields for long enough it seemed the plough furrows themselves were being torn from the land. Branches, hay bales, empty fertiliser sacks, old farm machinery and dead sheep. Anything too immobile to resist the gnawing of the stone circles was ground to paste and swallowed down hollow, echoing throats. Some of the masticated substance leaked out, pressed between millstone grit incisors to dry on the exposed sun-beaten rock. White ambergris was the popular name. For those brave enough to risk their lives collecting it from between the crushing orthostats, it was worth a lot of money. Feed a family for months. Much more than whale vomit. Our client's taste, however, was a little bit richer.

Pasha knew his work. I did not hear him slicing through the safety ropes of the rival collectors, fibres unwrapping like severed tendons as they were set free from the security of their horizontal tethers. He just slit the throats of the anchor men minding the ropes in the undergrowth, and tipped their unresisting bodies out onto the plough furrows.

It wasn't that I had a particular problem with killing, or that Pasha was better at taking lives. If necessary I could be as efficient as him. The other part of the job freaked him out. The collection. Me? I didn't mind getting up close to the crushing stones as they consumed the fields in which they stood. Maybe it was the relentless hunger that unnerved him. Too close to home. Saw too much of himself in the continuous grinding of those stone teeth.

Half an hour later he was sat next to me again with a black eye and cut across his face, rope tethered back around his waist.

"One of them put up a fight, but my knife was bigger than his," he said, and tapped the bloodstained wooden handle of the machete with a grin.

Next was the waiting game. Heavier objects like livestock, or dead bodies, got carried toward the stone circles quicker. Taking turns with the night-vision goggles, we watched ten bodies tumble across the field, like enthusiastic crowd surfers carried by an aggressive audience. We listened to the sound change as sand-stone crushed ribcages instead of soil and dead crops. We waited until the powdering of bone finished and the noise dulled back to a steady hum.

"You're up." Pasha said, patting me on the back. I nodded and rechecked my ropes, and checked them again, because you can't be too careful. I watched him roll a cigarette and light it, coal end glowing in the scratching twilight of the hedge, wondering, not for the first time, why I trusted him. Money. Money was the reason I trusted him. Money was the reason why I let such a cut-throat watch my back. Without me he got nothing.

I could have just let the tide of shifting dirt carry me to the stones, but that was uncontrolled, and slow. Instead, I dragged myself on all fours, using some of the momentum of the field to push off with each foot. Getting there was the easy bit.

Digging my steel toecaps into the constantly moving furrows I leant forward and scraped my fingers down the surface of the stones. White ambergris felt like congealed fat, peppered with splinters and grains of soil. I pushed my fingers deep into the paste trying not to gag at the smell. I'd only smelt it in two other places—abattoirs and battlefields. A mixture of fermented grass and warm clotting blood. Bone splinters stuck to my skin. This was what we wanted. I opened the first canvas bag and wiped the mixture inside.

Working my way around the outside of the circle, the danger was the rope snagging between the orthostats and severing, leaving nothing to drag myself to safety. Every couple of feet I checked the knots, checked the tension, and moved onto the next gap, trying not to think what might lie inside that stone mouth. What might be at the bottom of the throat. In the early days they tried sending men down. Experienced cavers. Then, when they did not come back, they tried drones. There were rumours the operators never recovered from what they saw on their monitors. I tried not to listen to rumours. They slowed you down.

In an hour I'd worked my way around one side, back to the

centre, then around the other, two full bags across my back. Two more tied to the rope.

Getting out was like walking up a down escalator. Several times I felt myself losing momentum. Several times I felt sure the churn of dirt would drag me like Pasha's victims between the stones, but over the next hour I made my way back to the hedge, landing exhausted in the ditch.

"How much?" Pasha said, turning on a torch and letting the beam scud across the haul.

"Four bags."

He shook his head.

"Doesn't seem much for ten people does it?"

"Not at all," I said, rested my head back against the branches behind me and closed my eyes.

Even in the dark the crane-like dragline was too large to comprehend. Over twenty-two storeys tall it looked as if a small city block had been dropped into the field. The boom stretched above overgrown hedges, immobile like a gallows pole.

We got out of the car and I opened the boot to take out the bags. Pasha locked up, not that there was anyone around to steal the thing. The air smelt of silicone grease and human sweat.

"That's just showing off," Pasha said, sounding more impressed than he meant to at the scale of the vast excavator. He grabbed two of the bags and I went to open the field-gate. Each cross piece had row upon row of small mammals nailed to it.

"What are those?" Pasha said, the note of disgust in his voice unexpected from a person who slit throats for petty change.

I knelt down for a closer look.

"Moles. Dozens of dead moles." I reached out and touched one, my finger brushing the desiccated skin of its paws. I wondered how many had ended up milled between the teeth of animated stone circles. Maybe these were the lucky ones.

All but the smallest draglines walked on feet, and this was

one of the largest, balanced on hydraulic pontoons each the size of a small truck. Few had been converted into private fiefdoms though. Even this far from any megaliths the ground rumbled with the constant, unyielding consumption. Maybe a walking fortress the size of a small village was a good idea.

A curve of arc lights pinned us in place. We put the bags on the ground and waited for the reception committee. I had no doubt that beyond those lights there was enough firepower to smear us to bone meal.

We stayed still. Footsteps rattled down the outside of the dragline until five men stood in front of us. The bodyguards bruised us in their thorough search for weapons, found our knives and showed them to each other, laughed and handed them back. A sixth figure stepped out of the shadows and stretched out his hand.

Even by the standard of high level drug dealers, Papa Yaga was pure evil, and the knowledge he'd personally requested to meet us made me very nervous. You survived in my industry by not being noticed. Mundane and average were the qualities for a long career. We'd been too good too quickly and we were now on the private property of one of the most dangerous men in the country.

"You're the team who have been so successful in harvesting high quality product for me?" He smiled, feldspar glittering in the greyed enamel of his teeth. So he was a user too.

He was short, only up to my shoulder, and slender, wearing heavy tweeds, mud-caked expensive hiking boots, with a shooting stick on a leather strap across his shoulder.

"We've been lucky," I said. Pasha normally left the talking to me. Not that he couldn't string a sentence together. He just never knew when to finish, his mouth finding more words than was good for the situation. I preferred to speak with precision and never for very long.

"In my experience luck is something crafted with chisels and hammers. Your acquisition has been too good to be pure luck," Papa Yaga said. He walked forward and rested a hand on Pasha's arm, his other on mine. "Let's walk to my office, and inspect your latest crop."

I expected us to go inside the dragline, and when his men turned in the direction of the boom I felt sure we were going to get powdered into the plough soil. He felt me tense.

"Don't be so nervous all the time. You two are my golden egg laying geese. My prize sows. My show-winning heifers. I have no intention of disposing of you just when you're making me so much money."

The bucket of the dragline was vast. We waited while one of Papa Yaga's men found a torch and led us inside.

The sheer scale started to sink in. The bucket was big enough to hold a large boardroom table, several bookcases and filing cabinets. The walls left bare metal, stained with rust and rain.

One of Papa Yaga's men wrenched down a heavy set of roller doors. We each pulled a chair up to the table and somewhere out of sight a generator started. Above us lights flickered like swallows. I glanced around the room. Cobbles and dirt accreted to the corners of the uppermost corners, making it more cave-like than industrial. Grains of soil shuddered loose with the dance of the generator, rattling and bouncing against the steel floor.

"Any questions before we start?" Papa Yaga said, sitting down opposite and folding his arms.

"What's with the moles?" Pasha said. I looked down at my hands and prayed to the gods that might still notice me.

"Moles?" Papa Yaga tensed. Behind him two of his bodyguards reached under their donkey jackets.

"He means on the gate. The skins nailed to the field-gate," I said, glancing over at Pasha. He was oblivious, staring up at the lights.

"Oh those," Papa Yaga said, laughing. He leant across the table. "Because the neighbours get too fucking upset if I nail the flayed torsos of my victims up in the lanes where the tourists can see."

I glanced over at Pasha and just hoped he realised how close he was to getting us decapitated, golden eggs or no golden eggs.

"I'm joking. They've been there for years. Some old gamekeeper folklore. Meant to scare away the rest of the moles. Hasn't fucking worked."

"Would you like to test the product?" I said, lifting one of the canvas bags into the centre of the table.

"Fee-fi-fo-fum," Papa Yaga said. Several of his men laughed. For a moment I was tempted to follow suit, but kept quiet.

"Fee-fi-fo-fum?" he continued. "I smell the blood of an Englishman? Grind his bones to make my bread?"

I shook my head. Clueless was better than cocky.

He pushed his hand inside the bag, pulling out a lump of the thick white paste. The smell was more subtle now, but still filled the room with the stench of wet hay and clotting. From the centre he dragged out a splinter of bone, a gobbet of muscle still attached.

"We call this Giant's Dough when we market it to clients. When it has the additions you work so hard to acquire. My little joke."

Dipping the bone back into the bag he came up with a strand of dirty white Giant's Dough, placed it in his mouth, and with the tip of his tongue rubbed it into his gums. The whites of his eyes turned autumn leaf russet, fading to the colour of stagnant water and dirty syringes. Infected wounds and seeping sores.

I'd never watched anyone use normal white ambergris, never mind the stuff we collected. Drugs weren't my interest, apart from the money to be made from them. I had no idea how long the effect would last, and glanced across to Pasha who, with a sense of etiquette I'd not seen from him before, shrugged so small it might not have been noticed by any of the guards stood around us.

Something shifted within Papa Yaga, and his eyes returned to their previous grey colour. He weighed the bag in his hand.

"How many went into this little mixture?"

"Ten," Pasha said. "Some still breathing, others not so much. Don't know if that makes a difference."

"Can't taste any as it unwraps inside you. Maybe the odd little gurgle of congealing blood around the edges, but I wouldn't be where I am today if I was put off by a little congealing blood."

"We don't know how much actually gets pushed out between the stones," I said quickly, making sure we didn't oversell ourselves.

"Of course," he said. "I know this isn't some Cordon Bleu recipe. More a one-pot, cook-it-all, see what comes out at the end."

"If you need more killing to improve the taste I'm happy to do that for you. Fifteen, twenty. Makes no odds to me."

There was a manic energy in Pasha's voice. Looking back I think that was the moment I decided to dissolve our partnership as soon as politic. Papa Yaga glanced over at me for a reaction. I distracted myself by lifting the other three bags onto the table.

"Canvas bags as your employee requested, to avoid contamination," I said.

Papa Yaga turned and spoke to one of his men who left, ducking under the roller doors. We all sat in silence until he came back with a set of scales and placed them in the middle of the table.

I watched Pasha while they weighed the white ambergris, or Giant's Dough, or whatever they wanted to call the crushed paste of several acres of English countryside and ten corpses. He couldn't keep his eyes still, gaze flicking from the piles on the scales to Papa Yaga and his men. There was a hunger there that was going to get us killed if I wasn't careful. I did not want to die because of his appetites.

One of the men noted down the quantities, did some conversions on an old desktop calculator and showed the total to Papa Yaga, waiting for approval which came with a slight nod.

"Do we get to see how much you're paying us?" Pasha said. I reached into my pocket for my knife. Maybe if I slit his throat first I might get out myself.

"You worry too much," Papa Yaga said. "As before, you will be well compensated for your work. I know how specialist your skills are. No need to worry about me conning you. I can pay you a very good rate and still make myself a small fucking fortune. Don't worry about that, little killing man. Follow me."

Papa Yaga walked out first, back to us, his men dropping in behind. It took a few moments for my eyes to adapt to the darkness. Until then I followed the sound of his footsteps. We stopped by one of the pontoons, a narrow ladder built into the giant hydraulic foot.

"I don't like to bring currency outside until it's leaving my possession," he said by way of explanation.

He climbed first. I followed. I had the feeling if I let Pasha go next he would get some stupid idea he could take advantage of that turned back. From the top of the dragline's foot we climbed a second ladder, then a third.

I'm only guessing, but I'm pretty sure when the dragline was tearing millions of years of geology from open cast mines there was no need for a panoramic penthouse.

In the centre was a small lounge. What wasn't covered in leather was coated in chrome. Two young half-naked models, one male, one female, draped over a white leather sofa the size of a family car.

"Please, take a seat," Papa Yaga said. He nodded to one of his men who returned a few minutes later with a holdall. I glanced in the top. Stacks of 500 Euro notes bulged against the open zip. I caught Pasha's eye and got a gut feeling he was going to say something. I shook my head and hoped no-one else noticed. Beside me one of the models smirked.

"That all looks fine," I said, the need to be somewhere else getting more intense by the minute.

"Another delivery soon?" Papa Yaga said, the glow from the in-floor lighting glittering off his igneous teeth.

"As soon as we can. We try to not harvest the same stone circles too often. We need tragic accidents, not rumours. If there are rumours there won't be any product."

"Of course," Papa Yaga said. "But not too long. I have a lot of buyers waiting."

I spent three more nights with Pasha, on the edges of stone circles consuming the land, while he severed throats and ropes. Three seemed like a good number to put distance between the audience at the dragline, while still getting out before Pasha got me killed.

My instincts were right. Each time we went out he got more erratic. More unpredictable. I could tell his attention was elsewhere. If I'd have known where, I'd have let the stones take him.

I went to see Papa Yaga in person, because he struck me as a man who believed in etiquette, and explained Pasha would be carrying on with a new partner. Explained I was retiring for family reasons.

"Families can be very problematic in our line of work," he said, and held out his hand. I moved to Hamburg where I had no family and knew no-one.

They caught me in Munich six months later, grabbing me as I left a small goth club in Kultfabrik. Whatever they injected into my arm cascaded me through a thousand personal hells. It was a long time before I smelt dry ice without checking to see if my skin was being scalded from my face. Waking to find both arms dislocated was a relief.

It was dusk and I was halfway along the dragline boom, legs a metre above the ground, arms wrenched out of my sockets behind my back. All my weight hung on narrow bracelets of gristle eroded into my wrists. I gritted my teeth and tried to stay still.

"I really appreciated your honesty in coming to speak to me in person, even though you were lying about family. It was an understandable, and acceptable, lie."

Papa Yaga was below me, sitting on his shooting stick, his tweed jacket thrown across his shoulder.

"If I'd found out my partner was so much of a liability I would have lied for a solution. The better lie would have been: 'I'm sorry Papa Yaga. My partner had an unfortunate accident where he impaled himself on an iron spike, and as I'm too old in the tooth to work with another partner I wish to retire.' I'd have tried to persuade you. You would have reluctantly, but politely, declined, and we'd have parted ways to never cross paths again."

He grabbed my bare foot and massaged the arch with his fingers, a soothing sensation going up my leg.

"I knew you weren't retiring to look after family. You struck me as far too sensible to work for me and have any relatives.

Your ex-colleague, it won't surprise you to find out, was not as bright. He decided to try and rip me off. Keep the Giant's Dough for himself and give me some white ambergris with cattle bone pushed in. As if I couldn't tell the difference. We caught his partner, some junkie amateur, and flayed the blistered skin from him over several days. Pasha must have got wind and ran. We had to pick up some cousin he stupidly visited a couple of months ago. The cousin didn't know anything."

Using my bare foot Papa Yaga slowly spun me around until I faced the main body of the dragline. The figure was pinioned just below the pelvis, steel cable on one side, pulley wheel on the other. Precision placed to prolong life. The early evening light was too faded to make out too many details. Even over the sound of my own torn tendons I heard the whimpering.

"It's rare theses day I have a reason to fire up this old darling. I felt finding your ex-colleague's cousin justified the cost in electricity."

The dragline came alive. Vibrations from the engine sent tears further into my tendons. I screamed despite myself. Above me, steel cable rattled against metal guides then started to move. The cousin was dragged further into the crush of the pulley, hoist ropes resisting the blockage.

Papa Yaga held me.

"Don't close your eyes or look away. I'll cut your eyelids off myself."

The air filled with the stench of friction, until momentum eroded through the cousin's pelvis. The two halves of torso tumbled into a patch of corn stubble, plumes of steam rose as the last of the body heat hit the cold air.

"If you're amenable, I would like you to track down your ex-colleague and give me the address. Then we really will never have to see each other again."

If this was a film I would have asked "And if I don't?" He'd have tortured me in increasingly inventive ways. It wasn't a film, and I had every intention of doing this last bit of dirty work for Papa Yaga. It wasn't like I had any lasting loyalty to Pasha.

Over the next few hours they gave me a few more scars, just to make sure I understood my place in the plan, but all the while they seemed almost apologetic.

Another syringe finished me off. When I woke I was in a nice, anonymous medical facility overlooking some rolling moorland. I was sure the purple heather was dancing and I couldn't help wondering where the nearest stone circle was, or how long it would be before the walls would be crushed to splinters between the orthostats molars.

I don't know what worried me more. Papa Yaga suspending me until my shoulders tore out of their sockets, or paying for the best healthcare money could buy to patch me up before I did his hunting for him.

I lost track of how many days I spent in that private room. At some nod from the consultant I was dressed in my own clothes, bundled into a van and dumped into the nearest town, a mobile in my pocket with a single phone number in the contacts.

Addicts are creatures of habit. Goes with the territory. Around other people Pasha was always too keen to impress to give any truths away. The truth was too mundane. He gave up trying with me a long time ago, and had slipped into his natural accent several times without realising. Specific enough to identify his home town, if you paid attention. Other occasions he talked about a club night here, or a landmark there. Enough detail to confirm my suspicions.

The town was small and too many people knew each other's business for Pasha's whereabouts to stay hidden for long. He'd splashed around stolen cash to try and find a hiding place, and I splashed around my own to find him.

The squat was on the edge of town. A large house, insides gutted by fire. Recent enough for the stonework to be blackened with soot, and the air still thick enough with ash to stick in my throat. The people living there didn't notice. They didn't notice me. They didn't notice what week it was. A bit of bad air wasn't going to bother them.

I found Pasha in the basement. Seeing his silhouette I thought he was praying, knelt in the far corner, away from the worst of the leaking pipes dripping verdigris water into stinking pools on the stone flags. The damp made my wrists ache, and I rubbed the still raw skin to ease the pain.

I thought about saying his name, but he was always faster than me. We were far beyond trust and loyalty now.

At first I thought the noise was a wasp nest in the room somewhere. The sound of constant chewing and tearing. I stilled my breath and listened. The grinding sounded too familiar. A memory of dead songbirds and decaying rubbish came back. I turned on the torch.

I don't know how much Giant's Dough Pasha had used. From the look of him I guessed we were talking kilos.

All his teeth had turned to stone, erupted vertically from his upturned face, and started grinding against each other. His skin was split by needle thin rips. Inch by inch, fat and capillaries were dragged over the tiny menhirs and ground to paste. Around his neck wet muscle fibres were exposed, stretched taut as they too were dragged upward to be crushed and gnawed.

I shone the beam of light into Pasha's face. His eyes were open, staring straight up at the ceiling. Feldspar glittered in his pupils. Clear gelatine seeped over his mineralised jaws and down his torn cheeks.

Wrapping my jacket around my hand I rolled up Pasha's trouser leg. Underneath all the dried blood it was impossible to tell where his ankle ended and the flagstones began. I dialled the number and waited for the call to connect.

Papa Yaga came into the basement by himself while his private army cleared the rest of the building.

I stood up from where I'd sat waiting on the damp steps.

"Weren't you worried it was a trap?"

He just smiled, and even in the dark I saw his teeth glitter. "Where is he?"

I took him over into the corner and turned the torch on Pasha, the chewing loud enough to drown out the sound of leaking pipes and footsteps on the floor above. He ran a finger over Pasha's face, collected a nail full of the pale gel and rubbed it into his gums. Reaching out, he steadied himself against the wall.

A woman came down the stairs, a saw in her gloved hands.

"You OK Papa?" she said, looking at me and placing the saw on the basement floor.

"I'm fine. You won't need that. Call our land agent and have him buy this building. When you've done that, bring our guests from the holding cells. As many as you think this place can hold," he paused, and nodded toward the stairs. "Bring down those individuals you found in the rest of the house. Let's give them a purpose in life. Also, bring our entire stock of Giant's Dough down here."

"Everything is already on contract and packaged to go out," she said, still looking at me, uncomfortable having this conversation in front of a witness. I knew I was uncomfortable being a witness to them having this conversation.

"Take samples of the white ambergris dribbling from that traitorous fuck in the corner, and get them out to our clients in the hour. First though make sure we have the deeds to this building."

The woman nodded and picked up the saw, leaving me alone in the cellar with Papa Yaga, and the constant sound of stone teeth grinding skin to paste.

"I'm sure you knew you weren't getting out of this room alive," Papa Yaga said, reaching out to take my hands in his. They felt warm and soft. Expensive. He massaged the back of my knuckles and leant in until his lips were against my ears. Peppermint on his breath stung my recently healed scars. "I hadn't decided whether to let my people take turns on you, or cut you up and feed you to our little crushing circle of stones in the corner. But considering the amount of money your ex-friend is going to make for me I'm giving you one chance to fucking run."

I looked at Pasha, now more self-consuming geology than man, and I did exactly what Papa Yaga suggested. I fucking ran.

Acknowledgements

A huge thank you to Michael Kelly, Carolyn Macdonell-Kelly, Courtney Kelly, and Vince Haig for bringing this collection to life.

Thank you to Stefan Koidl for his amazing artwork on the cover.

This collection wouldn't have happened without my critique group. Sending out love to the members of PAWS. Thank you Sarah Read, Chip Houser, Julie C. Day, Carina Bissett, Karen Bovenmyer, Marianne Kirby, Jordan Kurella, and Kathrin Köhler. You made late Sunday nights special times of easy friendship and good conversation.

To the Bavarian Fantasy Cocktail Club. Alexa, Lynn, Ranylt, and Simone, here's to the next round of Whiskey Sours, Basil Smashes, and Old Fashioneds.

Poems, Prose and Pints. Jem, Andy and Nicola, you gave me somewhere to share my weird fiction and have had my back over the years. Thank you for everything!

Thank you to my editors over the years, especially Val Stevenson, David Sutton, E. Catherine Tobler, and John Benson. Huge thanks to Ellen Datlow for supporting my writing.

A special thanks to Blue who first published my writing. You gave me a chance and started me on this path. You're an absolute star.

Hazel, your art is always an inspiration, and I feel so lucky to collaborate with you, finding the middle ground between your stunning paintings and my dark words.

To the UK horror community who made me so welcome. Special thanks to Priya Sharma who has supported my work, given feedback, encouraged me, and believed in me, as well introducing me to everyone within half an hour of arriving at Fantasycon so I had a whole new set of friends.

Whitechapel Prevails!

To Tessa Gordziejko and Becky Cherriman. Thank you for everything and making Haunt happen. Your empathy, care and enthusiasm made it a joy to work on.

To my family, you all have your own strength and inspire me in so many ways.

Trix, you're my brother. Whether whisky-soaked heart to hearts at 4am or eight hour conversations on site, you've kept me thinking and creating.

To Annie, I owe you a debt that can never be repaid. Over 25 years of adventures and hopefully the same to come. You are my world.

To Charlie. You'll probably be a lot older before reading this. Your creativity, humour and happiness inspires me every day.

Publication History

"Winter Home" is original to this collection.

"Beneath the Forest's Wilting Leaves" is original to this collection.

"Atelier" is original to this collection.

"Under the Banner of the Black Stamen" is original to this collection.

"Dancing Sober in the Dust" is original to this collection.

"Grenzen" is original to this collection.

"Call Out" originally appeared in *Innsmouth Magazine* #12, 2013. Reprinted in *The Best Horror of the Year*, Vol. 6.

"Streuobstwiese" originally appeared in *Shimmer* #46, 2018.

"The Kromlau Gambit" originally appeared in *Galileo's Theme Park*, (Juliana Rew, ed.) 2018.

"Dry Land" originally appeared as "Rising" on *Facebook*, 2018.

"Green Grows the Grief" originally appeared in *Shadows & Tall Trees*, Vol. 8, (Michael Kelly, ed.) 2020.

"Not All The Coal That Is Dug Warms The World" originally appeared in *Not One of Us* #54, 2015.

"Children of the Rotting Straw" originally appeared in *Weird Horror* #1, 2020.

"Ruby Red and Snowflake Cold" originally appeared in *Ruby Red and Snowflake Cold*, 2018.

"The Taste of Rot" originally appeared in *Nox Pareidolia*, (Robert S. Wilson, ed.) 2019.

"Flow to the Sea" originally appeared in *SYNTH #1: An Anthology of Dark SF*, (CM Muller, ed.) 2019.

"Mask" originally appeared in *BFS Horizons #5*, (Phil Lunt, ed.) 2017.

"Split Chain Stitch" originally appeared in *Mystery Weekly Magazine*, Nov. 2018. Reprinted in *The Best Horror of the Year*, #11.

"Skin Like Carapace" originally appeared in *Scheherezade's Bequest Presents: As You Wish* Vol. 1, Issue 1, *The Loathly Lady Issue*, 2013.

"Why the Sea Tastes of Salt and Why the Moon Always Looks Toward Us" originally appeared in *Typhon: A Monster Anthology*, Vol. 2, (Sarah Read, ed.) 2017.

"Dirt Upon My Skin" originally appeared in *Animal Day II*, 2018.

"No Sun To Guide The Way" originally appeared in *Speculative City* #8, 2020.

"Discarded Skins" originally appeared in *Gorgon: Stories of Emergence*, (Sarah Read, ed.) 2019.

"Verwelktag" originally appeared in *Lackington's* #17, 2018.

"Our Lady of the Tarpaulin" originally appeared in *Not One of Us* #60, 2018.

"The Jaws of Ouroboros" originally appeared in The Fiends in the Furrows, Vol. 1, (David T. Neal, Christine M. Scott, eds.) 2018. Reprinted in *The Best Horror of the Year*, #11.

About the Author

STEVE TOASE was born in North Yorkshire, England, and now lives in Munich, Germany.

He writes regularly for Fortean Times and Folklore Thursday. His fiction has appeared in Nightmare Magazine, *Shadows & Tall Trees 8*, *Nox Pareidolia*, Three Lobed Burning Eye, Shimmer, and Lackington's. In 2014 "Call Out" (first published in Innsmouth Magazine) was reprinted in *The Best Horror Of The Year 6*, and two of his stories were published in *Best Horror of the Year 11*.

He also likes old motorbikes and vintage cocktails.

You can find him at stevetoase.co.uk